Night and Day
Dottie Manderson mysteries:
Book 1

Caron Allan

Dedication

For Alan.

About the Author

Caron Allan writes cosy murder mysteries, both contemporary and also set in the 1930s. Caron lives in Derby, England with her husband and an endlessly varying quantity of cats and sparrows.

Caron Allan can be found on these social media channels and would love to hear from you:

Facebook:
https://www.facebook.com/pages/Caron-Allan/476029805792096?fref=ts

Twitter:
https://twitter.com/caron_allan

Also, if you're interested in news, snippets, Caron's ~~weird~~ quirky take on life or just want some sneak previews, please sign up to Caron's blog shown below:

caronallanfiction.com/

Also by Caron Allan:

Criss Cross: book 1 of the Friendship Can Be Murder trilogy
Cross Check: book 2 of the Friendship Can Be Murder trilogy
Check Mate: book 3 of the Friendship Can Be Murder trilogy

The Mantle of God: Dottie Manderson mysteries book 2
Scotch Mist: Dottie Manderson mysteries book 3: a novella
The Last Perfect Summer of Richard Dawlish: Dottie Manderson mysteries book 4
The Thief of St Martins: Dottie Manderson mysteries book 5
The Spy Within: Dottie Manderson mysteries book 6

Easy Living: a story about life after death, after death, after death.

Contents

Chapter One

Dottie Manderson had planned to walk the short distance to her sister's house, but as soon as she came out of the warm theatre and onto the pavement, she realised it was raining again. Hitching up the white chiffon and satin of her flowing gown, she put up her hand to hail one of the cabs. There were a dozen of them queuing to catch people as they came out into the miserable late November evening in London's West End. Obligingly, one pulled up. With a profound sense of relief, she got in.

'327 Mortlake Gardens, please,' she said and sank back against the leather. It was so nice to be out of the weather even though a moment ago she had been far too hot in the theatre, but the rain was coming down in torrents, and her fashionable but tiny hat being virtually useless, her hair was already dripping. It was also good to be off her feet. She stretched one elegant foot out in front of her and regarded her neat ankle with a mixture of satisfaction and concern. Being on your feet all day may be good for the figure, but it played havoc with your ankles. If she wasn't careful, by the time she was thirty she'd end up with fat, bulging ankles like Mrs Carmichael, and then the only models the old dragon would allow her to show would be the longest, most-covering up clothes, the floor-length gowns and the lounging pyjamas.

She looked out at the rainy street. It would be rather late by the time she arrived of course, but she had warned Flora about that. And Flora never cared about that sort of thing, she wouldn't throw anyone out before midnight at the earliest—later if they were all having too much fun.

In spite of the weather—or perhaps because of it—the normally quiet residential streets were just as busy now as they were at six o'clock in the evening. She gazed out of the window at the glistening world of night-time London, but her mind was elsewhere, remembering the show, remembering her companion. She hoped she would see Peter again. He was such a nice chap and danced beautifully. And he was the only chap she knew who didn't smoke cigars. Dottie abhorred the smell of cigars.

But Peter had been difficult to get rid of, wanting to escort her home. She had thought of asking him to come back with her to Flora's but in the end decided it would be better not to: she didn't want to make more of it than it was, and Flora was always the last person you introduced a young man to—unless you wanted her to start ordering the orange blossom and white satin. Just because she was married, she seemed to think everyone else ought to be married too. All the same, Mother would be furious if she knew Dottie was wandering around London in the middle of the night unescorted. But to Dottie's mind, travelling door-to-door by cab didn't count as being unescorted. The nice cabby would never let anything bad happen to her, she was certain.

'327 Mortlake Gardens, Miss,' the cabby called as they halted outside a tall fashionable villa. 'Mind your step now, the pavement's more like a river just here.'

And he came round to help her to descend. Dottie handed him his fare plus a modest tip. As she did so she looked about her properly. This wasn't it. The cabby slammed the door. And Dottie immediately realised what had happened. 'Oh my goodness, did I say 327? I'm such a fool—I meant 237. That's the second time I've done that this week. Really I shouldn't be allowed out on my own.'

'I can easily go back a bit Miss, you jump back in. It's no bother...'

'No, please don't worry about it. The rain's stopped and it's not far—I keep getting the number of my sister's house mixed up with my aunt's. Really, I must try to remember.'

'If you're sure Miss?'

'I am, thank you. Goodnight.'

'Goodnight Miss.'

Dottie stood there for a moment then set off back along the street. Although it wasn't so very late, the street felt deserted and a little unfriendly. One of the lamps was out a few yards away, and the stretch between the one behind her and the next one along seemed to yawn blackly in front of her. She bit her lip and told herself not to be a ninny. The canopy of a large tree added to the general gloom. But feeling determined, she fixed her gaze on Flora's house further along. The house was all lit up and even from here she could hear the sound of voices, laughter and music all spilling out on the night air.

If she hurried, she shouldn't get too wet. She had been hopelessly optimistic when she told the cabby the rain had stopped. It hadn't. Dottie drew her fur coat more tightly around her and held onto her hat, now not much more than a bit of limp lace and ribbon. But almost her first step took her an inch deep into a puddle and she couldn't help but give a little yelp at how cold the water was, and the shock of it.

'Blast it,' she grumbled, and leaning against a nearby gate-post, she shook the worst of the water from her silver sandals. Almost new, too, she thought ruefully, and almost certainly ruined. At least her dress hadn't seemed to suffer too badly. She hitched the skirt of it up a little higher and continued her short but eventful journey.

A sound came to her ears above the beating of raindrops and far-off traffic. A soft shushing sort of sound but almost melodic. She paused a moment. Listened. Her eyes, growing accustomed to the darkness, made out a shape on the pavement not ten yards ahead. Her heart gave an odd lurch, as if a cold hand gripped it.

'Idiot,' she muttered, and forced herself to keep going. She really shouldn't read gothic novels late at night, it made her jumpy. No doubt all she would find were the pages of a newspaper all spread about by the wind, and made to look odd by the streetlamp behind her creating shadows.

The sound came again. A little louder, a little more insistent. It sounded almost like...

There was someone—a man—lying on the pavement. She felt a little shimmer of fear. Could it be a drunk? Perhaps she ought to step into the road, walk round him very carefully, keeping her distance...

The head moved very slightly. His face was a pale oval in the dim lamplight. And she saw that the lips moved too. It was him making that odd noise. So it was a drunk, after all. He was singing to himself in a soft sibilant whisper. Her ear caught the rough melody of it, and even then, just as she saw the blood on his shirt-front, one part of her mind was saying, I know that song.

She forgot her fears and ran to his side.

'What happened? Are you all right?' she asked, then berated herself for asking such a stupid question. Because it was all too obvious he was *not* all right. She knelt beside him and put out a hand to take his groping one.

He was quite young, though older than her own nineteen years of age. But no more than perhaps his early thirties. Fairish hair, slightly receding, and dark from the rain. One of those little moustaches that were all the rage at the moment. Blue eyes, very blue like a child's, wide and astonished-looking. From his smart evening dress, he was clearly well-to-do, although she didn't recognise him. But the blood—oh the blood. So much...

'What h—happened?' she repeated but he seemed barely able to take in what she was saying. With infinite gentleness she lowered his head to the ground again, laid his hand across his chest, and picking up her skirts she raced the remaining distance to pound on Flora's door, screaming for help. And without waiting for a response, she hurried back to the man's side, kneeling in a puddle, taking his hand again. Then a thought came to her and she let go of his hand to open her evening bag. She took out a tiny cambric handkerchief, tried to hold it to his chest, but he kept clutching at her. The blood was spilling, spilling, all down his shirt, onto his coat, onto the ground.

'Someone will come,' she promised him, promised herself even more. 'They'll be here in a moment, just hold on a little longer. Wh-what's your name?'

The door was opening and George's head poked out. Thank God it was George. She yelled, 'Oh George! Help! There's been the most terrible... he needs a doctor. I c-can't stop the bleeding.'

George, bless him, was perfect in any crisis. 'Right ho, old girl,' he said, his voice carrying on the night air, and he disappeared back inside. She could almost hear him going around the house trying to find Someone Useful. No doubt there was a doctor present among his many cronies. George was not only a dear, he was a sensible man, and she could see perfectly well why Flora had married him.

The street seemed so quiet. The other houses were all mantled in darkness, not one light, not a sound. The houses along this part of the street might just as well have all been empty. The music and the laughter from Flora and George's party seemed worlds away beyond the other streetlamp, and here, in her little oasis of shadow, nothing touched her or the man on the ground. Dottie could hear the laboured sound of his breathing, gasping, as if he was snatching at air too thin to breathe. Yet he was still singing that song in that peculiar soundless whisper.

It came to her now what it was. She had been to see the show only last week at the theatre with George and Flora and a couple of other friends. *Gay Divorce.* The divine Fred Astaire, and Claire Luce in her gorgeous, flowing dresses of chiffon and lace, taffeta and lamé that Mrs Carmichael was already copying for her best clients.

Dottie looked into the man's wide blue eyes.

'What's your name? Can you tell me anything? Who did this to you? What's...' She heard the sound of a door slamming and running feet clattering on the wet pavement. 'Help's coming, hold on,' she said. He gripped her hand in a tight, painful grasp, and tried to raise his head a little. She thought he was about to speak, but he just continued to sing to her. His body heaved with the effort of finding the breath to form the words which came in stops and starts, singly and in pairs and threes. She found she was holding her breath, willing him to form each next word, even though in her mind she heard Fred Astaire's voice and saw his swirling coat-tails as he danced.

'Please, save your strength,' she begged the man on the ground. George and a couple of others were suddenly there beside her. Flora opened the door again and came out to stand on the steps, looking anxious, a little knot of guests crowding out behind her to see what was happening.

The man continued to sing the next line of the song. Dottie felt confused. If only he would tell her who he was, where he lived. Why did he just sing at her like that?

He wouldn't stop, he wouldn't let go of her hand even as the doctor tried to pull him back onto the ground so he could see to his injuries. They were asking her questions but she couldn't seem to take in what they were saying. The rain ran down her face, dripping off her ears, nose and chin. George's hand was under her elbow, trying to raise her and guide her away, but the man clutched at her, his fingers digging into her arm, refusing to let her go. She could see it in his eyes, the determination to hold onto her, there was something he simply had to tell her.

His voice was less than a whisper, she bent her head to catch the sound of it even though her memory was reminding her of the words of the song. In the middle of the last line of the chorus, his eyes lost their focus and glazed.

He was gone without finishing the line. A slight convulsion had him jerking then falling back onto the wet ground, and she sat back on her heels, her free hand covering her mouth, then George was wrenching her hand free, breaking the hold, pulling her up and leading her away, his arm warm about her shoulders, pulling off his jacket to place around her.

'Oh,' she said, and felt foolish for saying something so pointless. George waved to Flora who hurried over, gasping at the sight of the man. The pool of blood where he lay was huge. Dottie now saw the enormity of it as if for the first time. It ran across the width of the pavement, down into the gutter and was borne away by the rainwater, a long red line, stretching for yards and yards. The doctor and the other man were still with him, two pals of George's, she knew them so well and yet just for now their names were a mystery to her. Oh yes, Alistair—and...

'Come away, dear,' George was saying, and then he and Flora drew her into the house, past the staring guests.

'I just—f-found him,' she felt she had to explain. 'I was going to go around him—I thought he was a drunk, but then...'

'Come upstairs, Dottie dear,' Flora was saying. 'Let's get you out of those wet things.'

Dottie looked down at her dress in surprise. She really was wet through, and she hadn't even noticed.

*

Chapter Two

It was a relief to sit in an armchair in Flora's bedroom clutching a hot toddy between her frozen fingers.

Flora had tried to persuade Dottie to take off her wet things and get into bed, but Dottie had already made up her mind to go home. The hot drink was welcome and helped to calm her nerves as well as her stomach.

Downstairs in the hall, George was telephoning to Dottie and Flora's father, explaining what had happened and asking him to drive over to pick Dottie up. And as he was talking, the bell of the ambulance rang in the street outside and jangled her nerves. Flora was rubbing Dottie's back, sitting on the arm of her chair and fussing over her younger sister like a mother hen.

'Poor Archie Dunne,' Flora said. 'I can hardly believe it.'

'Who? W-what, you know him? That was his name?'

'Well, I couldn't see for myself, of course, but that's who George said it was.'

Dottie was silent, thinking. Somehow it was worse that they knew him. Flora took the empty glass from her, the toddy was all gone. Usually that kind of thing made her feel a little tipsy, Dottie thought, but not today. She still felt cold inside. That poor man...

George came into the room.

'Flossie dear, do you think we ought to tell everyone to go. It doesn't seem...'

Flora gasped. 'You're right—I'd forgotten all about them.' With a last pat of Dottie's back, she got up, saying over her shoulder, 'Shall I get rid of the guests whilst you telephone to the police? And I should think Charles and Alistair will be wet through and half frozen by now. I'll order some more hot toddies,' she added.

They hurried away, George saying, 'Lord yes, the police.'

A moment later, Dottie heard Flora clear her throat and say in a loud clear voice, 'I'm terribly sorry, everyone, but in the light of what's happened...'

Dottie didn't listen to any more. She could hear the murmuring and the sound of movement on the floor below. Feeling fidgety, she got to her feet and went across to the window. Twenty yards or so down the street Charles and Alistair were smoking cigarettes and standing beside the body of the man Flora had called Archie Dunne. Someone had covered his face with something white, a handkerchief perhaps, and Dottie felt glad about that. She didn't like to think of the rain pouring down on him. Not that it was so heavy now—barely even a drizzle, but all the same.

The ambulance drivers were bringing out a stretcher for him—the body—and beyond them, a little bunch of spectators had gathered, some holding their hats instead of wearing them, as a mark of respect. But the ambulance men didn't put him—it—onto the stretcher, they just stood there with George's friends, talking. At first she didn't know why, then she remembered they had to wait for the police.

Next, a car arrived and a gentleman in a smart suit, carrying a squat and heavy-looking medical bag got out. After a brief conference with Charles and Alistair, he went over and, putting down some newspaper, knelt beside the dead man, carefully checking his injury, feeling his wrist, and removing the handkerchief from his face. Just a few minutes later, he covered the man's face again, and went to join the ambulance-men and George's two friends, and settled in to wait for the police to arrive. After another brief word, Charles and Alistair shook hands with him and returned to the house.

Below her, almost as soon as the two young men had come in, the front door opened again, spilling a pool of yellow light onto the wet steps, and people began to leave, murmuring sympathetically to one another and pulling on coats, and she caught the odd words and phrases: 'How awful!' and 'Simply ghastly!' She heard the sound of footfalls on the stairs, and then Flora returned with another steaming glass for her. 'How are you holding up, darling?'

Dottie nodded and took the glass. She wouldn't drink any of it, but it would be nice to warm her hands. She couldn't seem to stop shivering.

As Flora bustled away to continue to see out her guests, Dottie said, 'Was he married, do you know?'

'Archie? Well yes, he married Susan Moyer last spring. You remember Susan, don't you? She was at our school, wasn't she?'

'Yes, she was.' Dottie turned back to the window. 'Poor Susan.' Outside it looked for all the world as if a street party was in full flow. Presently, when all the guests had gone excepting Charles and Alistair, she went down to the drawing-room and helped Flora tidy up all the glasses and plates and the overflowing ashtrays; anything to keep her hands busy. George, Charles and Alistair were all sitting about, morose and trying to get warm. Whatever they said didn't reach Dottie, her mind was seeing other scenes, hearing other words.

She was desperately tired. She had been persuaded to change out of her wet dress and was now wearing a pair of Flora's lounging pyjamas, with George's warm and sensible dressing-gown over them, and a pair of his socks to warm her feet. She still had to grit her teeth to prevent them from chattering. I wouldn't have been much use in the Great War, she thought, if this is how I go to pieces.

Her father arrived and had to be told everything all over again and he sat down with the rest of them to await the arrival of the police.

The police arrived half an hour later in a terribly noisy and attention-attracting manner. At the sound of the car's bell, lights went on all up and down the street, and people looked out of windows and doorways. Cooks and maids stood watching from area steps, their hair in curlers under headscarves. Well-to-do ladies in negligées leaned out of upstairs windows, their hair likewise arranged. One man stood in his undervest and trousers, his braces hanging down. Several uniformed policemen arrived on foot or on bicycles, presumably they had been out on the beat and been called in to help. They held back the rapidly increasing crowd. Dottie, standing by the drawing room window, saw a policeman in plain clothes—quite a young man, she thought to herself, and rather tall and thin—get out of the newly-arrived car and make his way over to where the body lay. He crouched beside the body, the hem of his overcoat trailing in the bloody puddle. What would his wife say about that when he got home? But perhaps she was used to it, Dottie thought. Perhaps policemen always went home from work with blood on their clothes. Then he stood and looked about him. After looking about him for a while, seemingly taking in the scene, he joined the medical chappie and had a chat with him.

Finally, the body was removed and the ambulance drove away, the urgency of its bell seeming a mockery. The crowd, with nothing left to gawp at, dispersed. The bicycle-riding and beat-walking bobbies soon followed suit, save one to watch over the scene. All was once again quiet in Mortlake Gardens. It seemed as though ice ages had come and gone before the policeman glanced in the direction of George and Flora's home, his face little more than a blur in the darkness. He nodded to the medical man and turned to walk in the direction of the Gascoignes's house. Dottie felt convinced that he had seen her standing there looking out, and she stepped back into the room, not wanting to be thought a ghoul.

Detective Sergeant William Hardy stood in the street and looked about him. Inwardly he cursed the rain. Why was it always at night, he thought, and always a wet night at that?

He had a quick word with the police doctor and ascertained that it was definitely not an accidental death or suicide. A knifing, he was told. Possible mugging. Nothing to be done for the poor fellow.

'Constable Maple? May I have a word?' Hardy called to the uniformed policeman who was standing back, overseeing the scene like a patient nursemaid. Constable Maple came over.

'Sir.' Maple said formally, but gave Hardy a matey grin.

'Evening Frank,' Hardy said.

'Bill. No Longden this evening?'

'The Inspector has a bridge evening, then he's off to stay with his in-laws in the country tomorrow,' Hardy told him.

'Nice enough for some!'

'Indeed. Who was it found the body?' Hardy asked. Maple pointed and then quickly outlined everything he knew. Glancing in the direction of the house, Hardy caught sight of a pale face at a window. As soon as she saw him looking, she drew back. Beside him, the other man was still putting him in the picture.

'Young slip of thing, she was, but they said she wouldn't let go of his hand, not till he'd gone.'

'Did she know him, then?'

'Apparently not. Some of 'em did, the men that tried to help him told me his name. Archie Dunne.'

'Hmm,' said Hardy. 'I'd better go and find out what else they know. See you in a bit, Frank.'

'So Longden's not going to show his face at all then? He's really too busy playing bridge to see to a murder?' Frank shook his head. 'Don't that beat all. I can't see the top brass liking a sergeant being left to run a murder case.'

'No doubt it'll all be different once they've had their breakfasts and thought about it. Stick about for a bit, will you? Just in case.'

It was a quarter to one in the morning when the detective sergeant was shown into the drawing room. It was the same young man Dottie had seen outside, as she had expected it would be, and up close he was every bit as young as she'd imagined him. Surely he couldn't know anything about solving crimes? Where was the senior officer?

He accepted the offer of a hot toddy with gratitude and settled down in an armchair with every appearance of a regular house guest. Not even a notebook, thought Dottie. He couldn't possibly have the slightest idea what he was doing, he was far too young. What were the police thinking, letting a sergeant conduct a murder enquiry?

He asked her to tell him in her own words what had happened. As succinctly as possible, she told him how she had come to find the man. George confirmed he had recognised the dead man. Flora produced an address from the little book she kept in the drawer of the bureau, and Alistair, the doctor, added his own evidence that the man had clearly been stabbed, and that he was already beyond help when Dottie and the rest of them had arrived.

None of this was written down, apart from the address, which Flora did herself.

After a cosy hour of sipping hot toddies and listening to what they all had to say, the detective sergeant rose, and with obvious reluctance, said his farewells.

'He asked us practically no questions, and made no notes. Surely a mere sergeant shouldn't be leading a case of this sort? I hope he's not that useless when he goes to see poor Susan,' Flora commented as she kissed Dottie goodbye ten minutes later. Dottie couldn't help but agree.

Her father led her down the steps to the car, and helped her tuck in the folds of George's dressing-gown before slamming the door.

When they arrived home, he had to wake her, and then

she had to endure her mother's interrogation and pronouncements that it didn't do a young woman any good at all to be mixed up with dead bodies. No doubt people would talk. Her reputation would be in tatters. Next time, she should be sure to step right round and keep going.

It was half past two before she was able to get into bed and fall almost immediately into blissful oblivion.

Towards morning Dottie's sleep lightened and she began to dream. In her dream she was wandering the streets of London, looking for Archie. She was calling for him as she ran down street after street, but all the streets looked the same and the cabby was running after her saying, 'He's down that way, Miss,' then, 'He's over there, Miss,' until she was completely confused, and the rain as pouring down, soaking her pyjamas, and the sheer stuff was clinging to her arms and legs, weighing her down and chilling her to the bone.

Every so often, in the distance she would catch just a glimpse of Susan Dunne, her face hidden under a heavy black veil, and Dottie had to hide, because Susan couldn't know Dottie was looking for Archie, there was a secret that Susan didn't know, and she wouldn't understand why Dottie was looking for her husband, so Dottie hid herself until Susan had gone by.

When she found him, she knew it was too late, and the road sloped sharply uphill, and somehow, even by holding onto railings, she couldn't pull herself up the hill. She couldn't reach him, and his blood was pouring out onto the ground, and running in rivulets down the hill towards her, and she knew she would never get to him in time. She woke herself sobbing, to find bright sunshine pouring in at the window and her bedclothes in a tumble on the floor. No wonder she was shivering.

There was a knock at the door, and the maid, Janet, came in with a breakfast tray, closely followed by Dottie's mother who carried the teapot. Her mother bustled over to the bedside, tsked at the state of the covers and with a nod of the head indicated Janet should help her replace and straighten them.

'Now Dorothy, I hope you won't be lounging in bed all day, because we're meeting the Angkatells and party for luncheon at the Royal Hotel, and there are a few things I need to get in Town first. You know, whenever you face adversity in life, I always say...'

'...put a smile on your face and your best foot forward, yes, Mother, I know,' Dottie said. She sat on the edge of the bed and felt thoroughly rotten. 'I suppose there isn't a chance you'd go without me?'

Her mother's scandalised look was enough to answer that question. With a sigh, Dottie promised to be downstairs in half an hour. Her mother left the room, evidently satisfied with that. Janet fidgeted with the tray, which was a sure sign she wanted to say something as soon as the coast was clear.

'So is it true then?' Janet asked, and her eyes were alight with excitement. Dottie nodded.

'Yes, and it wasn't the least bit like an adventure in a book. It was absolutely horrible. Whenever I think of that poor man, I just want to sob like a five-year-old.'

'And is it true you was at school with his wife?'

'Apparently. I didn't recognise him, but George did. Flora said so immediately, and that he was married to Susan Moyer. Not that I knew her all that well, I think she was a year or two older than me; it was really her sister I knew, Muriel. But poor Susan. Imagine sitting up in the evening at home, darning socks or reading a book, and thinking, he'll be home in a minute, then I shall hear all about it, and make him some nice cocoa or a whisky or something, and all the time...'

'The poor woman. No wonder you feel a bit queer. It don't bleeding do to think about it.'

'No it don't,' Dottie agreed. 'But I don't suppose my mother will have the faintest idea how I feel, so I might just as well get up and go out. She'll expect me to.'

'Well you just sit a bit longer and have your breakfast, you'll need it after what you've been through, and take some sugar in your tea for the shock. I'll put out your emerald wool. It looks a treat on you, and even though it's quite mild out, you need to wrap yourself up. Miss Flora sent your evening gown round early this morning, and it's a proper mess, I really don't think we can wear it again. It's just never going to look the same. There's quite a bit of blood on the front. And near enough the whole frock is soaking wet. Did you sit in a puddle or summat?'

Dottie thought back to the night before. 'Yes, I'm afraid I did. I—well I didn't feel I could leave him, so just I knelt by him, you know, and held his hand.'

'What, you held 'is hand while he died? Oh—my—oh Miss, you *never*!' And with that, in a flood of tears, Janet ran from the room. Feeling a tendency to go the same way, Dottie decided to be very stoical, as prescribed by her mother, and she made herself sit up, straighten her shoulders and hold her head up, drink her tea and eat her toast and egg. Then she washed her face, brushed her hair and put on her emerald wool dress. A few more minutes of this and that in front of the mirror and she went downstairs, receiving a brief nod of approval from her mother, and a kiss on the cheek and a 'Bearing up, kitten?' from her father. He put his hand out to take hers. For a moment her resolution wavered but then she caught her mother's gimlet eye, bit her lip and followed her to the door.

A maid, tall and ample in her proportions, showed Detective Sergeant Hardy into the drawing-room. He thought it odd that she appeared to have been weeping long and hard, and he felt a momentary annoyance that news of her master's death had clearly already reached the household by some means or another—probably a servant from somewhere else had heard about it and rushed round to tell everyone here.

He was annoyed because he'd wanted to observe Mrs Dunne's face and behaviour when he broke the news to her. So often in cases like these, those closest to the victim had perpetrated the crime, and he had wanted to be alert to any guilt in the face of Susan Dunne.

Mrs Dunne was already there in the drawing-room. She looked up from her sewing, showing him a composed though pale face, unburdened by any display of deep emotion. But the hand holding her needle trembled.

'Do sit down, Sergeant. I believe you wished to see me?'

'Mrs Dunne, it is my sad duty to deliver some tragic news. I'm afraid you must prepare yourself for a shock. I'm sorry to tell you that your husband, Mr Archibald Dunne was attacked last night as he was walking along Mortlake Gardens, and I am sorry to inform you that he died before help arrived.'

He observed Mrs Dunne closely as he said this. She dropped her sewing and gripped the arm of the sofa, the knuckles of that hand showing white. She gasped, then moaned, 'No! It cannot be true!' And fell back against the cushions in a swoon.

Hardy ran to call for the maid, seeing no bell-pull in the room. He could not be perfectly sure Mrs Dunne was unconscious. Everything about her seemed so controlled. In his limited experience—the women in his immediate family not being given to swoons—the body was apt to simply crumple and fall. Mrs Dunne had seemed rather to lay herself neatly back and close her eyes.

She rallied as soon as the maid loomed over her, and as Hardy left his card and his sympathies, he felt the looks both maid and widow sent after him were more calculating than grief-stricken.

At the front door, he turned and went back along the hall to the back stairs, and went down in the gloom, hoping to find a cook or other servants. Might as well speak to them now and get it out of the way, he thought. The kitchen was empty, although the boiling kettle indicated someone expected to be back there presently. He took a seat at the table and waited. Finally, the tall, red-eyed maid he'd already met returned. She was surprised to see him sitting there.

'I'd like to speak to the staff,' he told her. 'Just a few questions.'

'I'm all there is,' she said in a quiet, trembling voice. 'They don't keep no one else, I does it all, cleaning, cooking, errands, you name it.'

'How is Mrs Dunne?'

'She's gone to l-lie down.'

But as soon as he began to ask her questions she burst into tears, seemingly unable to hold herself in check a moment longer.

'Now then, there's no need to upset yourself. I just need to ask you a few questions.' His words seemed to have little impact and it was a few minutes before the sobbing began to subside.

The maid sniffed and scrubbed at her face with a damp cotton handkerchief she pulled from her sleeve.

'I'm sorry sir, I really am. It's—it's just been such a terrible shock.'

'I'm sure it has. Now then, have you worked for Mr and Mrs Dunne long?'

'Only six months or so. It's my second position. I was with a gentleman and his family what went to India and I didn't want to go with them, though they would of took me, they asked me to go, but I didn't want to go so far away from my mother as she's not as young as she was. Then I got this job.'

'And how is the job? Do you like it?' Hardy asked her. She shrugged her shoulders.

'It's all right. Not so hard as the other one, but then there's no children here.'

'And Mr and Mrs Dunne, are they easy people to work for?'

'Mrs Dunne, she's not very strong, sir, and she needs a bit of looking after. If I had anything to say it would just be that p'r'aps he doesn't look after her as well as he oughter. She's not very strong.'

Hardy hid a smile. The maid's manner of talking seemed to be a rather circular one.

'I see. And were Mr and Mrs Dunne on good terms?'

'Well. I don't really like to say, but...' the maid paused and looked down at her apron, her restless hands pleating and smoothing out the rather grey fabric. For a moment Hardy thought she had finished speaking but then in a quiet voice she said, 'To be honest, he has been staying at his club. It's because of a bit of a spat they had. They're regular ones for screaming at each other. Or was, I should say. But madam said he was coming home, though he was only back the two nights and away again that same night he...' The maid bit her lip but although tears welled up in her eyes again, this time she continued to speak. 'She said as they'd talked about things and he'd decided to come back home. But then he left again.'

'So he came back again, and was here for two nights, then the night he died he had decided to move back out again? Had they had another row?'

'That's right. Although I don't know about the row. They always did shout at each other something rotten and she was always one to pick up on every little thing. And very disrespectful to him, she was, even though she's my employer and I shouldn't say such things. But of course, I don't know nothing of what it was about—they wouldn't hardly talk to me about their private business, of course. But she was always on at him. I don't think he wanted to be here.'

'So what time did Mr Dunne leave? Did you see or hear him go?'

'Yes sir, I saw him coming down the stairs with his overnight bag at about half past six. He set the bag down so he could put on his coat, which I ran and held for him.'

'Did he say anything?'

She fixed her eyes on her hands in her lap, and Hardy saw the splash of tears on the back of one hand. Her shoulders shuddered briefly then she looked up at him, eyes swimming, and in a broken voice said, 'He said, 'Thank you Leonora. You are always there to help me out. Well, I'm afraid I'm off again. It didn't last long, did it?' And then he put on his hat, picked up his bag and out he went. I shut the door behind him and went back into the kitchen to see how the potatoes were getting on.'

Hardy waited a heartbeat or two then said, 'And Mrs

Dunne? Was she upset or angry over him leaving? Did she go out at all that evening? Did she perhaps visit a friend or have some other engagement?'

'Oh no, sir, madam never goes out after dark. She's a bit nervy, see, and well, she's not very strong. She never talks to me about what she's thinking, obviously.'

'I see.' Hardy felt a twinge of irritation. The Mrs Dunne he had seen so far seemed to be a rather determined, cold woman, and he wouldn't have associated that with nerves. 'So,' he said, determined to dot all Is and cross all Ts, 'you were both at home the whole evening and no one left the house after Mr Dunne went out and no one came to the house?'

'That's right, sir.'

'Does Mrs Dunne own an umbrella?'

Leonora stared at him 'An...? Beg pardon, sir. A brolly, would you be meaning? No sir. She's got one of those white lacy things for the summer but not a proper brolly.'

'Thank you, that will be all.'

As Hardy left he was aware of a deep sense of dissatisfaction with how that interview had gone.

*

Chapter Three

Dottie and her mother lunched in an hotel *almost* in the West End, but it was not one of Dottie's favourites.

The soup and the Dover sole were quite good, but the lemon meringue to follow was a dreadful disappointment, with the lemon being too runny and the meringue disintegrating into dust. Mrs Angkatell had declared she was too full for a lemon meringue, or even cheese or an ice, and would have nothing more apart from her coffee, and Dottie wished she could give in to a childish urge to sit there glaring at the woman. Because the lemon meringue was not the thrilling end to the meal it ought to have been and Dottie was convinced Mrs Angkatell had known full well that the Royal served an inadequate sweet.

Other than that, from Dottie's point of view, the whole meal as an event was a complete waste of time. No one had any really juicy gossip except Dottie herself, and even though the two young women on either side of her were clearly agog for as much gruesome detail as she could impart, Dottie didn't much feel like talking about what had happened to poor Archie Dunne. She felt angry at overhearing a niece of Mrs Angkatell say in a drawling, affected voice, 'How awfully vulgar, involving oneself in a common street brawl.'

But she clamped her teeth together and refused to allow this remark to provoke her. Although later she admitted to Flora, 'Oh I just wanted to slap her, the stupid woman!'

Finally, though, the meal came to an end and they left their table in the dining-room to wander into the hotel's drawing-room where coffee was being served, or tea for those who preferred it, and the guests, twelve in all, had the chance to move about and sub-divide into more satisfactory little groups for conversation.

Dottie found a place beside a person she had known at school, and proceeded to ask her if she remembered Susan Moyer. She did. Not only that but she had been to the wedding.

'Poor dear Archie,' she said. 'Perhaps he wasn't the most beautiful of men, and he was a *hopeless* dancer. But he was awfully sweet, always took the trouble to chat and make you feel welcome. And Susan—well, how will she ever recover from a shock of this kind? I'm sure I shouldn't.'

Dottie murmured in agreement and waiting for her companion to finish piling sugar into her coffee and get on with 'spilling the goods'.

'Of course, she's always been something of an oddity herself. Susan, I mean.'

'How so? I don't remember her all that well. I knew her sister Muriel a little better.'

'Oh Muriel, she's a perfect pet. In fact, I'm seeing her next week. Her people are giving a ball for her, it's her engagement party you know, to some boffin from one of the big universities, I can never remember which. Why don't I see if I can wangle you an invitation? There's always room for one more at those sorts of things. Or should I ask for two tickets? I believe I heard your name linked with the Honourable Peter St Clair St John, he's quite the catch,' she said with a sudden sharp sideways glance that took Dottie by surprise. She felt herself blushing.

'Oh well, I don't know, erm—perhaps two tickets would be a good idea. I'll drag someone along, even if it's only Flora.'

'That's quite all right, I'm sure no one will mind. Although...' She paused. 'I mean...' she said with a quick frown. 'It *will* go ahead, won't it, now that their other daughter's husband has been found dead in an alley?'

'It wasn't an alley, it was Mortlake Gardens, which is a perfectly pleasant neighbourhood. Or at least, it was until...'

And then Dottie was just about to add that no, on reflection she was convinced it wouldn't go ahead, what a shame, and her companion gave a huge smile and said happily, 'Oh of course it will go ahead, it's not as if they care too much about Susan's feelings, and anyway, they could hardly cancel something like that at such short notice.'

Dottie had her doubts, but they were not to be voiced. Her mother reminded her of the time and they made hurried farewells of Mrs Angkatell and the rest of the party.

It was just on half past four as Dottie climbed out of the bus and ran the forty or fifty feet to *Carmichael and Jennings, Exclusive Modes for Discerning Ladies.* Inside the door, Mrs Carmichael, proprietress and possessor of unsightly ankles, told Dottie she was late and not to dilly-dally as the Preview would be opening in less than half an hour. 'And half of them is here already, for Gawd's sake,' she pointed out.

Dottie dived into the back regions of the warehouse to find her spot amongst the other girls. Her first model was a smart two-piece costume in the finest, softest tweed. The main attraction of this outfit was the new lapel shape and the dainty peplum at the back. Dottie passionately craved such a creation for her own wardrobe, but her allowance had already been gobbled up by all the other things she just had to have and would not permit any further extravagance. And it wouldn't come out of her modest wage either, as she'd already spent that too.

She patted her hair into place and fixed her make-up, swiping a soft brush across her cheeks and nose to take care of any unfortunate shine, then regarded herself critically in the mirror. Not too bad, though she said it herself.

'It's the suit they've come to see, not you, missy,' grumbled Mrs Carmichael. 'Now you lot, stop chattering and giggling, there's work to be done.' And she chivvied the eight mannequins into position behind the curtain, and when she was absolutely satisfied, she stepped out in front of them to introduce the new mid-season range.

Later, when Dottie got home, she remembered she'd forgotten to ask her friend why Susan was considered odd. Or rather, she *had* asked, but the subject had been changed and she had somehow not managed to obtain an answer.

Poor Susan, Dottie thought, as she mounted the steps to the house. By now Susan would have been told that she was a widow. I wonder if there's anything I can do to help. She was about to hunt in her coat pocket for her latch-key, but the door opened and beyond it she saw Janet's smiling face, and the maid's expression told Dottie she had been keeping a look-out for her—she was clearly bursting to impart some news.

'What is it?' Dottie obligingly asked as she and Janet wrestled off her coat.

'Oh Miss. It's that nice Honourable Peter. He's been here, he hoped to take you dancing.'

'Blast! But I'm sure I told him I had the Preview this evening. I suppose Mother forced him to stay and have tea with her, or some such thing?'

'Oh yes, he was here a good hour. Poor bloke. He's ever so good-looking, Miss. And I think he's really keen on you, Miss. He was that disappointed you wasn't here, I could see it in his eyes. Lovely eyes he's got, has the Honourable Peter. He left his card for you.' Janet produced this now with a flourish and turned it over to show the message.

'He wants to meet you at the Savoy,' Janet went on to explain, turning the card towards the light to better read the elegant handwriting. 'On Wednesday next, says he'll meet you at eight-thirty in the lobby.'

'So I see,' Dottie commented wryly.

'But he said special to tell you it was because he had a late meeting somewhere with someone, and that's why he's hoping you won't mind making your own way there in a cab, though he said to be sure and tell you he'd bring you back home hisself after dinner. I told him you'd be happy with that, as I knew you were free on that evening.'

'Sounds like you had quite a chat.'

'Oh we did, Miss. He's just like what a young gentleman ought to be—so dreamy and romantic.'

'Not to mention having an important position at the Admiralty and a *very* nice house in Twickenham,' added the rather more prosaic Dottie.

'He's just perfect. And Miss, I was thinking, if you marries him, can I go with you and be your maid? Only I know Mrs Manderson has been really, really good to me, and I *am* really, *really* grateful. But I would so like to live in Twickenham, I really would, everyone says it's really, really nice there.'

'So I've heard. Janet, I'd love you to come with me, but one thing at a time—let's see if he still likes me after our dinner next week.'

'Is that you Dorothy? What on earth is taking you so long?' her mother bellowed. Dottie grimaced and quickly turned to the mirror to pat her hair into place. Why did it insist on sticking out in all directions like that?

'Yes, Mother, I'm back. I gather we had a visitor,' she said as she went in the direction of the great lady's voice.

'We *still* have a visitor, Dorothy,' her mother called back, sounding rather put out.

Her face alive with hope, Dottie turned an inquiring eyebrow upon Janet who sniffed and shook her head.

'It's only a policeman,' she said dismissively, and hurried away with Dottie's coat.

The detective sergeant from the previous day stood up as Dottie came into the room, and he held out his hand to her. She shook it automatically then wondered why. It was hardly a social occasion. Her mother sent a glare in her direction whilst her father handed her a glass of sherry.

Blushing furiously Dottie said, 'Good evening sergeant. I do hope I haven't kept you waiting?'

'Well in a way you have,' he replied, not looking at her. 'But it doesn't matter. After all, you weren't expecting me.'

She managed not to say the first retort that came to her lips, especially as her mother was present, and opted instead for a neutral smile. She waited.

'I'd just like to ask you once again whether you saw anything last night. I believe you said you had just been set down by a taxicab, and you were making your way to your sister's house?'

'Why on earth...?' her mother began crossly, but Dottie swiftly hissed in a low voice, 'Because I didn't want to take Peter to Flora's.'

To which her father immediately responded, 'Then why...?'

Repressing a sigh, she said, 'Because I told the cabby the wrong house number! I was thinking of Aunt Adelaide's. Then I thought I might as well walk and enjoy the fresh air, that's all.'

She turned back to smile at the sergeant. 'Yes, that's right. I noticed one of the streetlamps was out—it was quite dark just there so I didn't see the man at first.'

'But then you did see him, and you attempted to help him?'

'That's correct.'

'What did you do?'

'I thought I told you all this...' She hadn't meant to sound so haughty, but she was embarrassed to be discussing it in front of her parents.

'Yes, I'm sorry, I just wanted to hear it again.'

'Perhaps you'd like a pencil and a piece of paper, sergeant?' her mother asked in what Dottie and Flora called her Imperial Tone.

'No thank you, madam. So what did you do?'

'Well, at first I thought he was drunk, but then I saw that he had some kind of injury; there was blood all over his chest and on the pavement. A-and so I knelt beside him to try to h-help.'

'No wonder your dress was ruined, you silly girl! How many times have I told you to have a little more care of your clothes?'

'Excuse me, madam. Perhaps I might make use of your dining-room in order to speak with Miss Manderson in private?'

Her mother stared, whilst her father hid a smirk behind his sherry glass.

'My dear sergeant, I hardly think...'

'Then please madam, it would be a tremendous help if you could keep your comments until the end of the interview. Your daughter must be allowed to answer the questions as accurately as possible without any distractions. This is, after all, a murder investigation.'

Dottie's mother was torn between taking umbrage and a reluctant admiration for his gall. It was a brave man who called her 'madam' in that tone and got away with it. Her momentary surprise gave Dottie the precious seconds she needed.

She hurried on, 'I knelt beside him, and straight away saw how much blood he was losing, and I ran to my sister's house—it's only a few dozen yards from where he was lying—I called for a doctor. I knew it was quite likely that one of Flora and George's cronies would be a doctor, they have so many professional people amongst their acquaintance. Then I ran back to the man—Mr Dunne. I—well—I suppose I didn't like the thought of him being on his own. I asked him if he could tell me his name, but—but he didn't. I told him a doctor was on his way. I thought that might be a comfort to him. He—he—clutched my hand.'

The room was very quiet, apart from the crackle of the fire. Her mother was still looking a little put out, but her father—Dottie had the impression he approved of her actions. She felt as if she had a supporter in the room.

'And did he say anything? Tell you his name, for instance?'

'No. It was George who told me his name—or rather— George told Flora and she told me. Later on, I mean. No, the man was singing. I mean, he was in evening dress, so I thought perhaps he'd just come from the theatre and had been set upon by thieves. Or—or—something.' She bit her lip. She felt foolish, ignorant. If only she'd been a little bit more useful, Archie Dunne might still...

'And what was he singing?'

'Oh, a song from that Astaire show. *Gay Divorce*. Do you know it?'

He did, but said only, 'And how did that go?'

She looked at him. 'What—you want me to sing it for you?'

'If you don't mind. It might be helpful.'

'Oh.' She was blushing again. She hesitated for a moment then rather haltingly began to sing. She felt herself blushing as she sang the rather romantic words. As she came to the end of the line, to the bit where Archie Dunne had halted, she faltered and stopped singing. The clock ticked. No one spoke for a moment. Although her parents were there, she felt quite alone with him. He was watching her with an odd look in his eyes. I bet he thinks I'm a rotten singer, she thought, and looked away, uncomfortable, wishing he would just leave. Aloud, she said, 'Well anyway, I think those are the words. Except he didn't say that last word 'day', he—er—well—before he could...Um, that's all he said. And then...'

'He passed away? Very well, thank you, Miss Manderson, you've been very helpful.' He stood up, and reached out his hand to shake hers again, then seemed to think he'd better shake hands with both her parents too. In the doorway he stepped aside to allow Mr Manderson to precede him, and he turned back to Dottie.

'I forgot to ask, you didn't see anyone hanging around, or running from the scene, or hear anything other than what you've already told me? Or did you notice an umbrella lying about?'

She shook her head, unable to speak. He left, and suddenly she felt—full—overfull in some way and she had to get out of the room. Her face felt hot, she felt trembling and weak. She had to get out. And upstairs to her own quiet cool bedroom.

'Seems an odd sort of chap to be a policeman. Obviously had a decent education. But hardly a fitting profession for a man of his background,' Her father remarked upon returning to the room. Dottie made a non-committal agreeing sound. Then they listened as Mrs Manderson gave her views on the subject, rather at length and with a good deal of emphasis on the twin subjects of Good Manners To A Lady and How Things Were Done When I Was A Girl.

After a couple of minutes Dottie made a point of exclaiming at the time and added, 'I must have a bath and get to bed, I'm shopping with Flora tomorrow, and she's picking me up at ten.'

She said her goodnights and fairly raced up the stairs to lock herself in the bathroom.

At a public house not too far from the Mandersons' home, Sergeant Hardy sat over a beer and thought about the case. Inspector Longden had gone away to a weekend in the country with his wife's family, and once again, Hardy found himself bearing the brunt of not only the investigation but also the wrath of their superiors, which he felt would have been more properly directed at the Inspector rather than himself.

But Inspector Longden had little interest in crime solving. His main motivation in his work was to raise himself through the ranks of the police force as rapidly as possible in the hopes of achieving a life peerage by the time he was fifty, and thus earning some respect at last from his wife's family. Quite what happened with regard to the case of the murder of Archie Dunne was of little interest to an Inspector who aspired to be a country gentleman.

Sergeant Hardy continued to turn over in his mind what he had learned thus far. However, into his thoughts there intruded the pale, beautiful face, the large brown, anxious eyes and the dark wavy hair of a certain young lady. He recalled the scene in her mother's drawing-room this evening. How brave Miss Manderson had been to try to help the dying man. And what a pretty voice she had.

*

Chapter Four

A young policeman ran down the hall from the front desk to call Sergeant Hardy to the phone.

'We have your connection through now, Sir,' he said. 'I'll put it through to old Longden's office.' That said, he vanished again almost immediately.

'At last,' said Hardy to himself, and he hurried after the messenger. When he reached the Inspector's office, he took up the receiver and shortly after that, the call was put through.

'Hardy? That you? What is it you want? I hardly need remind you that I'm very busy.'

'I'm sorry, sir, I just wanted to let you know how the investigation is proceeding.' He went on to lay out for his superior officer the details of Archie Dunne's murder, and all the information he had thus far accumulated. It took a few minutes. He paused at the end of this long speech, searching through his notebook in case he had missed anything. At the other end of the line, he distinctly heard the sound of a champagne cork popping, and people cheering. It wasn't even mid-morning.

'Sir?' he asked, fearful Inspector Longden had actually

left the telephone to join a party.

'Yes, yes, I'm still here,' Longden growled at him. 'Look, why don't you get on with some work instead of pestering me with your quibbles. Good God, man, what do you think we pay you for if not to get on with the job?'

For a few seconds the sergeant said nothing. He reflected that it was a good thing the Inspector was far away, as Hardy felt there was a chance he might have forgotten himself and told Longden exactly what he thought of him. As it was, he managed to sound perfectly polite as he said, 'I had expected you to return this morning sir, after your weekend away. May I ask how long you expect to remain with your wife's family?'

Longden, clearly both offended and feeling guilty, treated Sergeant Hardy to a stream of invective, punctuated with a few fake-sounding sneezes and snuffles which culminated in the response: 'As soon as I am well enough to travel I shall return. I trust that meets with your approval, Sergeant! Now get on with your job or I shall report you to the Chief Superintendent.'

Hardy's reply of 'Yes sir' was lost on the Inspector: he'd already hung up the phone.

'I was thinking we might pop in and condole with Susan Dunne,' Flora said as soon as Dottie opened the door.

'Hello to you too!' Dottie kissed her sister on the cheek and turned to take her coat from Janet. They were about to go, when Flora hesitated.

'Sorry, Darling, do you think I'd better just run in and say hello to Mother?'

'If you don't, we'll both be in trouble. We'll never hear the end of it. By the way, do you think we'll be dining out?'

'I hadn't planned to.'

'Blast. Are you sure you can't dine out?'

'If *you* want to dine out, you can always tell Mother I pressed you to come back with me. Anyway, you go and get in the car, and I'll go and see the old...'

'Good morning Florence.' Their mother's voice boomed

from the dim recesses of the hall and made them both jump guiltily, and Flora rolled her eyes and whispered to Dottie, 'Oh God!' before hurrying to greet her mother with a bright smile.

Dottie made good her escape with a quick, 'Bye Mother,' and after a conspiratorial grin at Janet, she ran down the steps to the car. It was almost fifteen minutes before Flora returned. Dottie remarked on this fact as Flora slid into the driving seat, rolling her eyes in exasperation.

'Your fastest time ever! You're getting good at this.'

'Having a husband is excellent training for learning the skills required to handle one's mother. It's such a shame that one has to put up with the latter for twenty-odd years before one finally acquires the former.' She pressed the self-starter and soon they roared away.

'By the way, I told her you had to come to dinner with us as I had invited a young bachelor vicar especially for you.'

'What! How could you? I thought we were united in this fight?'

'Don't worry. Just tell her he had bad teeth, you know what she's like about teeth. Or he could be bald. She hates bald men.'

'I know. Poor Father. But still, Flora, a vicar!'

'So what do you think? Shall we go and see Susan? Would it be too much of an imposition, do you think?'

'I'm not sure. Why do you want to? I mean, it's not as if we know her.'

'Oh let's do it. We don't need to stay long. As you were with him when he died, you could say he tasked you with delivering a final, death-bed message. Just tell her he wanted her to know he loved her.'

'Really? Flora, I hardly think...'

'If there's a crowd of people, we won't stay. If there's no one, she will doubtless be glad of the company. If all else fails, we could reminisce about Lady Margaret's.'

No one else was there.

When they climbed the tall flight of narrow steps to

ring the bell, they both felt the neglect of the place. The front door was dusty and its paint was chipped. The house was a large, rambling villa surrounded by an overgrown garden barely held in check by a fence of broken railings. The door was eventually opened by a tall, pale-faced, shabbily-dressed maid.

The maid led them to a drawing-room facing towards the street, but nevertheless a dim, gloomy space. Just before they entered through the doorway, on an impulse, Dottie put her hand on the maid's arm and in a quiet voice, asked, 'Are you quite all right? You don't look at all well.'

The maid was clearly surprised. She managed a weak smile. 'Thank you, ma'am, I'm quite well. Just—you know—it's been such a...'

'Of course,' Dottie agreed with a sympathetic smile.

In the drawing-room, a small, slight young woman clad in rusty black came to meet them, a hand outstretched first towards Flora and then to Dottie.

'I remember you both from school, naturally, although you were a year or two above me, Mrs Gascoigne, and you Miss Manderson were, I believe a year or two below me.' Susan Dunne had a low, dragging voice, as if it too was suffering from years of neglect.

'That's right,' Dottie agreed. 'I was in the same year as your sister Muriel.'

'Of course.' Mrs Dunne invited them to sit, and folded her hands before her and looked at them with an air of expectation. 'Now what can I do for you, ladies?'

Flora and Dottie exchanged a look. Flora said, 'Well, I— er—we—that is to say...'

'Ah I see. You came to pay your respects,' Mrs Dunne said with half a smile. They nodded and waited.

'We are so terribly sorry about poor Archie,' Dottie added. As soon as she spoke, she knew she'd been too informal. His widow noticeably bridled.

'I didn't realise you knew my husband so very well,' she said. 'Excuse me, I'll just order tea. Or would you prefer coffee?'

A little bemused, they agreed tea would be lovely. Mrs Dunne called to the maid along the hallway, then resumed her seat and turned an inquiring look on them which indicated she was still waiting for a response to her previous question.

'We didn't exactly know him,' Flora explained. 'He was an acquaintance of my husband.'

'I thought I knew all my husband's acquaintances, but clearly that was not the case.'

Silence fell on the room. Tea was brought in by the same maid who had opened the front door, and who now bore every sign of having been weeping afresh. Once she had served everyone with their tea and departed, Dottie turned back to Susan Dunne and said, 'Erm—I feel I should—that is, he asked me to...'

'My husband spoke to you?'

Flora and Dottie exchanged a look. Dottie, searching for a delicate way to explain, said, 'Well yes. He—er—he was still—c—clinging onto life when I...'

'*You*? It was you who found him?' For the first time Susan appeared slightly animated. In fact she actually seemed quite shaken. She said, almost as if to herself, 'So it was you who was with him at the end?' She rose from her seat and went to the window, still murmuring and practically wringing her hands.

'Yes, yes it was,' Dottie tried to find a happy medium between sounding overly excited at her adventure and looking suitably sorrowful and respectful of the deceased.

'That's why we're here,' Flora added, raising her voice a little to reach the woman still standing gazing out at the street. 'To let you know that right up to the last minute, he was thinking only of you.'

Dottie nodded earnestly.

Turning back to face them, Mrs Dunne seemed to be completely and utterly bewildered. She half-shook her head as if to deny their words. She came back to her seat, and groped in her sleeve for a black-edged handkerchief then pressed it to her eyes. Dottie leaned over and patted Susan's arm a trifle awkwardly. 'I'm so sorry,' she said in a low voice. 'I'm sure things must seem very grim now, but I hope it will comfort you to know that he was thinking of you when he—at the end. He wanted me to tell you...'

Susan stared at her in complete astonishment. 'What—what did he say?'

'Just that he loved you. He wanted you to know that.' Now that Dottie had imparted to Susan the fictitious message of love from the dying Archie, it seemed horribly inadequate. Should she perhaps embellish a little more, she wondered, if a few simple words could bring comfort to a grieving...

'Get out!' Susan shouted, surging to her feet, the handkerchief falling to the floor.

Flora and Dottie stared at Susan as if she had two heads, completely unable to fathom her reaction.

'Of course, you're upset and—erm, grief-stricken—no doubt—but we just wanted to let you know...' Flora said soothingly.

A strange, strangled cry issued from Susan's lips and she ran from the room. Dottie, frozen in the act of rising from her chair, stood in that attitude for several seconds, half-risen, one hand on the arm of the chair, the other poised in the air. Then it occurred to her that she should resume her seat. She sank back, hardly able to believe what had just happened. Her eyes sought her sister's. Flora bent to retrieve Susan's handkerchief from the floor. She folded it neatly and placed it on the little side-table. Neither of them spoke.

Above their heads, a door slammed and they heard the sound of hurrying feet and the groan of bed springs.

'Oh dear,' said Flora.

The maid appeared in the doorway, and she looked if possible, even paler than before and was visibly shaking. She seemed to be feeling about her for the right thing to say and finally came out with, 'I'm so sorry Miss, and—er—Miss, I'm afraid Mrs Dunne isn't feeling very well. I do hope you understand...'

'Of course,' Dottie said, and together they followed the maid from the room. She helped them on with their coats and ran to open the front door.

Dottie noticed an unusual picture on the wall, depicting a young woman in a long gold cloak, much decorated at the hem. 'What a gorgeous cloak,' she commented.

'That's meant to be Esther out of the Bible, Miss. I think she was a queen or summat.'

'This is my card,' Flora was saying. 'If it's all right, could you possibly let me know when Mr Dunne's funeral is to be held, my husband and I would very much like to be there to offer our respect and our support.'

'Of course, ma'am,' the maid said and dropped a slight curtsey, taking the card and putting it in the drawer of the hall table. She was hugging herself as if cold. 'I'll tell madam when she's feeling—a bit—better.' As they went out she added, 'Thank you so much for taking the trouble. I know it meant a lot to Mrs Dunne. I'll let you know about the—erm—*arrangements*. I'm sure Mrs Dunne will be pleased to have your company.'

'I wouldn't bet on it myself,' Flora said in an aside to Dottie once they were out on the pavement again. The door had closed behind them, and they crossed the empty road to reach Flora's car.

'I suppose to be fair, one could hardly expect her to be jumping for joy,' Dottie remarked. 'She didn't seem to know about me being with him at the end though. I'd have thought the police would have told her everything that happened.'

She glanced back at the house and noticed a curtain at an upstairs window twitch. 'My friend was right, you know,' she said to Flora as they got into the car. 'She is definitely a bit odd.'

'Oh definitely. That handkerchief was bone dry.'

They lunched at Claridge's. There they met some friends who had heard all about the murder, and who were very keen to ask Dottie about her 'ghastly ordeal'.

'I'm sure I should have swooned,' one said, while the other laughed.

'You would have 'swooned' as you put it, if you'd so much as seen a spider. You're the biggest scaredy-cat of all time.'

'True. Last time I was at the Royal, I went into the ladies' cloakroom, and on the vanity unit I saw the largest spider I've ever seen. When Jennie came to find me half an hour later, I was still out cold on the floor. *Anything* could have happened!' she added with a delicious shiver.

Dottie smiled and avoided catching Flora's eye in case they made each other laugh. 'We've just been to pay a call of condolence on Susan Dunne,' Dottie said. Laughter followed this.

'Gosh, well, now you know everything!' the scaredy-cat one said.

'She was a little—she wasn't really quite ready to receive visitors,' Dottie added, employing the new tact her sister had been attempting to teach her.

'Oh goodness! Is Susan Dunne ever ready to receive visitors? I should think they have very few. That house! I know Archie could never invite people for dinner, or even just for drinks. What an odd stick she is.'

That word again.

'Why is she considered so odd? In what way?' Flora asked, leaning forward so she could keep her voice down.

'Well you know her, so you're probably better informed than I. She has some strange religious ideas. At least, they're sort of religious, but rather out of the normal way. This is something new, secretive. Doesn't she think she's the reincarnation of ancient high priestess or something?'

'No silly,' said Jennie. 'It was Archie himself. Something to do with the Freemasons or—well I don't really know, to be honest, it's just the whispers one hears.'

'No, it's definitely her,' insisted Scaredy Cat. Jennie rolled her eyes. 'No seriously, Jen, I mean everyone knows they were a bit unusual. Didn't go in for visitors, and she never goes out to parties or dinners or the like.'

'He was wearing evening dress,' Dottie remembered suddenly. 'And although we told Susan that he asked me to tell her he loved her, actually when he—died—he was humming that tune from that show that's on at the Palace. The one with Fred Astaire.'

'*Gay Divorce* you mean, we've been to see it three times, it's just wonderful.' Jennie sipped her tea, then asked, 'Which song, by the way?'

'*Night and Day*,' Dottie said, and involuntarily blushed as she remembered singing it for the sergeant. There was a silence at their two tables. Dottie assumed that the others, like her, were mentally singing their way through the verses, trying to find something to link Archie and his manner of death with the song he had been singing as he lay dying.

But unlike her, they could not visualise the scene—the cold, dark night, the rain, the droplets pattering all round and splashing into the puddles. The man in smart evening dress, lying on the wet ground, the tails of his coat spread out, and again, the ever-present rain, soaking through the stuff of his coat. Running into the blood that seeped through his shirt and trickled away down the road and into the gutter. The blood. Neither would they feel the cold, pinching grip of his fingers as they dug into her arm. Absent-mindedly she pushed back her sleeve to look at her arm, and was not in the least surprised to see several round, purplish-yellow, three-day-old bruises on her skin.

Jennie leaned forward and grabbed Dottie's hand, stretching her arm out across the aisle and commenting loudly, 'My heavens, did *he* do that to you?'

Around the restaurant, heads turned towards them. Now they all think I'm a victim of marital cruelty, Dottie thought. She snatched her hand back and tugged down her sleeve.

'Yes, poor man. He was so desperate to make me listen. Which is why it makes no sense at all that he just sang at me, instead of telling me who had attacked him or something a bit more useful.'

'Perhaps he was mad?' Scaredy Cat suggested. 'Or perhaps he thought you were Susan? You are a similar colouring. Though obviously she's a good deal shorter than you.'

'Everyone's a good deal shorter than Dottie,' Flora laughed.

'I simply felt he was trying to tell me something, and he seemed very insistent, and at such a time,' Dottie said. 'I just can't understand what he was thinking. It was so thoroughly peculiar.'

'Perhaps it's a kind of code,' Jennie suggested. 'Perhaps he was really a spy for a secret organisation and he thought you were his thingy—his contact? Perhaps you were supposed to sing the next line back at him.'

'Well, you'd think he could say something that made sense,' Dottie said, and Flora nodded.

'Oh yes. Absolutely. Because then we went to see Susan Dunne and made up that stupid message about him sending her his undying love, when in fact...'

'I don't suppose she'd have swallowed that for a minute,' Jennie's friend said. 'Everyone knows he was the most notorious womaniser. He's been threatening to leave her practically since the honeymoon, always taking up with some new girl or another. In fact, Susan almost called the wedding off because it was widely known—and talked about—that he was carrying on with some young girl.'

Flora and Dottie looked at each other.

'That would seem to explain why she behaved so oddly,' Flora commented.

'You mean, she didn't believe he would say he loved her?'

'No, you idiot, because she probably thinks you are his latest floozie. Otherwise how do you explain 'just happening' to be with him when he died? And at that time of night. Also in evening wear?'

'Oh!' Dumbfounded, Dottie thought about that for a moment. That certainly seemed to make sense. It explained Susan's manner, at least. Archie's singing was still inexplicable. As a farewell message it was somewhat lacking in actual information.

'More tea?' Flora asked her. She shook her head.

'Not for me. You go ahead if you want some. Can we go

to Liberty's in a bit? I want to see if I can get some gold fabric for an evening cloak.'

'Gold?' Flora asked, astonished.

'Well, a sort of bright mustard colour, if they have it. It was that picture at the Dunnes' that gave me the idea.'

'Oh Queen Esther?'

'Yes, it looked—unusual, I suppose, but very effective with her dark hair. I thought I might try something like that.'

'Why not? I need some gabardine for a new costume myself. If you like, I'll take your stuff back with me and ask my needlewoman to make it up for you. She's very good.'

'I'm coming back with you, remember? The bald vicar with the bad teeth?'

'Lord yes, I'd forgotten. Well in fact a couple of George's colleagues will be there, so you never know, one of them might do for you.'

'Shut up Flora, or I'll tell Mother you've started smoking again.'

Sergeant Hardy felt a keen interest in how Susan Dunne would behave now that the first shock of her grief had begun to subside.

As before, the large maid, still pale but no longer red-eyed, showed him into the drawing-room. Susan Dunne was seated as before at one end of the sofa, and Hardy couldn't help wondering if she had been there for the whole of the intervening time. She too was remarkably composed, although her cheeks were their usual greyish white. Her hands were folded neatly in her lap, her back ramrod straight. She neither smiled nor greeted Hardy. Beside her sat a grey-haired man of a military bearing. He looked up as Hardy entered the room, and gave the sergeant a brief nod.

Without preamble the gentleman said, 'I hardly think this is necessary. My daughter is not well enough to be questioned. Perhaps the police would do better to press forward with their investigation into how this terrible business came about, rather than coming here upsetting a grief-stricken widow.'

'I'm very sorry for the intrusion on Mrs Dunne's grief, and I am extremely grateful for your forbearance in this matter. I would like to ask Mrs Dunne a few questions which I hope will enable me to proceed with my enquiries.'

'*Your* enquiries? I think not. The name of your superior officer, if you please.'

With an inward sigh, Hardy told Mrs Dunne's father the name of his chief superintendent, the assistant chief constable and the chief constable.

'Wait in the hall whilst I verify this.' The angry ex-soldier marched into the hall and along the corridor. Somewhere in the back of the house, a door slammed.

Possibly this might be his chance, Hardy thought. He glanced at Mrs Dunne who still sat demurely clasping her hands together, her eyes fixed on the uninspiring brown carpet.

'Mrs Dunne,' Hardy began, keeping his voice soft and sympathetic.

She barely lifted her eyes to look at him. 'The hall, sergeant, if you please.' The chill of her voice killed any sympathy he might have felt. Without another word he got up and went to stand in the gloomy hall. As he waited he noticed an intriguing and unusual picture.

It was almost half an hour before Hardy was called back into the drawing-room. He was not invited to sit, nor did he receive either apology for being kept waiting, or for the lack of courtesy. His temper was fairly put out by this time and it was with great effort that he achieved a neutral expression.

Mrs Dunne's father, also standing and trying to make the best of his extra inch or two, said in a stroppy voice, 'Right. Let me get a few things clear. We are not about to be hounded by some jumped-up bobby with an axe to grind. I shall make a statement and you shall leave. Any further contact will be through my solicitor. Do I make myself clear?'

'Perfectly so.'

'Very well. My daughter has no knowledge of her husband's whereabouts nor of his companions for the night in question. That is all we have to say.'

'Thank you, sir. Unfortunately, that is not what I wanted to ask.'

Mrs Dunne's father paused in the act of turning away. As far as he was concerned, the business was now concluded. The expression on his face made it clear he had no intention of responding.

Hardy continued, 'I'd like to know why you are acting this way. Surely Mrs Dunne and yourself want to ensure justice is done, and want to help me to apprehend Mr Dunne's killer. There have been no accusations, not even the slightest slur has been cast upon Mrs Dunne's good name, so I am interested in knowing...'

'I knew your father, Hardy. He was a fool and a coward, and if you think you can...'

'Where was your husband going on the night he was killed, Mrs Dunne? Where had he been? Whom did he see in the evenings?'

'How dare you! I've made our position perfectly clear. You have nothing more to do here. Kindly leave at once.'

Hardy could see it was pointless. The father had worked himself up into a royal rage, and his daughter was icy and uncommunicative. He couldn't arrest either of them for that, much as he would like to. Clearly he would get neither help nor information from either one.

'I am sure that you have ascertained that I am here with both the knowledge and the support of my superiors. Yet still you decline to be transparent. Therefore, I can now only assume that you are concealing some guilty knowledge. Your attitude and behaviour will be mentioned in my report, and you will find yourselves subjected to very careful scrutiny.'

Forced to be content with that, Hardy turned and walked to the door. There may have been exclamations or admonishments, even threats, but Hardy was aware only of a deep sense of relief as he opened the front door and went out into the cold winter air.

*

Chapter Five

It was only ten o'clock but it had already been a very long day for Sergeant Hardy. He had been up late the night before, mulling over the details of the crime. He had arrived early at his desk and had immediately typed up numerous reports regarding the victim, the circumstances of the crime, and his subsequent interviews with witnesses and related persons. He was still feeling irked by his conversation the previous day with Inspector Longden. He still didn't quite know what to do about the Inspector's absence.

At eight o'clock that morning he had gone to the mortuary and discussed the case with the police medical examiner, and had been told what kind of weapon had been used to perpetrate the crime. He made a note in his book to the effect that they were looking for a long, narrow-bladed knife, with a blade approximately eight and a half inches in length.

The mortuary assistant handed two paper bags to Hardy.

'Is this everything he had on him?' Hardy asked the medical examiner, who was busy scrutinising a tray of instruments.

'Yes, quite literally. The large one underneath contains all his clothes and his shoes, and in the smaller one you will find all the personal items from his pockets, and also a watch and a signet ring. That's the second bag the clothes have been in, the first one got so wet it tore, and so we tried to dry the clothes out a bit for you. Anything to help our colleagues in the police force.'

Hardy thanked him with a grin, and turned to a table behind him and emptied the contents of the smaller bag out.

The signet ring appeared to be a valuable one, gold, and with a fairly large diamond set in the centre of a smooth rectangle; grooves radiated from the diamond like the rays of the sun.

The watch was a surprisingly ordinary one, however, with a worn leather strap and a plain face. There was no inscription on the back.

In addition to these, there was a wallet, and a silver cigar case and a lighter of the new Zippo variety. The cigar case was almost full. The cigar case was inscribed to Archie Dunne from his parents on the occasion of his twenty-first birthday.

The wallet looked fairly new, was good quality leather lined with silk, and contained forty pounds, a number of betting slips, a photograph of a scantily-clad young woman who was most definitely not Mrs Dunne, and a few other bits of paper.

Finally, having replaced all these in the bag, Hardy was left with the smaller items: a handkerchief, more or less clean, a small ordinary penknife the handle of which was inlaid with mother-of-pearl, a shilling and a sixpence, a diary with the pencil in the spine, and the usual type of latchkey.

The clothes, apart from being still slightly damp from the rain and somewhat bloodied, were not especially remarkable. There were no tailors' labels.

'You can take them with you if you like,' the medic told him. 'I've done all I need to do.'

Hardy thanked him and gathered everything up once again, and took it back to the police station here he sat and looked through it all much more carefully. Then he began to log each item on a large sheet of paper to add to the case notes.

The diary showed that for the last several months before Archie Dunne's death, he'd been meeting two people each week on an average of two occasions each. At least, Hardy surmised they were people. The dates in question merely showed an initial D or V, followed by a time. Hardy felt reasonably sure these were indications of Dunne's liaisons with women. There were few other entries. Even Dunne's own wedding only warranted a brief note: 'April 4th, Wedding 2pm', and the other details of his life were treated equally briefly, 'May 1st, return from Honeymoon', 'May 12th, Susan's birthday, 26'. There were other birthdays marked, and the Grand National horse race, but nothing that helped to enlighten the policeman.

With a sigh, Hardy set the diary to one side, and entered it into his list. Reflecting on the initials D and V he had seen in the diary, he wondered if the D might stand for Dottie. He hoped very much that it might stand for something else. He didn't want to believe it could be Dottie. He realised that he would have to go back through all the statements and notes he had to try and find a V. What women's names began with V, he asked himself. He got as far as Victoria and Violet, and then was stumped.

At eleven o'clock, Hardy was summoned to a meeting with his superiors: Superintendent Edward Williams, Chief Superintendent William Smithers, and Assistant Chief Constable Henry Rhys-Meadowes. Required to give an account of his actions, he explained what he had done both on the night in question and in the hours since the murder had been reported; he succinctly informed them of all the information he had gathered thus far and gave them an account of his conversations with the medical examiner and other policemen. He outlined the witness testimony he had gathered and expressed his dissatisfaction with the behaviour of Mrs Dunne and her father. There was an indefinable something in the air in the Assistant Chief Constable's meeting room. An air which did not emanate from the highly polished table or the comfortable leather-upholstered seats.

At the end of this account, at a nod from the Assistant Chief Constable, the Superintendent leaned forward and said to Hardy, 'Very well, wait outside if you would, Sergeant. I shall call you in a moment.' Puzzled, the young sergeant got to his feet, briefly half-bowed to the gentlemen and left the room. In the hall, a dozen or so feet from the door, he spotted a chair, and settled himself on it, wondering why they wanted him to wait. What did it all mean? Were they going to take him off the case and give it to a more senior officer? Had Longden returned from his holiday? Did Longden know what was going on? Did he even care?

By the time the door opened and Superintendent Williams looked out and nodded to him, a somewhat depressed Sergeant Hardy had drifted off into thoughts of Dorothy Manderson. Dottie, as he had heard her called. Dottie, as he already called her in his mind whenever he thought of her. Which was often.

At Liberty's, Dottie was thrilled to find some gloriously soft, gold-coloured extra-fine wool that would make a lovely cloak. The saleswoman helped her to find a pattern, and some matching satin to make a beautiful edging. Dottie relished the fresh smell of the fabrics as she and Flora waited whilst the saleswoman cut the stuff, then parcelled everything up together in brown paper, tying it with string. Dottie told her the name of the account and the saleswoman remarked, 'That stuff will look a treat on you, Miss, when it's made up, it really will. Most elegant, and lovely and warm. Just right for this awful damp weather we've been having. We've sold quite a bit of it for cloaks lately, and the ladies have all been very pleased with the results, or so I've been told.'

'Oh! Who else has bought some?' Flora asked, exchanging a glance with Dottie.

The saleswoman cautiously looked about her before leaning towards them and saying, 'Why that poor lady as lost her husband. Drunk I expect he was, though it didn't say so in the papers. Stabbed in the street like a common beggar. Like Russia this place is now, you're not safe in your own home.'

Ignoring this, Flora said, 'Mrs Dunne? She bought some of that same fabric for a cloak?'

'Two lots, Miss. Some for her and a length for her friend Mrs Penterman. And since then there's been two more. Quite a craze, it seems, but a very becoming colour, especially on you Miss. That poor Mrs Dunne doesn't have your nice complexion, sadly.'

In the street, they hurried back to where Flora had parked the car, their packages clutched close against a sudden squally shower. On the way home, they talked about what they had learned.

'Perhaps she just wanted to brighten herself up a bit, perhaps she felt dowdy and depressed and thought she'd win back his affections with a new, brightly-coloured cloak...' Dottie said.

'Well he'd only see it if they went out, and he was on his own when you found him, so...Besides we've been told they didn't go in for socialising. Or at least, she didn't.'

'Do you think he really was with another woman? This young girl we've heard about? Perhaps he had already walked her home, or perhaps she was frightened of getting caught up in a scandal and when he was attacked, she ran away?' Dottie asked.

'Possibly. Some women can be that selfish. Personally if I was with a man and he was attacked, I would stay with him until help arrived.'

'But what if he was a married man? What about your reputation?' Dottie responded.

'Hmm. Tricky. But then I wouldn't carry on with a married man. Do you mind if we go straight home? I'm really not in the mood for any more shopping.'

'That's all right. I've got all the bits and pieces I wanted. And my lovely fabric.'

'Leave it with me and I'll ask Mrs Green to get it made up for you.'

It was the following day. The room was hot and crowded, the noise of voices and scraping chairs was deafening, and that a large number of the spectators had been gathered for some time was evident by the pall of blue-grey smoke hanging just below the ceiling, making the room appear almost three feet shallower than it really was. Dottie felt claustrophobic and wished she hadn't worn her fox-fur wrap.

She squeezed into a gap on the bench next to Flora, George and George's pals Charles and Alistair. Across the way she saw the odious police sergeant sitting between two other men, both in police uniform. The sergeant was in a shiny new suit with a collar that irritated him. Dottie could see the back of his neck was red.

Susan Dunne was accompanied by an older gentleman of an imposing military bearing whom Dottie assumed was her father. Susan was wearing that same tired black costume she had been wearing when they had visited her, although this time she had added a black hat-and-veil combination that partially hid her features. No attempt had been made to soften her appearance with jewellery or a corsage, or indeed any make-up, from what Dottie could see of Susan's mouth and chin. In one hand she clutched her black-edged handkerchief, but as Dottie later realised, at no point during the afternoon's offices did Mrs Dunne feel the need to make use of it. She's acting, Dottie thought. None of it is real.

Dottie herself was both excited at the prospect of giving evidence and extremely nervous. But the proceedings were performed in such a dull manner by the authorities as to rob the occasion of most of its terrifying aspect. It was almost as boring as going to the dentist.

Dottie was called upon to explain how she had happened upon Mr Archibald Dunne, the thirty-one-year-old stockbroker of 191 Ryton Gardens, South West London. She told the gathering that she had returned from the theatre intending to visit her sister's house, as they kept late hours when they had guests and wouldn't mind her turning up so late. She explained how she had got out of the taxi, only to find she had given the wrong house number and that she would have to walk the forty or fifty yards or so back along the road to reach her sister's house. No, she hadn't recognised the gentleman she found lying on the pavement, but her brother-in-law had known him and told her his name later. Bearing in mind not only that she was under oath, but that she felt a moral obligation to continue with the very slight deception she and Flora had perpetrated, Dottie was then forced to add not only that the deceased had sung to her a song she recognised from a particular West End show, but also that he had, moments before dying, clutched her hand and begged her to pass on his message of love to his dear wife.

Dottie felt rather guilty about the lie, especially as she was under oath, and she hoped no one other than Flora— who knew her so well and was obviously also acquainted with the truth—would recognise her deception. She found it hard to look the coroner in the eye as she gave this part of her 'evidence' and was glad she had thought to bring a handkerchief with her, so she was able to cover her guilt by lowering her head modestly and dabbing the handkerchief to her eyes two or three times. She knew that her slender, apparently fragile build, and her youth would create a favourable impression in the minds of all those present. They would see her as a poor brave little thing happening on a desperate but unavoidable situation and keenly affected by the experience.

However, as she glanced around the room, she noted that not only was Susan Dunne frowning in puzzlement but the sergeant was absolutely glaring at her. She faltered as she replied to a question posed by the coroner, and a general murmur of sympathy and approval went around the room. She stammered a response that no, she hadn't seen anyone in the vicinity nor had she seen a weapon. She was excused with a kind smile.

Next the coroner called forward the widow, Mrs Susan Dunne, and he offered her the court's sympathy and asked her to state her name and address for the record. She sat leaning slightly forward. Her small, thin frame and black ensemble gave her the appearance of a gaunt crow hunched against the weather. Her gloved hands gripped one another in her lap as she perched on the upright chair placed in front of the audience.

Through questions put to her by the coroner, she told the court that she and Archibald Dunne had been married for almost a year, since the previous April, and that they had no children. There were a couple more 'background' questions as Dottie termed them to herself, then the coroner asked about the night Archie died. Mrs Dunne said she had seen him leave the house at about seven o'clock that evening, but that he had said nothing about where he was going or with whom, or at what time he expected to return home.

'And after a year of marriage, I knew better than to ask my husband questions,' Susan Dunne said with an air of suffering. Dottie and Flora shared a look and another general murmur went around the room, accompanied by some shaking of heads and pursing of lips.

'Did your husband frequently go out of an evening?'

'Fairly frequently,' she said. 'Usually two or three times a week. He generally left at about the same time of the evening. He normally returned home at about one o'clock, although sometimes he stayed out all night. He used to say that he had been at his club. However, I am not aware which club that was or whether he was there.'

She was thanked and excused. The audience had continued to murmur, but now fell quiet as Alistair came forward, took his oath and began to give his evidence. He had a warm strong voice that carried effortlessly to the back of the room. He told the court he was a medical doctor and that he had been a visitor at the home of Mr and Mrs Gascoigne who were dear friends of his, when

Mrs Gascoigne's sister had raised the alarm. He and his friend Mr Charles Holt, had gone out into the street and had tried to help the deceased as he lay dying but it was immediately obvious that his wound was mortal.

Charles was called to verify what Alistair had already said, and excused again almost immediately.

Next, in the absence of a more senior officer, the police sergeant stood at the front and told the coroner that Mr Dunne had no financial worries and that thus far, it had not been possible to determine a particular motive behind the attack on him. He did not incline to the belief that the attack had been an attempted theft, as the deceased still carried a silver cigar case, his watch, a valuable signet ring and his pocket book which upon examination as found to contain a fairly large sum of money. No one had been seen fleeing the scene, and no weapon or other evidence had yet been obtained. Mr Dunne was not known to have any enemies, nor was he known to have fallen out with anyone of late.

Apart from his wife, everyone will be saying, Dottie thought. It seemed to her that Susan couldn't have made a better or a more subtle accusation against the dead man's character. Clearly everyone's sympathy would be with the plain young wife who stayed fearfully at home whilst her husband went out gallivanting of an evening. But that sympathy would quickly turn to suspicion.

Then the police medical examiner gave his findings. The deceased, a thirty-one-year-old man in good health and with no other injuries, had been stabbed in the chest in such a way as to pierce through the ribs and into the heart. The weapon was a long, thin and extremely sharp blade, perhaps eight to nine inches in length, broader than a stiletto but narrower than a common kitchen knife, and with a very slight curve to the blade. Upon examination he found that the deceased had eaten a light meal and had consumed a pint of beer approximately three hours before he was killed.

The police sergeant stood to request more time to conduct enquiries and the coroner stated that he had no hesitation whatever in acceding this request. Therefore, he adjourned the inquest until such time as the police had all the facts of the case in their hands.

Outside, Dottie, Flora and George were debating the pros of going with Charles and Alistair to lunch at a nearby hotel and the cons of having a few brief words with Susan Dunne once more in an attempt to convey their sympathy. In the midst of all this, Dottie found a hand beneath her elbow and she was abruptly steered away from the group.

'I want a word with you, Miss Manderson.'

'Sergeant—er—whatever-your-name-is. How very pleasant to see you again.' Dottie forced herself to smile even though her heart had plummeted to her shoes. He looked furious.

'What was that you said in there about him sending a message to his wife to tell her he loved her? You haven't mentioned that before.'

'Oh dear. Well, promise me you won't be cross, now will you, sergeant. But the thing is, we felt so awful when we went to see Mrs Dunne, that we just felt we simply had to...'

'You made it up,' he stated in a dangerous tone. Dottie flashed him a brilliant smile to which it seemed he was sadly immune.

'Not exactly...I mean, not to say...well all right, yes we did.'

'You were under oath in there.' He pointed back to the door behind them.

'Yes, but...'

'You were giving evidence in a court of law, namely a coroner's inquest. I could have you charged with attempting to pervert the course of justice. Or at the very least, with perjury.'

'Yes, but you see, having told Susan Dunne that Archie sent his undying love, obviously I had to carry that through or she would have known something was fishy.'

He stared at her.

'I didn't even know you were acquainted with Mrs

Dunne.'

'We were at the same school,' she said, and attempted another bright smile to appease him.

'Of course you were,' he said, and began to walk away. Dottie thought he looked and sounded very tired. He turned back and called, 'Do me a favour—don't make up anything else. Understand?'

She bit her lip and nodded. He turned on his heel and stormed off.

Flora hurried over to grab her arm. 'You know, I think he likes you. George says he's a perfectly decent chap. They were up at Oxford together.'

'Oh?' Dottie's expression was one of studied indifference. 'What a small world. Right ho, I must get home. Got to make myself ravishing for dinner with dear Peter tonight. Wish me luck!'

'Don't be silly, darling, we'll drop you. You can't go home on a bus. Mother would have a fit, and think what the neighbours would say!'

'I always go by bus, it's perfectly all right,' Dottie grumbled, but when the heavens opened and the rain began to pelt down, she shrieked and raced to the car.

'Thank you for seeing me. I'm sorry if I'm disrupting your evening, there are just a few quick questions I need to ask.'

'Of course, Bill, old chap. Er—I mean—Sergeant Hardy,' George hastily corrected himself.

Flora offered Hardy a drink, which he declined. They sat on sofas on opposite sides of a large rug and stared at one another for a few moments, the silence broken only by the occasional sound of a voice or a motor car from the street.

'Erm—look, I do hate to ask you this, but I'm sure you understand that in a police investigation, we are bound to ask questions of a highly personal and sensitive nature.'

'Of course we do,' Flora murmured, and George nodded, but Hardy fancied they both appeared a little more wary. A distance appeared to grow between them.

He cleared his throat.

'Er—so, if I could just ask you about your sister, Mrs Gascoigne. I suppose Miss Manderson—that is to say—was Miss Manderson at all acquainted with Mr Dunne?'

They exchanged a look then Flora immediately said, 'No, she'd never met him.'

'You're quite certain?'

'Quite certain.'

'She couldn't possibly know him, without you being aware of the fact?'

'I'm quite certain she didn't.'

'I see.' He paused, feeling breathless, as though he'd run upstairs. 'And did she know Mrs Dunne at all?'

'Not really. Susan Dunne went to our school, but she was in a different year. We both knew her by sight, nothing more.'

'And Miss Manderson had never spent any time with Mr Dunne, didn't know him, didn't know his wife, in fact had no relations with the couple whatsoever?'

'None,' said Flora, looking mildly irritated now. There was a protracted and uncomfortable silence.

'Well, thank you. That's all I needed to know. Thank you for your time.' Hardy got to his feet, his trembling fingers struggling to fasten the buttons of his jacket.

George also stood up, ready to see Hardy out. Hardy turned at the door.

'Do you know anyone, possibly a young lady, whose name begins with either a D or a V?'

They'd both shaken their heads before Flora added, 'Well of course there's George's sister Diana.'

'And is she acquainted with the Dunnes at all?'

'Oh no, Sergeant, she went to a completely different school to the one Dottie and I attended. She went to Blackheath. We went to Lady Margaret's.'

On his way home from the Gascoignes', Hardy decided, quite on impulse, to take a detour and go to the Dunnes' home. It wasn't late, after all. But there were a few things he needed, so he took a further detour to the police station.

It was almost an hour later when he finally knocked on the door. If no one had answered, or he had been denied admittance, he wouldn't have been particularly surprised, but as it was, the maid opened almost immediately and he was invited to step into the drawing-room.

Susan Dunne, still clad in that one black suit that seemed to be the only clothes she possessed, looked up from a magazine. In a rather bored than annoyed tone she said, 'What is it, sergeant?'

'I wonder if you recognise these?' And he drew from his inside pocket the small jewellery box, opened it and held it out for her to see. She looked. And he caught a flicker of surprise and possibly something else—fear? Then she turned back to her magazine.

'Yes, they were my husband's. You'd have thought he would give his family heirlooms to his lawful wife, but no, he gave them to his mistress. Is that all, sergeant?'

Her tone pricked him and he said, rather curtly, 'No, Mrs Dunne. It is now Inspector Hardy. And I may have further questions to put to you at a later stage.'

Her gaze shifted but she didn't look at him. She said nothing. He left the room without another word. The maid was hovering in the hall, uncertain whether she was needed or not. Hardy ignored her, and turned to the front door. He took out the latch-key that had been in Archie Dunne's pocket, and attempted to insert it into the keyhole. It didn't fit.

*

Chapter Six

The rain had finally stopped by the time they arrived at the rather grand Moyer family seat in Hertfordshire on the evening of Muriel Moyer's engagement ball. Privately, Dottie was still rather astonished that the ball was going ahead in the light of the recent family bereavement. As they entered the galleried reception hall and stood with the other guests waiting to be greeted by the betrothed couple and the bride-to-be's parents, she couldn't help wondering if Susan Dunne herself would attend. Surely she wouldn't? She couldn't, could she? Dottie told herself Archie's widow couldn't *possibly* attend but felt a frisson of excitement. What if she *did* attend? What would that say about her marriage, about her relationship with Archie? Would it be a scandal, or not? Was society so inured these days to the breakdown of marriage or to a lack of observance of the traditions of mourning?

Dottie had put on the new cloak in view of the cold evening and the long journey, and was pleased to find it delightfully warm and the colour was every bit as vibrant and cheering as she had hoped.

'She's here!' Flora, two steps in front of her, turned to

hiss at her.

'No!' Dottie craned her neck to see, and thought she caught a glimpse of a bony, black-clad figure. The sea of bodies swayed and parted, and sure enough there was Susan Dunne, pale as ever but smiling as she shook hands with guests, standing between her parents and the affianced couple.

Dottie whispered in Flora's ear, 'I really hadn't expected to see her...now I don't know what to think.'

'Nor I,' Flora whispered. 'Mother will be scandalised.'

'I'm quite scandalised myself,' Dottie whispered back, and her sister nodded in agreement. And then they were being introduced, and the ladies all smiled and bobbed and the gentlemen shook hands. George, handsome in his evening attire, shook hands with Colonel Moyer and the beaming groom-to-be.

Susan Dunne took Dottie and Flora's hands and, with animosity gleaming in her eyes, she leaned forward, much to Dottie's surprise, to kiss each of them on the cheek as she had the ladies before them. Her lips, barely grazing Dottie's cheek, were cold. Was the woman never warm?

'So nice to see you again,' Susan murmured, but her eyes were already scanning the next arrivals.

'And to see you too,' Dottie responded with feeling. Susan's eyes came back to her from the horizons, and surveyed her with distaste. Dottie added, 'How marvellous to see you so well recovered.'

'One must keep up appearances,' Susan countered with a certain amount of frost. She turned to speak to the couple behind them and they were thus dismissed.

Fortunately, Muriel was very excited to see them. They were introduced to the tall young man who looked considerably younger than she, although in actuality he couldn't have been much younger, Dottie calculated, as Muriel was only twenty years old, and clearly they both had to be old enough to marry. Nor was it to be expected that her parents would permit her to marry a penniless student, although in any other setting Dottie would have put his age at fifteen or sixteen. Periodically he ran a finger around the inside of his collar as if it irked him. Clearly formal wear was a new experience for him.

'This is Clive,' Muriel said, a giggle in her voice. She clutched his arm with the possessiveness of a limpet and appeared to be in her element. Dottie and her party congratulated the happy young lovers and moved on, but then, a thought suddenly occurring to Dottie, she darted back to take Muriel by the arm and led her to one side.

'Muriel,' she began, 'I hate to ask on such a happy occasion, but do you have any idea when poor Archie's funeral will take place?'

Muriel stared at her for a few seconds, and Dottie began to fear she had given offence, but then Muriel said, 'Oh but...you didn't know? The funeral was yesterday. It had to be, or Susan wouldn't have liked to come this evening. Had you wanted to attend?'

Dottie found it almost impossible to hide her surprise. She shook her head to try to pull herself together. 'Well, yes,' she said. 'We specifically asked Susan's—er, excuse me—Mrs Dunne's maid to let us know. When we called on her, your sister was—er—somewhat unwell and had to retire to her room. So Flora particularly asked the maid to let us know about the arrangements.'

'Susan was unwell?' Muriel asked in surprise. She glanced back to where her frosty sister was offering a cool reception to another young couple.

'Yes, I'm afraid she became upset. I expect it was too soon for her to be having visitors. But the maid...'

'Oh dear. Well I'm afraid Leonora is not terribly reliable. I suppose she simply forgot to pass your message on to Susan. I'm so sorry you missed it, although of course it was hardly a happy occasion.'

'No of course not. Very sad. Well, congratulations again, I'd better not keep you any longer from your guests. Thanks so much for inviting us this evening. Can't wait for your special day!'

Dottie hurried back to Flora and George. Flora immediately said, 'And what was all that about?'

'Tell you later.'

For Dottie it was a long and tedious evening. She was neither in the mood for dancing, nor for making witty conversation, nor for toasting the future of the happy couple. It seemed as if the evening would never end. On two occasions she attempted to get close enough to Susan Dunne to engage her in conversation, but both times, Susan mysteriously seemed to get lost in the crowds and reappear on the other side of the room, Dottie's aim frustrated.

At long last they, and almost everyone else it seemed, were claiming their outer garments from the long table in the upstairs gallery that had served as cloakroom. As Dottie wrapped her cloak around herself, once again enjoying the warm soft feel of the golden stuff, a voice behind her hissed in her ear,

'You show your colours openly, sister.'

But when Dottie attempted to turn in the throng to look about her, the only people nearby were women she didn't recognise and she had no way of knowing who had spoken. No one was looking at her or speaking, there was nothing to say the words had existed outside her own imagination. But it shook her all the same.

'What on earth?' she muttered, but had no more time as Flora hurried her away to the entrance hall and out to the car, George having taken his leave of their hosts.

It was raining once more, and Dottie longed for the light clear evenings of summer when you could come out in the evening and look about you. Everywhere there were shadows. She felt the eyes of the darkened windows of the upper reaches of the house staring down at her. She was on edge, feeling as if she were being observed secretly from behind some wall or tree. George shielded them as best he could with an umbrella, as the three of them ran the short distance to the vehicle.

'We're giving old Evesham a lift, girls, hope you don't mind. Sit in the back, will you darling?' Flora replied in the affirmative and just then, the heavens appeared to open that little bit more.

Dottie shivered and pulled the cloak's folds still closer

about her, and immediately felt something sharp prick her finger.

George held the door open and Flora jumped in, sliding across the seat to make room, and glancing back to see what was taking Dottie so long.

'Your dressmaker left a pin in my cloak,' Dottie protested, and quickly shrugged the garment off and jumped inside the car. 'Old Evesham' turned out to be an attractive young man in his early thirties. He jumped into the passenger side and slammed the door against the elements, uttering an oath as he did so. He turned to beam apologetically at the ladies behind him. George hurried round to the driver's seat and leapt in and started the engine. Dottie was still rummaging amongst the folds of her cloak.

'What?' Flora said, then, 'No silly, look—that piece of paper—looks like an admirer has been leaving you love-notes pinned inside your cloak. How awfully romantic! George darling, you never do that for me. Mother said a young man once secretly pinned a note to her shawl at the end of her coming-out ball. What does it say? Perhaps we ought to let George read it first, in case it's something not suitable for a young lady's eyes.'

'Shut up,' Dottie said and she stooped to gather up the scrap of paper from the floor. She unfolded it, her fingertips at once divining by the tiny holes that the paper had indeed been pinned inside her cloak. 'How very melodramatic!' Then she added, 'it's no good, it's too dark to see what it says.'

'You'll just have to wait until we get home, then.' George said. And he and Old Evesham began a dreary discussion about golf clubs.

For the next hour and forty minutes, she was forced to fidget and fret in the back of the car. What on earth was going on? She found it difficult to believe the paper contained the romantic outpourings of some would-be suitor's heart. She had never been the kind of girl to excite such passions in the opposite sex.

'I can't believe they didn't let us know about the

funeral,' Flora said. Then had to repeat it a little louder for the sake of her husband who couldn't hear what she was saying.

'Yes, I know, it's all a bit odd, isn't it? And Mrs Dunne avoided me all the evening. It's very sad to feel so disliked. Surely she doesn't really think I'm the one he was carrying on with?' Dottie commented.

'They're awfully odd, though, the Moyers.' That was the entirety of 'Old' Evesham's contribution. Dottie assumed the young man had a first name, but she was never to discover what it was.

She leaned back into the leather of the car seat, the folds of the cloak arranged over her knees and pulled across to cover Flora's too. The warm heavy air in the car and the throb of the engine began to lull Dottie's restless mind. It seemed like only minutes later George was opening the door and Flora was nudging her and saying, 'Come on, Sleepyhead, we're not carrying you inside.'

Looking about her in confusion, she saw that Evesham had already been despatched and they were parked outside Flora and George's home in Mortlake Gardens.

As soon as they got indoors, George took himself off to his study for a quiet smoke and a read of his newspaper. Flora and Dottie changed into pyjamas and sat in the drawing-room, with a pot of cocoa and a plate of sandwiches. Dottie produced the piece of paper and they stared at it together. It took no time at all to read, but would they ever understand what it meant? The paper contained words written hurriedly in black ink by some unknown but probably feminine hand:

How dare you flaunt the colour of the Queen and her daughters.

'It has to be something to do with the cloak, and me wearing it.' Dottie said. She then told Flora about the whispered comment she had heard when she was collecting her cloak. 'It must have been the same person.'

'I don't think so. Why would they take the trouble to write the message and pin it to the cloak, and risk being seen, if all the time they were going to whisper in your ear when you picked it up? Besides there was no desk in the gallery, no pen and ink or paper or pins. That had to have been done separately. And there were too many people around. Imagine trying to find the cloak you want, write then pin the message onto it, all with so many people there jostling you? And presumably they wouldn't risk being seen, they'd want to remain anonymous too, so...No, that had to have been done earlier, and separately.'

'Flora, that makes things worse. That means there are two of these odd—that dratted word again—women who attended the party and saw me in the cloak. It's all very unsettling. I'm quite upset by it.'

'Yes, I would be too. But there are some strange people in the world, and unhappily, two of them seem to have been at Muriel Moyer's engagement party. I think you're right about it—them—being women though, this is definitely not a man's handwriting. It's too small and neat. George can write neatly, but in a much larger hand. And there's that word 'sister'.'

'I still can't believe Susan was there. I bet Mother will be horrified when we tell her. I'm surprised Colonel and Mrs Moyer would permit such a thing. I mean, I thought it wasn't very nice to allow the ball to go ahead, but one can understand that—such a lot of work would have gone into the preparations, and with so many people invited...but for Susan herself to actually attend a bare week after her husband was murdered...I can't seem to believe it really happened,' Dottie said, and Flora murmured her agreement.

Flora poured them both a cup of cocoa, and handed a cup and saucer to Dottie, then she offered her the sandwiches. Dottie selected two and handed them back. Flora poured a third cup and getting to her feet, said, 'I'll just take this to His Nibs, he always complains if I have cocoa but don't take him any.'

A moment later she was back and she said, 'You know, we were told by your pals in Claridge's that Susan has these odd religious ideas. And then there was that picture we saw, the one which started this whole craze of yours for gold cloaks. And clearly someone was upset by you wearing such a cloak yourself. Do you think this all goes together somehow?'

'The maid, Muriel told me her name was Leonora, said the picture was Queen Esther. Wasn't she the beautiful but ordinary girl who became the King's consort? Do you think that's the Queen the note-writer was referring to?'

'It seems likely, Dottie, what other Queen would make sense in this context?'

'Well who were her daughters? Did they do anything special?'

Flora shook her head. 'Sorry, I'm afraid I am a deep well of Biblical ignorance. If you like I can try to find out.' She yawned. 'But it won't be today. I'm exhausted.'

'I don't think I'm going to wear that cloak again. Not for a while at least.'

'Hmm. I should think not, if people are going to start hissing at you and leaving you messages.'

Dottie gave a sigh. Without really thinking about what she was doing, she reached for a magazine and started leafing through it. Her mind though, was still furiously working to unravel the puzzle. After a few minutes she said, 'I'm rather disappointed to have missed the funeral.'

'Oh quite,' Flora said. 'It's as if they deliberately forgot to invite us to that, too. Which is a shame as I'd really wanted to see who else was there.'

'The other woman?'

'She might have attended. No one can stop you from going to a funeral.'

'Unless they just don't tell you when it's taking place,' Dottie pointed out, somewhat bitterly. 'Muriel said that the maid was unreliable and forgot to give Susan our message about wanting to know when the funeral would be held. But I believe she deliberately didn't tell us, so we couldn't attend. You saw how offhand she was with us when we arrived. I wouldn't put it past Susan to have written that note herself.'

'Possibly. Oh darling, I'm going up, I'm all in. See you

in the morning.' Flora kissed her cheek then left the room.

Dottie continued to sit there for a while, listening to the sounds of the house. She heard her sister go into the study and the soft murmur of her voice as she said goodnight to George. She heard Flora go upstairs, the soft sound of her footsteps as she went to and fro in her room, taking off her things and putting on her nightgown, washing, and the creak of her bedsprings as she got into bed. Dottie sipped her lukewarm cocoa and nibbled distractedly at another sandwich. She thought about Susan Dunne whom she only knew slightly, about Archie Dunne whom she had never known but whose hand she had held as he died, and the dim, cold interior of what had been the Dunnes' family home, and how unhomely and unwelcoming it had seemed.

She herself knew nothing of creating a family home as she lived with her parents, who made all the decisions about the furnishings and the conventions and routines of the house, but she also spent a lot of time in her sister's home, and so she knew the difference between a home and a house where two people simply lived together. She hoped one day, she might herself have her own home. She knew that like her mother, and like her sister, she would have to compromise on the choice of this curtain or that item of furniture because that was what a real home was, a marrying together not just of two people but of two viewpoints and two tastes. In Dottie's opinion, Susan Dunne had not made a home, and Flora had. And she knew she would have to learn as much as possible from both in order to avoid making the same mistake as Susan Dunne, of creating merely a house and not a home.

She had spent almost as much time in Flora and George's home as she had in her parents' this last year and a half. And she was fully aware of the generous nature of her brother-in-law in allowing her to be there so much and not seeming to resent her intrusion on his privacy, especially in the first weeks and months of their marriage. She declined to think about any physical intimacy between her sister and her brother-in-law, it was one of those things you knew happened but it was better not to think about. She could certainly not imagine herself engaged in anything of *that* nature. Holding Archie Dunne's hand as he lay dying was the most intimate she had ever been with a man, apart from wrestling with the Honourable Peter on the doorstep as he 'said goodnight' to her. His lips had been horribly wet and slobbery. She had been reminded of Aunt Adelaide's Labrador. She would definitely need to marry a man who would not practically attack her at her mother's front door and who was a good dancer and had nice warm, dry lips.

Crossly she pushed out of her mind the image of that odious policeman, and instead attempted to force herself to dwell on the prospect of a hitherto unknown young man who would woo her. If only George had a brother! And with these thoughts, a deep sense of relaxation stole over her, and she knew she had to move or she would still be there when everyone got up in the morning.

*

Chapter Seven

Hardy handed over the receipt. The elderly jeweller leaning forward to take it from him with fingers gnarled and bent. Bent from long hours spent carefully piecing, turning and burnishing precious metals. From forming delicate ornaments to adorn the fingers, bosoms and heads of the great and the wealthy.

'Yes, it's one of mine. Hold on.' The old man stooped to retrieve a vast leather-bound tome from under the counter, and leafing through dog-eared pages, he finally paused. Pulling out a loupe from his coat pocket, he huddled over the page, his lips moving as he read the entry.

'Ah yes, I remember. Mr Dunne, of Flat 4, Richmond Villas, College Avenue, to clean and repair a set. Earrings, a ladies' dress ring, and a brooch. I think there may have been a necklace, too, but he didn't bring me that, though I would have liked to take a look at it, purely out of interest. Lovely work. Quite old. Very dirty of course, but still really quite lovely. He should have collected them yesterday as a matter of fact. Hold on,' he said again, and he turned to go through a curtained doorway to the rear of the premises.

A few minutes later he returned with a small wicker basket, velvet folds of cloth sticking out of the top of it.

He separated the folds of velvet to reveal a neat wooden box. The box was removed, set upon the counter and opened. Inside, a pair of pendant earrings and a small ring gleamed softly against a background of more velvet. The stones appeared to Hardy's untrained eye to be sapphires and diamonds, and the gold was very yellow.

'Are they real?' he asked the jeweller, and couldn't help lowering his voice.

'Oh yes.'

Hardy let out a long whistle. 'Worth a few bob.'

'Oh definitely. Very handsome set. Very, very good craftsmanship. About two hundred years old. Quite the loveliest items I have even seen in my career. They were rather grubby. But now, as you can see...'

'I suppose he owes you a packet?'

'No, all paid for. I always take the money up front. One never knows in this line of work...'

'Very wise,' said Hardy. 'I thought you mentioned a brooch?'

'Ah yes.' He turned back to the ledger. 'It says here—I do remember it now, this has reminded me—he came to collect the brooch early. Told me to do that piece first as he needed it for a particular occasion. Tall chap, I seem to recall, modern appearance, youngish fellow. Fair hair, slicked back. One of those ridiculous little moustaches. Not very remarkable apart from that.'

'Thank you, sir. Of course, I'm afraid I'm going to have to take these with me.'

'Very well, sir. I'll just wrap them up for you.'

'It's not a gift,' Hardy reminded him. 'Just some newspaper will do. It's going in my inside pocket. Let me just copy down the entry in your ledger, please.'

'Of course, sir.'

When the Honourable Peter St Clair St John arrived at the Savoy, all the staff snapped to attention and vied with one another to give him the best possible service. He was known as a generous tipper. Dottie, observing his arrival, wondered if his arrival had the same effect as that of the visitation of Kings or Popes in the past. It seemed to her that everything was polished just that little bit shinier for his advent, and the flowers were just a little fresher, the smiles on the faces of the waiters and doormen just that little wider and brighter. The Honourable Peter smiled and beamed and nodded at all who appeared on his horizon. Dottie sighed, and rose from her seat in the foyer to go to meet him. Let's not pretend, Dottie my love, she told herself, Peter is a dear, but he enjoys seeing himself adored by others far more than he adores you!

The Honourable Peter greeted her with pleasure, smiling and hugging her and kissing her gloved hand. And that was the end of his adulation. He glanced about in a calculatedly bewildered manner and immediately the maître d'hôtel was at his elbow, craving to know where the esteemed gentleman would prefer to be seated. Peter waved a vague hand and tables were rearranged, other diners moved, and all was rendered perfect for the Honourable Gentleman.

Almost at the last minute, Peter remembered to wait until Dottie had been seated before taking his own seat. She felt like an amused onlooker as Peter and the maître d' went through the rigmarole of selecting appropriate wines before the discussion of the dishes took place. At no point was she consulted about her choice so she was at liberty to sit back and watch the performance rather as she had done at the theatre. It was a grand spectacle whenever she went out with the Honourable Peter, and she didn't mind too much that she was so greatly overshadowed by his splendour.

Usually.

Tonight she felt a little irked. Possibly it was the way Peter leaned slightly to the left so as to catch his own reflection in the mirrored wall. Or it may have been the way he smoothed his hair down and ran his tongue over his teeth. She felt a little petulant, and resisted the urge to clear her throat very loudly to get his attention. There was no point, she realised. He just wouldn't understand. To him, she was only slightly elevated above the charming floral table decoration between them.

Eventually, having approved the wine, he turned to her and said, 'So I hear you stumbled quite literally on a dead body last week?'

It was not a topic of conversation that she wanted to revive, as it seemed as if no one had wanted to talk of anything else since it happened. But she obliged him with the bare bones of the story.

'Archie Dunne. Poor old sod.'

Dottie did not approve of what her mother termed 'language', especially not in a smart setting such as the Savoy, therefore she treated him to a frown, which he did not notice. The Honourable Peter went on to say, 'I was at school with him, you know.'

'I'm beginning to think everyone was,' she responded. 'Flora's George was too.'

'Oh yes, George Albert Gascoigne de la Gascoigne, yes I remember dear Georgie. A weasly little fellow.'

'So you've said before. He's certainly turned out jolly nicely since then, I'm happy to say.' She didn't know why she wasted a perfectly good snap on him, because once again, he simply didn't notice, and she had been the only one to hear the annoyance in the tone of her voice. He lounged an elbow on the table cloth and failed to notice her withering look. In her mind, Peter had slipped from nice chap and excellent dancer to utter bore. Inwardly she sighed in disappointment.

'Old Archie was a bit of a rum sort, though, what? Very bookish. Very bookish,' he added again, as if he'd enjoyed hearing himself say it. 'Didn't know the wife. Bit dowdy from what I've heard. And very rum too, by all accounts.'

'Yes,' Dottie said. 'But no one seems to know what it is that makes her so—erm—rum.' She despised these common phrases, but hoped that the idea of 'if you can't beat 'em, join 'em' would pay off in further information.

'No, can't say as I know.' Peter agreed.

'But why was he so odd? Apart from being bookish,' she

quickly added, seeing he was about to repeat his new favourite phrase.

'It was just he was always reading some old philosophy or stuff like that. It was all about thoughts and ideas. History. Dusty religious tomes. All airy-fairy stuff you couldn't get hold of.'

'And her? Susan?'

Their first course arrived and she was afraid her attempt to get information out of him would be frustrated by the commencement of the meal, but as soon as the waiter had slipped away with an ingratiating smile, Peter turned back to the topic.

'From what I hear, she was a bit the same. Old Archie always used to say we were living in an artificial way, that it was time for mankind to get back to their true lifestyle, to a better, more real time. Got to return to our natural order.'

'Natural? How so?'

'Search me, Dot, like the primitive tribes, I suppose, all hunter-gatherer stuff. Living off the land and close to nature. Moon tides. Communing with the seasons, and all that rot. Have you seen the new show at the National?'

'Gallery or theatre?' she asked waspishly. She abhorred being called Dot.

'Theatre, you idiot, you can't have a show at a gallery.'

Inwardly she sighed yet again, and outwardly she put on a smile. 'No, Peter, I haven't seen it. Have you?'

'Rather! Excellent stuff, farce you know, terrifically funny. Want to go? I wouldn't mind sitting through it again.'

She didn't really want to, but couldn't think of an excuse so she agreed. Perhaps next time he wouldn't seem such a fool. 'Perhaps we could invite George and Flora to make up a four?'

He wrinkled his nose. 'If we must. You know, old George is as dull as ditchwater.'

'He is not!' she said hotly.

'If you say so. Only I think I'd know as I know lots of the top people, been rubbing shoulders with them since I was born, and so I can pick out a dull one as easy as anything. But I suppose your sister chose to marry the chump, so...'

'Yes, she did,' Dottie said, and clenched her fist in her lap so as not to hit him with it.

'She could have had my brother,' Peter pointed out.

Now there was a man who could bore for England, Dottie thought, but smiled again and remarked that the restaurant was very quiet this evening. It was always like this. She liked the idea of seeing him, and in fact there were occasions when she adored him but sometimes, increasingly of late, he was quite simply an idiot, and she was unsure of making it to the end of the meal without screaming at him or throwing something at him. It just went to show that having the best of everything including education, could not buy good manners, common sense or intelligence.

Peter stated that they were not interested in dessert, and would go straight to the cheese and port. Dottie, who detested port and wasn't overly fond of cheese, called the waiter back, and said she would very much like some dessert, and a coffee to follow. It was difficult to know who was the most surprised by her temerity, Peter, the waiter or Dottie herself. The waiter actually looked at Peter for confirmation, and Peter gave a shrug, which the waiter took as approval and hurried away. As she looked across the table at her companion, a man she had once harboured romantic hopes of, she saw his bloodshot little piggy eyes as if for the first time, the hint of future high blood pressure in his red face and thickening waistline, and in his previously-admired confident manner, a future overbearing pompous bore, and she told herself, remember this, and next time he invites you, turn him down. Flat.

Eventually he took her home. She briefly wrestled with him on the doorstep again and sent him away irritable and feeling unloved. She went inside and leant against the door, eyes closed, and breathed a sigh of relief. She would have to invent some excuse not to see him as she had agreed. She couldn't bear the thought of another evening in his company.

'Dorothy? Is that you? Didn't the Honourable Peter want to come in for a night cap? I hope he won't think we're being inhospitable. He's always welcome in this house, even without an invitation,' her mother yelled.

Not quite as honourable as one might think, from his behaviour just now, Dottie decided. She went to join her parents in the drawing-room. 'No Mother, I'm afraid not. He said he had to get home for an early start in the morning.'

Her mother frowned. 'I'm beginning to think his intentions are not serious at all.'

In spite of her gloomy mood Dottie had to laugh at this. 'No, I don't think they are. Which suits me perfectly. I don't think he's quite my type.'

Her father rustled behind his newspaper. 'Bit of a chinless wonder if you ask me.'

'Well, we didn't ask you, Herbert,' her mother said waspishly. 'And as for you, young lady, you're proving to be far too particular. You could hardly hope to land a better catch than an Honourable.' There was a calming pause, then her mother said, 'Well. Then goodnight dear, I only stayed up to see you when you got home.'

Dottie kissed her mother's cheek and said goodnight. Once her mother was safely upstairs her father emerged and offered Dottie a whisky and soda. She declined but he poured a generous one for himself.

'So he's not your type, eh? Glad to hear it, my love.'

'I wish I could find a nice chap, Father, someone a bit like George. Peter dismissed George as weasly and a bore. But I think George is terribly sweet. One can always turn to him in a crisis. And he and Flora are so madly in love—unlike most of the couples one meets.'

'Ah well,' her father said, 'George and Flora do two things that guarantee they will be happy forever.'

'What's that?' Dottie asked in surprise. This wasn't the sort of thing her father usually came out with.

'They treat one another with respect, and they have

time apart from one another.'

'Gosh. So they do.'

Several miles away, in a different part of London, Sergeant William Hardy sat down to dinner with his mother and sister.

In the relatively short time since Mr Hardy senior had died and left the family practically penniless, Mrs Isabel Hardy had acquired skills she had hitherto never needed. And she had ensured that her daughter had also learned useful, practical skills that had once been considered unnecessary to her future. Mrs Hardy had expected her daughter Eleanor would go to a respectable finishing school in Switzerland, and then come home to marry well. Now, Mrs Hardy thought as she looked across the small table at her seventeen-year-old daughter, she was more than a little concerned about the class of young man her daughter might nowadays suit.

They dined on a clear soup, followed by pork chops with roast potatoes and then apple pie with custard.

'That was very tasty, Mother,' William Hardy said, as his sister removed the dinner plates and brought in the apple pie.

Isabel reached across to pat her son's hand. She gave him a smile. At night, when she was alone in her room, she wept, still, over the necessity of her eldest son giving up his studies and having to work for a living at what she considered a menial job. That he had provided for his sister and her in this way, kept a decent if humble roof over their heads and food on their table was a source of great comfort to her, and she was immensely grateful, but it hurt her very much that he, and his sister, had been so abruptly denied the lifestyle they had been used to living, and the loss of a small but profitable, and eminently respectable private estate.

Eleanor seated herself and cut the pie and served a slice to each of them. 'I'm getting quite good at pastry, too,' she said with a grin, 'I believe this one will be almost edible!'

'I shall reserve judgement,' Hardy laughed, and took a

piece. He pulled several faces of disgust and revulsion before saying, in a teasing voice, 'It's very good, Ellie. Very good indeed. Even Mrs Jeffries didn't used to give us such a good pie. You'll make some lucky chap a wonderful wife one day.'

Eleanor beamed with pride, and their mother managed a smile, though said nothing, but kept her eyes on her plate. It was true. Her daughter was becoming a good little housewife. A good cook. A hard worker in doing the housework. Less inclined to be concerned about her lack of fashion or connections or parties or inability to dine out or go to shows. Very much the suitable life-partner for an office worker or a policeman, or—and fighting back the tears—Mrs Hardy ran through the list in her mind of occupations that would not mean too harsh a life for her daughter. Mrs Hardy dare not think too much about the future and what it might bring.

*

Chapter Eight

Christmas was rapidly approaching. The weather continued to be wet and squally, and very unChristmassy.

Dottie had commitments for the next two afternoons and evenings. The preview had gone so well that Mrs Carmichael was expecting a capacity crowd all eager to spend their money on clothes for their parties and dinners during the festive season, and accordingly, Mrs Carmichael wanted all her girls at the warehouse ready to show all the outfits on both days. By the time Dottie got home at the end of the final session on the second day, she was exhausted and wanted nothing more than to fall into bed.

However, her mother had other ideas.

Mrs Manderson had ambitions for her younger daughter. She considered that Dottie's looks were of an unfashionable, modern type, despite the fact that her daughter earned an excellent living as a mannequin, or 'pin money' as Mrs Manderson herself termed it, and she therefore felt that it was unlikely a successful match would be contracted in the usual way. Dorothy was rather over-tall, at five feet seven inches, which gentlemen often found unappealing, preferring all too often a smaller, more delicate, ladylike build. Not only that, but she was far too bookish and well-informed politically which again, many true gentlemen also found off-putting; she was inclined to be rather serious, and although her figure wasn't too bad, she possessed none of the alluring curves that drew the eye of wealthy young gentlemen, as Florence's had done.

But here Mrs Manderson declined to ponder too long. George Gascoigne, who had not been Mrs Manderson's preferred choice for her eldest daughter, might be a pleasant enough, well set-up young fellow who could trace, if he chose to exert himself that far, his family line back to William the Conqueror, but he had no drive, no ambition; he lacked that ruthless determination to succeed that she felt necessary to a true gentleman. She would never see that young man raised to the peerage. If only Florence could have been prevailed upon to accept Viscount Greenwood.

Setting aside past disappointments, Mrs Manderson returned to a contemplation of her younger daughter's situation. No, she decided, Dorothy could not be relied upon to draw in a suitable admirer under her own steam, so to speak. Her failure to lure in the Honourable Peter was evidence of that. Therefore, Mrs Manderson supposed, the matter of ensuring a proper attachment for her younger daughter would rest entirely in her own hands.

Fortunately, she was up to the task. She had compiled a list, and as soon as Dorothy returned home from her evening out, they would sit down together and go through the list. For she had decided upon the most advantageous and efficient manner of interviewing for the most eligible candidates: The Mandersons were to have a Christmas Party.

In her own day, one was a debutante and 'came out', and this was attended by a wonderful, but business-like, season of balls, dinners, card evenings and theatre parties. And although Dorothy was not yet twenty years old, she had already declined any interest in 'coming out'. Mrs

Manderson knew from past disappointments that Dorothy was not the sort of girl to change her mind. But it was how her own mother had made the Mandersons' match, and if it was good enough for her mother and herself, it ought to be good enough for Dorothy.

Not that it signified in any case, thought his lady as she gazed upon the sleeping countenance of Mr Manderson. He had sat down to 'read the paper' more than an hour earlier, and was now snoring softly; his spectacles had slipped from his nose, his hands still clutched the edges of his crumpled newspaper in his lap, and his head tipped right back to rest on the antimacassar created by Mrs Manderson's great aunt Agnes in the 1890s as part of her own trousseau. Whatever a young man promised in his 20s and 30s to become, in his 50s and 60s he would go the way of all husbands: comfortably napping behind his newspaper. At least, Mrs Manderson consoled herself, she knew where her husband was of an evening, which was more than could be said for her sister Cecilia, all alone in that great big house in Crawley.

Mrs Manderson heard the sound of the front door opening and at that moment the clock in the drawing-room chimed eleven o'clock. Dottie's face appeared around the door. She looked awfully tired, her mother thought, her face was pale and she had shadows under her eyes. She'd never catch a future cabinet minister or a captain of industry looking like that.

'Dorothy, dear, you're terribly late. Your father and I have been worried.'

Dottie cast a disbelieving look at her father who was yawning and rubbing his eyes, pulling himself upright in his chair. His paper was still concertinaed on the floor.

'But Mother, I told you I would be late, although admittedly I hadn't expected to be quite this late, but one of the other girls runs a car, and she had said she'd bring me home. So you needn't have worried.'

'You really shouldn't go about with these fast girls dashing about from place to place in motor cars, Dorothy, think of your reputation. However old-fashioned you may think it, these things reflect badly on a young woman.'

'Mother, she's hardly fast. She's a married woman.'

'Then all I can say is, I'm greatly surprised her husband permits her to gallivant about at all hours doing this modelling thing.'

It was the old argument, and one Dottie knew she had no chance of winning. She came forward to kiss her mother's cheek, about to say goodnight, but her mother held up a hand and said, 'I have something I wish to speak to you about. Let's go into the morning-room to avoid disturbing your father.'

Her heart sinking to her boots, Dottie trailed in her mother's wake. Now what had she done? Her mother held a piece of paper. Dottie's eyes widened in horror. It was The List, she just knew it was. She hardly dared to breathe.

'Well, sit down, dear,' her mother said with a smile. A crocodile smile, thought Dottie. And now she's calling me dear. It's finally happened. She's sold me to a sheikh. Dottie felt rather sick and stared at her mother from her perch on the edge of the sofa.

'Darling, your father and I have been thinking about your Future. And—don't look like that, Dorothy—it is not a death sentence!' her mother snapped, then smoothed out the piece of paper on her knee. It was! It was The List. Dottie could see the long column of spidery black writing. The Suitors.

Oh

Damn

And

Blast

It.

'Mother, I'm afraid I...'

'Nonsense, dear. Now listen. We've decided we shall have a party this Christmas. This is a list of young men who are—well, eligible—for want of a better word, and I'd like you to cast your eye over it, to see if there's anyone you particularly feel you'd like to include, someone you may wish to take the opportunity to get to know a little better. I'm also considering a few other social events during the Christmas and New Year season. And of course there will be the usual New Year ball to attend at the Gascoignes'.'

She held out the list, and without intending to do so, Dottie found that she had taken it and was now holding it at arm's length in front of her, like a dead rat. Her hand shook.

'Mother, really I've the most awful headache, so perhaps...'

Her mother, unconvinced, observed her daughter coldly for a few moments then tutting with annoyance, said, 'Oh very well. Show it to Florence and tell her to help you with it. I want to know within the next few days so there's enough time to send out the invitations.'

Dottie had just thought that there was her key to avoiding this most unpleasant of situations, when her mother added those most terrifying of words, 'If you don't choose, I shall make the selection for you.' At the door, she turned and added, 'No more than six single young men.'

With that, Mrs Manderson swept through the doorway and across the hall as if clothed in imperial robes. At the foot of the stairs she paused, turned again and said, 'As your Loving Mother, naturally I only want to see my Youngest Child happy before I Die.' And she swept on, calling in a terse voice, 'Come along, Herbert.'

Gosh, thought Dottie, full of admiration. That was the best performance yet of Martyred Mother Of Ungrateful Child. I must tell Flora tomorrow. She shook her head, still in grudging respect. Her mother was the only woman on the planet who could enunciate capital letters with such devastating effect.

She heard her father go upstairs. Dottie got up and went into the warmer drawing-room, and kicking off her shoes, curled up on a sofa, her only light that which came from the dying embers of the fire. The house about her creaked into slumber, and Dottie's eyes grew heavy. She didn't want to go up just yet, though, this was her favourite time of day. She glanced at the list of names without really seeing them.

It had been fabled between the two sisters that their mother had drawn up a list of acceptable potential sons-in-law whilst they were both still in the nursery. Luckily Flora had quickly met George, so she had avoided that particular torture, but clearly although still not of full age, Dottie had run out of time. At the head of the list was The Honourable Peter St Clair St John.

'Well we can scratch him, straight away,' murmured the drowsy Dottie. She got no further. In the morning her mother found her there sleeping, the list still clutched in her hand. At least it convinced her that Dorothy was taking her efforts to find her a suitor seriously.

'Darling girl,' Lavinia Manderson whispered and she bent to smooth Dottie's hair out of her eyes, then dropped a soft kiss on her hair before clearing her throat briskly and, in a no-nonsense manner demanding that Dottie get up at once and go upstairs and dress.

'So how are things coming along, Hardy?' Superintendent Edward Williams asked, and indicated a chair.

Hardy sat, and, unsure of the correct way to proceed, pulled out a notebook and quickly outlined the results of his enquiries to date. After a few minutes, the Superintendent's eyes seemed to be dulling over slightly and Hardy felt sure his words were falling on deaf ears.

As soon as he paused, Williams took the opportunity to say heartily, 'Excellent work, very good. Clearly you are making progress. Well, I must tell you that we have been talking, the higher-ups and I, about the fine job you're doing with this investigation. I want you to know we have every faith in you. And as a result of our deliberations, we have decided to award you with a promotion to the rank of Detective Inspector, with the concomitant raise in salary, with immediate effect. You'll need an assistant, I'll let you choose a chap for yourself, someone reliable, make sure he's a good fellow, someone who's got your back. And completely beyond reproach, goes almost without saying,

I should hope. If you don't know of anyone, we'll fix something up for you. See my assistant on the way out, he's got a few other bits and pieces for you, and a letter of promotion, of course, keep things official. Well, well, I won't keep you, but congratulations, young fellow, very well done.'

It was clear that he wasn't expected to linger. Pausing, Hardy said, 'If I might just ask, sir, what about Inspector Longden?'

'Who? Oh Longden? Yes, well you know. Retired. Put out to grass.'

A sobering thought, Hardy decided.

And with that, the Superintendent was extending his hand to shake Hardy's whilst simultaneously propelling him towards the door. A last vigorous handshake and a 'Jolly good show,' and Hardy was in the outer office and the door was already closing behind him.

It took a few minutes for the Superintendent's assistant to put the finishing flourish to the great man's signature then neatly blot, fold and envelope the letter before handing it to Hardy with a smile and a brief, 'Congratulations.' There was a larger, brown envelope of other papers.

Hardy was back in the crowded room he shared with several other sergeants less than ten minutes after leaving it. He drew out the letter, unfolded it, and nearly choked when he saw the salary. Any pity he felt for Longden faded. This would make a huge difference to himself and his family. And possibly to someone else too.

After a moment, he went in search of his pal from the beat, Constable Maple.

'Here, Frank, got much on at the moment?'

'Bill. No, just got this drunk and disorderly to finish off. Why, need a hand?'

'In a manner of speaking.'

'What you need,' Flora said to her sister upon hearing about Dottie's interview with their mother the previous evening, 'is a sort of progressive type, but one with pots of money.'

Dottie wrinkled her nose. 'Progressive?'

'Well you don't want some stuffy old club-bore conventional type.'

'Hopefully he won't be old at all,' Dottie said, 'but I'm only nineteen, why can't I just be left alone to enjoy my life? Why do I have to be married off?'

'You just do,' said her sister. 'It's the only way to get away from Mother, and she would die of shame if you simply went and shared a flat with some girls. It may be very modern and all, but you know Mother doesn't approve of girls who are independent. And with you not getting your trust fund until you're twenty-five or married, it's better to give in now and enjoy the money as soon as poss.'

'I earn enough from my modelling. In fact, Mrs Carmichael is really quite generous.'

'I'm surprised you get away with it. If I'd ever wanted to do that sort of thing Mother would have had forty fits. She was far stricter with me than she ever was with you.'

'It's because I'm the baby,' Dottie said smugly. 'I'm the one who was spoiled rotten. You were the one raised when she still had noble ideals about how a young woman of a good family should be brought up. You were the gold standard, I'm the product of disillusionment and compromise. And I'm the one who usually finds a way to not do as she's told.'

'You're certainly the bad egg. So let's have a look at this list then. I told you she would have one.'

'I really didn't believe it, not until last night, but as soon as I saw the paper in her hand, I just knew...Peter's at the top, obviously.'

'Obviously. So we'll scratch him, then. Oh God, not Gerald Billington! You certainly can't marry him, he can't dance to save his life. And Algernon Stamford-Hughes is a bore. *Very* old school. George's father detests him.'

'George's father is very astute when it comes to young men. Perhaps he should be the one to fix me up? I might suggest it to Mother.'

Flora snorted and cackled loudly. Heads turned in their direction in the Lyon's Corner House. Then she became very solemn again. 'Darling, remember, this is really only a list of guests to invite to the Christmas bun fight, you don't actually have to marry any or all of them. Just ask yourself if you can bear any of them for one evening. That's really all Mother requires.' Then she said, 'Oh my goodness, she's even got Montague Montague on here.'

'I don't think...' said Dottie screwing up her face in an effort to remember.

'You *do* know him—the limp, the monocle, the shooting stories—all blood and guts and stuff. Hideous man. Even his own mother cringes when he starts in on one of his interminable anecdotes.'

'Oh, M'Dear Monty!' Dottie said. 'How could I have forgotten?' She finished her coffee and felt business-like. She pushed away the crockery, produced a pencil and handed it to her sister. 'Right let's sort this out once and for all. Then perhaps Mother will leave me alone. Cross off everyone who is boring, stuffy, antiquated, bald, has bad teeth or calls everyone M'Dear. Oh and if they can't dance, they've got to go, too. I must at least get a dance now and then.'

With a number of decisive strokes, Flora went to work. After thirty seconds, she surveyed her handiwork.

'Who's left?' Dottie asked.

'See for yourself.' Flora said, and Dottie saw that she was laughing. She took the paper, glanced at it and groaned.

'Really? Only Peter? And he may not be bald or boring and I know he can dance, but really, *surely*, marriage should be the bringing together of two loving souls, not three. There's no room in a marriage where the man loves himself even more than you do.' By the time she'd finished, Dottie was near tears. Flora took her hand, surprised by her sister's sudden emotion.

'Don't fret, Dottie dear, it's not so hopeless. Look I'm sure there are lots of nice men we could invite, and you know, some of these might not be so bad once you get to know them...'

Dottie hiccupped, and carefully dabbed at her eyes. 'I'm sorry, I don't know what came over me. I suddenly felt I was going to be an old spinster all alone like Miss Havisham, all bitter in a smelly old wedding dress and no one to marry and piles of mouldy food.' Her chin quivered again and Flora hurriedly poured her some more coffee.

'Have another drink, and let's try to cheer up a bit. Cake?'

Dottie took another petit fours. 'And a fat Miss Havisham, at that.'

'Nonsense, you're skin and bone. With fabulous limpid fairy-pool eyes. And hair. Lovely hair, Darling, any man would love you just for your hair. When I get home I'll ring up George's mother and get her to have a think about someone nice to invite. And there's always George's cousin Francis. I know he's a bit on the portly side but he's terribly jolly and fun, and very generous and sweet. And he *adores* dancing.'

'Yes he's lovely, but,' Dottie dropped her voice. 'I don't think he likes ladies if you catch my drift.'

Flora looked at her in surprise. 'Really? Are you sure? Hmm, yes, you could be right, thinking about those silk handkerchiefs he always has in his breast pocket. And he is quite *careful* about his appearance...' She paused for a moment's thought then nodded, 'Yes, so probably not Francis then. Cheer up, Dottie, we'll think of something. You're not quite on the shelf yet. And when you are too old to marry off, you can always come and live with us. You can be a governess to my children.'

'Thanks a million! Give me that list.'

'Good afternoon Miss Manderson, Mrs Gascoigne.'

Dottie and Flora glanced up to see the man who was addressing them. Dottie felt a wave of irritation go over her.

'Oh for goodness sake, sergeant! Can't you see my sister and I are having afternoon tea? What is it *this* time?'

The policeman looked quite taken aback. He performed an odd stiff bow and said, 'Please excuse me, I was passing by on my way to a table and saw you sitting here. I thought it would be rude to ignore you completely. I see that I was wrong.'

Dottie flushed red to the roots of her hair. Flora covered her mouth with a gloved hand and concentrated on her plate.

'I-I'm so terribly sorry, sergeant, for a moment I thought, I-I...'

He nodded and walked on, taking a seat at a table further towards the rear of the room. His companion was a well-dressed young woman who leaned in to say something to him, her eyes fixed on Dottie. Dottie saw him say something to the woman, and the woman bit her lip in the same way Dottie did, when she felt a need to prevent herself from laughing inappropriately.

'Oh I feel terrible,' Dottie said to her sister, who was still smiling.

'You're definitely a bad person. That poor man! Honestly Dottie,' Flora teased. 'How could you?'

'Well in my defence he has crept up on us several times now. I thought it was another of those times. Should I go over and apologise, do you think?'

'No dear, you've already apologised. I'm sure he wants to forget the whole thing.' Flora changed the subject and for a few minutes they conversed about her and George's plans for the Christmas season.

As they waited for more coffee to arrive, Flora pulled the list over for another look. 'Now look at this. At the bottom of the list. The Honourable Cyril Penterman. Why do I know that name?'

'One of the women who had some of that gold-coloured material was a Mrs Penterman. The saleswoman at Liberty's told us she was a friend of Susan Dunne's.' The policeman completely forgotten, Dottie looked at Flora in excitement.

'Hmm. Perhaps it's the same family. It's hardly a common name. Perhaps we should get Mother to invite him, then we can try and get something out of him.'

'If she's a friend of Susan's,' Dottie said, 'she may have

been at the engagement party the other evening.'

'Yes, and it may even have been her who hissed in your ear, or who pinned the note to your cloak—anxious to preserve the fabric for her sole use. Or rather their sole use, as they've both got some. I think you should suggest him to Mother.'

'You crossed him off as unsuitable.'

'Only because I didn't know him and he was the last one on the list so I thought he may as well go too.'

'Well you didn't cross off Peter,' Dottie pointed out irritably. 'I suppose you think he'd make me a fine husband!' A shadow fell across their table and she glanced up to see the police sergeant and his companion were walking past. The sergeant nodded curtly and his companion smiled at them.

Dottie put her head in her hands. 'He heard me, didn't he? He'll think I'm a gold digger or something. Oh Flora it's a nightmare!'

Flora frowned at her. 'What's the matter? Why does it matter what he thinks? He doesn't even know you.' She hesitated a moment, staring after the retreating couple. Her eyes came back to rest on her sister thoughtfully. 'You like him. You...'

'No, I most certainly do not,' Dottie said hotly, and got to her feet. 'I'm going to the cloakroom. When I come back I think we should not only change the subject but you should take me home.' She hurried away without waiting for a response, leaving her sister watching her with a knowing look.

*

Chapter Nine

'What do you think?' Maple asked. He tugged at the front of his waistcoat and straightened his tie.

'Very smart. Brother-in-law?' Hardy tried to hide a smile but failed dismally. Maple's enthusiasm was not to be dented, however.

'In a way it's lucky he died when he did,' Maple said with a broad grin. 'Otherwise what'd I wear for this new job?'

'I don't suppose your sister is able to take quite such an optimistic view of things.'

'Every cloud,' Maple said with a shrug. 'At least she's getting the insurance. And with what she'll save with him not being out every night down the boozer, I think she'll be all right. In fact, she says she only sees him a little bit less since they buried him than she did before, and at least he don't come home at all hours and frighten the children.'

'The suit is very smart,' Hardy said, 'How many did you get?'

'Just the three. But she says I've got to save the dark grey one for best, so that leaves me two for work. Should be enough.' He did a little pirouette as he tried to see himself from every angle in the glass of the office window. He stopped, aware of Hardy's look, and added, 'I can't thank you enough. I don't know what you said, but you must of made me sound like bloomin' Sherlock Holmes. So thank you, Bill. It means the world to me, I wouldn't have got this chance without you.'

'No need for that. They asked who I thought was ready for promotion and I told them, in all honesty, that I thought you would be excellent for the job. I need someone I know I can trust.'

Maple held out his hand and Hardy shook it. It was a solemn moment broken only by Maple belching then saying, 'Must be time to get down to the pub.'

'You're buying,' Hardy told him.

'Steady on, I haven't had me pay rise yet, you know.'

Hardy opened the front door, and as he came into the hall, his mother called out, 'We're in the kitchen. A cup of tea, dear?'

He paused outside the kitchen door, thrust the bouquet of flowers around the jamb and waited. He smiled when he heard her gasp, heard her hurrying steps and then she grabbed the bouquet with one hand and put the other up to his cheek.

'Oh William! Dearest! They're beautiful!'

He bent to kiss her. 'Happy birthday, Mother.'

'Oh William!' Tears filled her eyes. She put her nose deep into the midst of the flowers and inhaled the scent.

'Oh William!' she said again, tearful yet smiling. 'Darling, you shouldn't have. How can you afford...'

'Ah now!' he said, putting up his hand to stop her, He kissed her cheek again. 'It's your birthday, after all.'

His sister came over from the stove, her apron covered in the various blobs and smudges she had acquired during the preparation of their dinner. She looked at William, surprised by the extravagance, and puzzled by his enigmatic smile.

'It smells good,' he said with a nod towards the stove.

'Unless that's the laundry.'

'Beast!' she laughed, punching his arm.

'These roses remind me of the ones on the terrace at our old house,' he said.

His mother nodded, her eyes cloudy with the memory of her beloved home of over twenty years. She gave a sigh, set her shoulders back, as if pushing the memories away, and in a brisk voice, said, 'Yes, dear, they were lovely. And these are lovely too, but it's really very naughty of you. Now then, your tea.'

They all sat around the kitchen table, and she poured his tea and set a plate of rock buns within reach. Then, before anyone could say anything else, Hardy put his hand over his mother's and said, 'I don't want you to be upset, Mother, but I'm afraid we're going to have to move from here.'

She looked at him, and there was fear in her eyes. 'Oh, William, I don't think...'

'I'm sorry, Mother. I know that you've got settled now, and you're used to this place, and I know that it wasn't easy for you. But it really can't be helped. You're going to have to make up your mind to it, I'm afraid. We shall be moving to a four-room house with a daily maid. I'm sorry.'

She stared at him; they both did. He felt some compunction at seeing the tears start into his sister's eyes, at seeing their confusion and dismay. Gradually they realised he was teasing, and confusion and fear gave way to hope and a tentative joy.

'Four rooms? Are you mad?' Eleanor said scornfully, but she began to smile at him.

'A maid? *Daily*?' Mrs Hardy said, and at the same time, Eleanor said again, 'Bill, what on earth are you talking about?'

He pulled the letter from his pocket. 'Read that.'

They read it. Twice. His mother looked up, tears again in her eyes.

'But—but...William, it says here that you've been promoted to the rank of Detective *Inspector*.' Her voice fell away to a whisper.

'With immediate effect!' his sister added, her eyes round with excitement. 'Look at that salary!'

'Yes, and I have my own office; my name shall be on the door—eventually,' he told them, and then setting aside his teasing manner, took their hands again and said more soberly, 'Things have been difficult, we all know that, and the two of you have been through so much. And I've been so proud of how both of you have just got on with things and adjusted to our new lives, without the slightest complaint. But things are going to get better for us. I've been given a substantial pay rise to go with the promotion, and the sooner we get out of this damp, dreary hovel, the better I shall like it. And I'm perfectly serious about the daily maid and the four rooms. We shall find a lovely home in a nice area, and we will be much more comfortable.'

'Oh William!' his mother said yet again, her eyes glistening.

The following week Flora and George collected Dottie in a taxicab and took her to the theatre. The sisters had hatched a plot to see *Gay Divorce* yet again, but this time they were going to pay careful attention throughout, just in case they were able to spot a previously unseen connection with the dead man.

'Although,' Flora remarked as they waited for the curtain to go up, 'perhaps it's just the whole divorce thing—we've already been told they were not happily married—what if she'd actually threatened or even begun divorce proceedings? What if it's just the word divorce that is the key to this?'

'From what we've heard she'd already threatened to leave him a dozen times before,' Dottie hissed back. The orchestra struck up with enthusiasm, the curtain rose and the audience applauded wildly.

'Perhaps she paid someone to do him in?' George suggested with relish, leaning across his Beloved to talk to her sister.

Throughout the first part of the show Dottie ruminated on his suggestion. At the interval, George found them seats at the last empty table in the corner of the bar-lounge, and was then dispatched to procure the drinks he'd ordered when they first arrived at the theatre, the waiters taking too long to get to them.

'Gosh it's warm,' Flora commented and flapped her programme to cool her face. They talked about the show, agreeing that although it was wonderful—even after seeing it four times already—nothing really struck them as being relevant to Archie Dunne's death, nor especially noteworthy.

'What is taking George so long? I'm absolutely gasping. And it'll be time to go back to our seats soon!' Flora complained.

A minute later Dottie spotted him pushing his way through the throng, cocktails bounced madly in his hands, his elbows out to fend off anyone who got too close and a broad grin on his face. Dottie recognised the look. 'He's found something out,' she warned her sister. They watched his approach and could tell he was excited about something. He looked like a schoolboy bursting to tell a secret.

'You'll never guess what!' he said at the top of his voice when he was twenty yards away.

'Good evening, Miss Manderson,' a voice spoke, much closer to hand. Dottie jumped half out of her skin and turned to see the man she thought of as 'that odious policeman' standing there.

'S-sergeant, I'm afraid you startled me. Do you always sneak up on people like that?' she said, giving herself a few minutes to recover her poise. 'Erm...of course you know my sister and her husband, Mr and Mrs George Gascoigne. Here comes George now.'

'Coming through!' George called cheerily as he negotiated several plump ladies, and set the glasses in front of Flora and Dottie. He quickly shook hands with the sergeant and to Dottie's intense amazement, gestured to the policeman to join them at the table.

Dottie couldn't think of anything to say, and it seemed she wasn't the only one as no one spoke for a full minute. George pulled a glass from the pocket of his evening coat, and then a small bottle of something strong from the other, and proceeded to put together his own drink. The ladies occupied themselves with taking dainty sips of their cocktails and making appreciative sounds.

'So what brings you here, Bill, old chap? Or should I call you sergeant? Are you on duty or just taking a well-earned night off?' George asked.

Dottie, still recovering from her annoyance at having the policeman sitting next to her, recalled then that George and the sergeant had been up at Oxford at the same time. It still felt a little strange to think of Hardy as a real person who did normal things such as going to university or to the theatre. As a policeman he was terrifying yet so annoying, and the policeman persona tended to eclipse all else. The policeman in question fidgeted and replied to George,

'No indeed. I'm here in pursuit of my enquiries, trying to obtain information pertaining to the case.'

'Oh by Jove, so are we!' George said, and Dottie was tempted to kick him under the table to make him shut up, but decided against it, as she knew he wouldn't understand what she meant, and she was worried about the possibility of kicking the wrong person. Not that she wouldn't like to kick the policeman sitting next to her like a sack of potatoes in that horrid old overcoat.

The sergeant observed them through narrowed eyes, and seemed about to say something repressive or cautionary when the bell rang for the end of the intermission, and unable to stop herself, Dottie snatched up her evening purse, pushed back her chair and said in an overly bright voice, 'Oh good, time to get back! I can't wait for it to start again!'

And grabbing her sister's arm, she hastened back to their box, leaving the two gentlemen scarcely enough time to stand up as they hurried away. The men followed at a more leisurely pace, parting at the head of the stairs, and

George followed the ladies along the hall to their box whilst the sergeant ran lightly down the stairs and into the main theatre, pushing his way along a row in the stalls to reach his own seat.

'What on earth was all that about?' George asked when they were finally all in their seats.

'Sorry, George dear, I just had to get away from that dratted policeman. I was sure he wouldn't be particularly pleased to hear we are conducting our own investigation. Plus, there's just something about him that makes me squirm with discomfort,' Dottie said. Then, 'So George, what did you find out?'

'Sounds like you've a guilty conscience, Dottie. Ladies, you will be very proud. I'm definitely a sleuth of the finest order. A well-placed pound note enabled me to discover that our deceased friend had been in pursuit of a certain young lady who sells cigarettes in this very establishment.'

'A whole pound!' Flora grumbled.

'A cigarette girl?' Dottie said, and felt a twinge of disappointment. 'If that's true, Archie Dunne wasn't the nice man I'd hoped he was.'

'I know what you mean,' Flora agreed. 'I had such high hopes that the rumours of his philandering were spurious. How sad. Poor Susan. And well, you know, what a shame. So it was just a cigarette girl all along.'

'Do we know which one?' Dottie asked. 'Would it be possible to ask her a few questions? Well, obviously it would have to be you who did that, George.'

'Talk to a pretty girl? Oh well, if I simply must. I'll try to catch her when she comes round. No, by the way, I don't know which one, but I will courageously interrogate them all until I find the right one. Give it another half an hour and no doubt there'll be a girl in the corridor outside.'

And so the show recommenced. Dottie, leaning forward with her elbow resting on the parapet of the box, and her chin in her hand, remained completely oblivious to what was taking place on the stage. The actors moved, spoke their lines, sang and danced, but all she could think about was that odious policeman, and the fact that, after all,

Archie had been nothing more than a womanising cad. And all this time, she thought to herself, I've imagined him as a noble and tragic figure, when in fact the whole thing is merely sordid and horrible. No doubt Archie was killed by the cigarette girl's jealous boyfriend with a sword-stick. Dottie shook herself and tried to concentrate on the rest of the show, unaware that below them in the shadow of the stalls, the sergeant had been watching her the whole time.

About half an hour into the second act, George wandered out into the hallway and sure enough a pretty young woman of about twenty was there, holding a box of smoking requisites suspended from her shoulders by broad straps. Upon his approach she whisked out her little electric torch and played the beam over her range of wares.

'Good evening sir, what would you like?' She fixed him with a bright smile and George felt embarrassed. She looked like a sweet little thing. He hesitated, trying to think of the best way to proceed. It was difficult to find the right words.

'Perhaps a nice cigar?' she suggested, seeing his diffidence. 'We have several different brands including some really special Cuban ones in this corner, or if you prefer, we have some miniatures and cigarettes.'

'Actually, if you don't mind, Miss—er...'

'Valerie.'

'Oh, er, Miss—Valerie. Er—gosh that's an awfully nice name...'

'Thank you, sir. What was it you were wanting, sir?' She smiled still, but her eyes were wary.

'It's a bit awkward, Valerie, and I'm not terribly sure of the best way to go about it, so I'm just going to come out with it, and I hope you won't be cross with me. Um—a friend of mine recently passed away and I'm sort of wondering if he might possibly have been a friend of yours too. Um—his—er—his name was Archie Dunne.'

She looked at him with cool eyes. Whatever she'd been

expecting, it wasn't this. Her eyes seemed suddenly much more mature than the rest of her, he thought. She said nothing. Panicking slightly, he ploughed on, 'Of course you mightn't know him after all, I was just sort of hoping. You see, I've been told he had a friend who sold cigarettes here and I was rather hoping it might be you.'

'It wasn't,' she said. 'At least, well I suppose it sort of was.' She was wrinkling her nose up, trying to find the words to explain what she meant. 'He came to me and asked me if I'd help him out. I thought it was going to be the usual, you know, but it wasn't. Usually when a certain type of gentleman sees me, he thinks he can buy me at the same time as he buys his fancy cigars, but I'm not that sort of girl.'

'No, no, of course you're not, Miss—er—Valerie,' George said and he blushed as an elderly couple pushed past them in the hallway and continued on towards the stairs, glancing back once or twice to direct looks of disgust at him.

'Oh dear,' said George. He bit his lip. 'I suppose you wouldn't come into the box, would you, only...'

'Certainly not! I told you, I'm not...'

'My wife and my sister-in-law are there, they'd be chaperones, if you like.'

'I can't, I've got these bloody cigarettes to sell. There's not much more I can tell you anyhow. I met him here, a couple of months ago, when he came to buy some cigarettes and we got talking. Archie, he wanted me to help him with something. He wanted me to pretend to be his bit on the side, so's he'd have an excuse to pop out from home of an evening. He was convinced his wife was carrying on with someone, and he wanted to be able to follow her without her knowing. So a couple of times he'd say he was going to the theatre, and she'd think he was with me. But then, he just stayed outside in the street and watched the house. Like I said, he was just trying to find out where she went, and what she was up to.'

'Did he tell you what he found out?'

'Not really, but I know he found out something. It fairly

upset him. He said it wasn't what he thought it was and that it would mean changes to his domestic—what-d'you-call-'em—arrangements. His home life. I took that to mean he was slinging her out. But I don't really know what really happened. He only came back to see me the second time, and he paid me twenty quid for helping him out, not that I even did anything. And if she or anyone was to ask me about him, he wanted me to just pretend I was new and didn't know anything about it. I had to say I'd been brought in to replace a girl who got the sack for carrying on with the clientele. He said to tell her we're all called Valerie, it's part of the job. That way his wife wouldn't think it was actually me and make things difficult for me. That's it, the whole thing. It's a real shame he's dead, he seemed like such a nice chap. Really upset he was, at the thought of his wife carrying on with someone else behind his back. Are you sure you don't want anything from the box, sir?'

'No, sorry, I'm afraid not. Erm—look you've been very helpful, Valerie, I do hope you'll keep our conversation to yourself. I wouldn't want anyone to misunderstand our friend's motive, or to cause any embarrassment to the family now that he's...I've got to dash. Thank you so much.' George deftly transferred two neatly folded ten-pound notes into her hand and hastened back to the box to tell Flora and Dottie what he had learned.

It was difficult to talk during the show, however, as the people in the box next to theirs kept shushing them, and then during the second intermission the noise was just too much to make themselves heard. He promised to tell them everything in the taxi on the way home, and meanwhile they'd just have to be patient, which was easier said than done.

Dottie was greatly relieved that she didn't see the police sergeant again during their trip to the refreshments lounge during intermission, as for some mysterious reason of his own, he stayed away, and she felt able to relax and enjoy the spectacle of the people in all their finery standing around her. She didn't even see him once she came back to her seat. When she leaned on the parapet and looked down into the stalls she could see that someone else was now occupying his seat and the policeman was nowhere to be seen.

'Thank goodness,' she said. 'He seems to have gone.'

'Who, darling?' Flora asked.

'That odious policeman,' Dottie said, and didn't understand why her sister suddenly turned to smile at her husband.

George snoozed through the majority of the final part of the show, and it was a relief all round to just pile out of the theatre and into their taxi and collapse back against the seats.

And then he told them everything.

The two women sat back and exchanged knowing smiles.

'What?' George demanded. 'What is it?'

'She's having a baby,' Flora said shaking her head in realisation. 'Of course. How could I have been so dense? That explains why she is so emotional, and not feeling well. And those mysterious visits, or whatever Archie thought she was up to, that he followed her for...'

'...were just her visits to her doctor!' Dottie finished. 'Yes, of course!' Her smile faded. 'Gosh, poor Susan, left a widow when she's just found out she's expecting. How absolutely horrible for her. And for the poor little baby. Perhaps that's why she's been so determined to soldier on as if nothing has happened? Perhaps she feels she's got to keep going for the sake of the baby?'

'Oh it's awful! Poor Susan. Do you think anyone else knows?'

'I bet her parents do, and probably Muriel too,' Dottie said. 'Perhaps we'd better not let on we know, if we should see her again. Which I doubt, seeing as she went to so much trouble to avoid us at Muriel's engagement bash.'

'In any case, we can't give Archie away,' George pointed out, and they both nodded in agreement. 'It's quite nice to know there wasn't anything untoward going on, just a little case of marital misunderstanding.'

'I'm surprised she doesn't look pregnant,' Dottie said. Flora, older and wiser, smiled and said,

'Well it won't show for a few more weeks yet, and if she's only just found out, she must be still in the very early stages. Besides she's such a stick, I don't suppose she'll ever balloon up the way some women do. I bet I shall get huge when it's my turn.'

'Don't worry, darling,' said George, right on cue, 'I'll still love you no matter how enormous you get.'

'Oh you're so adorable,' she said leaning over to kiss him. Dottie made protesting sounds until they stopped.

*

Chapter Ten

'There he is,' hissed Flora behind her hand.

'George? With our drinks?'

'No you fool, the Honourable Cyril Penterman. He's not as awful as I'd expected,' she added.

Dottie turned and regarded the newly-arrived gentleman critically. He appeared to have a full head of hair, but as he was most agreeably tall, it was hard to be completely sure. She made a mental note to walk behind his chair during the buffet supper to get a proper look at his crown. 'And,' she said, continuing her train of thought out loud, 'until he smiles we shan't know the state of his teeth, either.'

'Don't forget that in spite of all his apparent good looks, he might prove to be a truly dreadful dancer. Could you live with that?' Flora asked.

'Definitely not. Just imagine never being able to dance with one's husband,' Dottie said. 'It's all right for you, George is a *divine* dancer, you're so lucky. Are you sure he doesn't have any single brothers or cousins we don't know about?'

'Oh look out, here comes Mother. Battle stations!'

'Dorothy! Florence! For goodness' sake, girls, mingle. Circulate.' Their mother bustled by, her pearls bouncing wildly on her ample bosom.

'Oh come along, Florence, do. Circulate!' said Dottie.

'Very well, Dorothy, just so long as you ensure you mingle.' Flora leaned close to Dottie's ear. 'Try to mingle in the direction of Cyril the Potential.'

'I'll try,' Dottie said. By the time she'd walked in Cyril's direction, apparently intent on finding Someone In Particular, he had succeeded in dropping his cigarette case and on bending to retrieve it, afforded her an excellent view of the top of his head.

'So far so good,' she muttered. She put a hand out to greet the elderly lady standing beside him.

'Mrs Gerard, how lovely to see you again. It must be at least a year since we last met. How is your Pekinese?'

'Dottie, my dear girl! How lovely you're looking this evening.' The elderly woman stretched up to kiss Dottie's cheek. 'Poor Flopsy! She isn't with us any longer, you know, I do miss her terribly.'

'I'm so sorry, what a shame, she was a sweetie. Will you get another?'

'Bless you dear, I may be getting a pup in the spring, I'm waiting to hear from my friend who breeds them. Do you know the Honourable Cyril Penterman? He's my nephew, my brother's eldest boy. Cyril, dear, this is Dottie Manderson.'

Cyril's eyes were hazel and merry. His mouth widened in a smile, and without any hint of British embarrassment, he seized Dottie's hand and placed a kiss on its back. Dottie felt herself turning crimson but was absurdly pleased. Nice teeth too, she noted. His attributes were stacking up...

'Miss Manderson, it's a pleasure to meet you. Tell me, do you like to dance?' He gave her a dazzling smile.

...nicely.

'Oh Mr Penterman, I love to dance!'

'Perhaps a foxtrot? Or a quickstep?'

'Lovely.' She beamed at him happily. Cyril the Potential

was certainly scoring well on the approval scale.

'Then may I request the foxtrot and lead you out onto the floor?'

'I'd be delighted.'

He hurried away. Mrs Gerard clutched Dottie's arm and put her head close to Dottie's.

'He's an Honourable, single, got pots of money and although he's my nephew so I've got to say it, he is quite the nicest young man I know. I really think you should give him every encouragement. He couldn't find a sweeter or lovelier girl than you, dear.'

'Bless you, Mrs Gerard, he's just the breath of fresh air we need this evening.' She lowered her voice to a whisper, adding confidentially, 'There are quite a few stuffed shirts here, I'm afraid.' Dottie paused then said, 'I believe he takes after his mother?' She thought she was being exceedingly clever and terribly subtle.

'Eh? Gloria? Well, I suppose...'

And then the band struck up a foxtrot, and Cyril Penterman materialised at her side, and tucking her hand into the crook of his elbow, he led her away to the dancefloor.

He was the most divine dancer—light on his feet—and hers—intuitive, fluid and best of all, inclined to add in a few improvisations of his own. Never had Dottie enjoyed herself so much. Best of all, towards the close of the dance, he said softly in her ear, 'Would you do me the honour of accompanying me to the theatre? I'm thinking of going to see that Astaire thing, *Gay Divorce*. Have you seen it?'

The dance had ended, and they all stood about applauding the band. And the band then stuck up a chord and without even asking, he swept Dottie into his arms once more, this time for a waltz, and their conversation continued as if there had been no interruption.

She told him with genuine regret that she had already seen the show several times and that she didn't feel able to see it again. She liked his old-fashioned courtesy, and on impulse told him, 'I'm afraid that show doesn't have the happiest of associations for me now.' And she went on to explain about finding Archie Dunne dying. She watched his reaction carefully.

'Good Lord!' he exclaimed. 'I knew about poor Archie, of course. We are acquainted with the family. And I knew that a young woman had discovered the body and summoned help, but I had absolutely no idea...It must have been a horrifying experience for you.'

'It was awful,' she admitted. 'I have never felt so helpless in my life. And even though I had never met him and didn't know him, I couldn't bear to leave him alone...it just felt so—so wrong.'

'I think a lot of people wouldn't have had your courage. I must say, I tremendously admire the fact that, oblivious to your own comfort and convenience, you remained with him, not only until help came, but until his own end came. That takes real strength of character.'

He was so earnest, so forthright, she was overcome with shyness and couldn't meet his eyes. Yet her heart sang. After this, she thought, I shall never complain or disoblige my mother again. Well, she mentally added, not for a little while anyway.

As they moved around the floor with all the other couples, she caught sight of her sister and brother-in-law a few couples away from them, entwined in each other's arms, heads close together as they whispered. She thought how wonderful it was to find that perfect someone, that soulmate, to never be alone again. And then there was her mother, watching from the sidelines, a satisfied smile taking in her youngest daughter and her eminently eligible partner.

As the second dance came to an end, annoyingly her father cut in, and Dottie was hugely disappointed. Then the dance turned out to be a tango, and that was not her father's forte, so by mutual consent they moved on into the next room for a glass of punch. Dottie saw Cyril go by clutched in the embrace of a blonde woman she knew nothing about other than that she was from New York, and tremendously wealthy. She certainly looked like the cat with the cream, Dottie thought, and detested the very sight of her.

Janet, Dottie's maid was serving the punch, and she poured Dottie and Mr Manderson an extra-large glass each. As she handed Dottie hers, Janet leaned forward to whisper loudly, 'He's a nice one, and quite a catch.' She directed a knowing look in the direction of the dancefloor, then turned back and added, 'bet he's loaded, too.' And gave Dottie a broad wink. Dottie smiled and quickly turned away.

Flora grabbed her arm, and drew her out of the room. Dottie, feeling guilty, turned back but her father was already deep in conversation with an old friend. Flora and Dottie hurried into the little lobby at the back of the house, between the morning room and their father's study.

'So?'

'He dances divinely, and his teeth are beyond reproach. Oh, and he's got hair. Even Mother would approve,' Dottie confirmed.

'I knew it!' Flora laughed.

'In fact she does approve, I caught sight of her watching us, and she couldn't have looked happier. He wanted me to go with him to the theatre but I told him about seeing *Gay Divorce* so many times already, and then I told him all about finding Archie. I wanted to see how he responded. But then Father interrupted us. I could have been dancing the tango with Cyril by now, but instead, thanks to Your Father, he's with that blonde piece from New York. I could spit.'

But Dottie needn't have despaired. Half an hour later, the buffet was served, and as everyone sat or stood about talking and eating, Cyril once more found his way to her side. He handed her a glass of champagne. He clinked his own glass against hers, and his eyes locked on her eyes, and he said softly, 'To meetings, to possibilities.'

She whispered the toast back to him, the moment suddenly seeming solemn and portentous. I shall remember this moment even when I'm an old woman, she thought. Then he laughed, and taking her by the arm, steered her back to the long row of buffet tables to pile up her plate. She felt a delicious thrill of coupledom as he added a few items and said, 'That's for me,' and whether the combination of the evening and too much wine, or champagne, or just being in his company, whatever it was she felt marvellously reckless and smiled at him with complete unreserve. And right at that moment, out of the corner of her eye she caught sight of the head and shoulders of a man, and for a moment it seemed as though her heart had actually failed. Gasping for breath, she turned to get a proper look, but the man had turned and now she could see him more clearly, she realised it was not who she had thought it was.

Relief flooded through her but was quickly displaced by—she didn't know what name to give the way she felt. But in any case, it didn't deserve to be noticed, she was perfectly happy, thank you, with the very charming company of a very charming new acquaintance. She was in Cyril's company and he was everything admirable in a young man. She forced herself to attend to what Cyril was saying.

He talked and talked. He had an endless supply of humorous anecdotes, stories and tall tales, and Dottie felt as though she did nothing but laugh for the next hour. Later, when the dancing resumed, he hardly left her side. They even finally managed a perfect tango, which caused a few raised eyebrows and her mother's look told her it was too much. But Dottie had no regrets.

As she said goodbye to him at the front door, watching him go down the steps to the street, she felt she could see her future, rosy and certain, all laid out before her. And then he bounded up the steps again, and right in front of her mother, swept her into his arms and kissed her actually on the mouth, then kissed her hand and ran back to his car again, laughing and waving. Her joy was complete.

'You really ought not to permit such impertinence,' her mother said in her ear, but there was an indulgent twinkle in her eye. Dottie put her arm through her mother's as they returned to the stragglers.

'Mother, I know I was difficult about this party, but I'm so grateful really. And Cyril Penterman is such a delightful young man. I think he and I will be great friends. We're dining together this week.'

Her mother said nothing but smiled again and patted her hand, then trotted off to bid farewell to more guests who were on the point of departing.

As Dottie went through to get herself a final glass of punch, she walked directly into the police sergeant.

Words failed her. She couldn't even feel angry. She just quite simply stared at him in confusion.

He looked equally ill at ease. Finally he said, 'Well, goodnight, Miss Manderson. I think the evening was a great success.'

He had been here the whole time. How had she not seen him? And yet, somehow, she had known he was there. When she had seen that other man...

Her sense of correct etiquette came to her aid. She realised he was in evening dress. So he was clearly there as an invited guest and not as a policeman. But this still bewildered her. However, she had been brought up to show courtesy at all times, and now she held out her hand to him. He took it briefly in his own warm clasp then released it.

'I'm glad you enjoyed yourself,' Dottie heard herself say, 'Thank you for coming.'

He hesitated then murmured something indistinct and moved on. Only now did she realise he was in the company of an older woman, and the same young woman she had seen him with at the Lyon's Corner House.

Catching the young woman's eye, Dottie advanced, her hand outstretched.

'I'm so sorry,' she said. 'I'm afraid that's the second time we have almost met, but not quite managed to be introduced. I'm Dottie Manderson. How do you do?'

The young woman seemed a little embarrassed, alarmed even, by the attention, and Dottie now saw she was somewhat younger than she'd at first appeared, Dottie estimated her age to be sixteen or seventeen. She took Dottie's hand in a soft brief clasp.

'Um—well—I'm very pleased—I'm Eleanor Hardy. And this is our mother, Mrs Isabel Hardy. My late father was an acquaintance of Mr Manderson's and it was he who so kindly invited us this evening.'

Dottie had heard of Major Garfield Hardy, a great wartime associate of her father. She smiled and turned to speak to the older woman, a softly spoken person, but later had no recollection of what she said; all her energy and wits were intent upon Eleanor Hardy's use of that word 'our' and her awareness of the fact that the young woman in front of her was clearly either his wife or his sister. For some reason, Dottie hoped she was his sister. She thought she had to be his sister. She was very young, surely she was his sister? And then the older woman spoke, and this time, Dottie was able to attend to what she said.

'I understand you actually met my son during the course of his work on that most distressing case.'

'Yes indeed,' Dottie said, proud to be in charge of her wits once more. 'And a very—um, efficient—officer he is too. I'm sure the case will be resolved in no time.' She smiled again, although afraid she had sounded patronising or insincere. But she couldn't think of anything else to say. Had he really been here the whole evening? It seemed certain he had. Had she somehow caught sight of him without realising she had done so? That would explain the other thing... She became aware that he—and they—were watching her closely, and she was overcome once more, having no idea if anyone had spoken since her last comment, or whether they were awaiting a response from her. She had no clue what to say or do.

'Oh hello again, Mr Hardy! How lovely to see you, and looking so dashing in your evening attire! George was just telling me he'd seen you.' Flora was there by her side, her hand warm and reassuring on Dottie's arm, her smile directed first to Mrs Hardy and then her daughter, and Flora had so many of the right things to say.

Dottie found herself at leisure to look at him then. His eyes met hers, and when after a few moments of conversation his mother said, 'Well, William, I think we ought to be going,' he physically started like a guilty lover, and Dottie was angry and upset to find that she had done the same.

*

Chapter Eleven

An invitation to tea with the Pentermans a week later was cause for both joy and alarm in Dottie. After her recent dinner with Cyril she was so eager to see him again, but was somewhat daunted by the prospect of her meeting him in the company of his parents and their guests at their home. She was glad her mother had also been invited, although her father's absence might put a few noses out of joint, but Dottie was glad he wouldn't be there. His presence might tend to make the occasion seem more important than it was, and Dottie felt nervous enough already without feeling as though she were being interviewed for a position as daughter-in-law.

She was wearing one of Mrs Carmichael's newest creations in a soft rose-coloured wool and knew that she looked absolutely at her best. A girl could do no more than that when meeting the formidable mother of a young man she liked rather a lot.

Mrs Penterman's maid showed them into what she termed 'Madam's private sitting-room', which Dottie knew would vex her mother, as this was, no matter how extensive or beautifully furnished, nevertheless still a home: rendering all the rooms private, in Mother's opinion. However, there was no time for Mrs Manderson to quibble. Dottie was disconcerted to find there were already at least a dozen people there before them, mainly ladies, but with a few men amongst them, and to Dottie's great relief, one of whom was Cyril.

On the threshold of the room, he bounded over to greet them, and after clasping Dottie's hand firmly in his warm grip for what seemed like a very long time, and smiling into her eyes, he went away to fetch them some tea. Meanwhile, his mother, a tall woman with a rather cold, stern demeanour, and the same fair hair as her son, came over to introduce herself, and drew them into the room, saying she had a pair of seats saved for them.

They followed Mrs Penterman dutifully, but Dottie was desperately disappointed to find they were to be placed at one end of the long room, with Cyril at the opposite end. Nevertheless, they smiled at the matriarch and took their seats, nodding to those ladies nearest to them, whilst Mrs Penterman peered at them through her old-fashioned lorgnette then said something vague about ringing for more hot water, and left them. Conversation with Cyril, Dottie realised, would be all but impossible. She felt as though she and her mother had been tucked away out of sight. Her mother expressed the same view in an angry whisper, adding, 'It's a public set-down, that's what it is. She's telling us we're not good enough.'

Dottie demurred, but a delicate ripple of laughter from the other end of the room made her lean forward to see the owner of the laugh and she saw the young woman who sat on one side of Cyril enjoying a conversation with his watchful mother who sat on his other side. The woman's fine features, slender frame and carefully dressed fair hair proved Dottie's suspicions correct. It was the New York heiress. Cyril was leaning back against his chair, nodding and smiling, their tea clearly forgotten; but to Dottie's eye, there was something wooden about his responses that made her relax and feel no concern, even when her mother hissed in her ear, 'See, that's the lady his Mama has chosen for him. I'm afraid you've lost him, Dorothy.'

The next two hours were two of the dullest Dottie could remember ever having endured. Everyone else seemed to be intimately acquainted whilst having no particular interest in getting to know Dottie or her mother. They had almost no conversation, the lady the other side of her mother politely agreeing with a couple of Mrs Manderson's observations about the weather and the lightness of the Victoria sponge, but taking the matter no further.

The long narrow room was decorated in a style fifty years out of date, and the profusion of side tables and plant pots on stands kept them separated, so that Dottie was too distant to be included even in this poor excuse for an exchange, and she was obliged to sit in silence for the majority of the visit. She wrestled with her longing to either turn over the tea-tables and storm out of the room, banging the door behind her, or to march the length of the room to speak with Cyril. Or perhaps to inform his sour-looking mother that he had kissed her, and that she wasn't giving him up to that scrawny fair-haired thing.

'Thou painted maypole,' Dottie murmured under her breath, remembering her favourite Shakespeare, and feeling better for it. Nevertheless, she gripped her hands tightly in her lap and did nothing, and realised sorrowfully that she had certainly grown up a good deal of late.

'Well,' her mother began in the cab on the way home. 'I don't at all care for the woman's way of receiving visitors, no matter how grand the Pentermans may be. If I were her, I'd have got rid of all those little whatnots and plants, and arranged the chairs in more of a circle, to enable my guests to converse comfortably with one another and so that no one was left out. Mark my words, she did it on purpose. Anyone would think we'd turned up without an invitation. Very rude. Very improper.'

And on and on Mrs Manderson went, unfolding her own preferred and approved method for setting guests at their ease and ensuring a pleasant flow of conversation.

Dottie said nothing, but listened—and agreed—in silence. She had entertained such hopes of a lovely afternoon, even though she had been nervous. Now she seriously doubted they would ever receive another invitation again, and in the incredible event that they did, she knew beyond a doubt that she would have to invent a dreadful cold to get out of it. She couldn't wait to vent all her frustration on her sister.

'Cyril, this lobster is absolutely scrumptious. You must try some,' Dottie said the following evening, and placed a piece of it on the edge of his plate. In the present rather superior dining-room, she didn't quite have the courage to hold her fork out for him to take the lobster from it, though it would have been lovely to be so grown-up and couple-like, she thought regretfully.

He speared the piece of lobster with his own fork and wolfed it down, nodding as he did so. When he had finally disposed of it, he said, 'Hmm, yes, delicious. Have one of my *moules*.'

He was not so shy. He leaned across, one mussel impaled on the tines of his fork and he practically shoved it into Dottie's mouth with an encouraging nod and a 'What?'

She was acutely embarrassed, which spoiled the flavour of the mussel and she was all too aware of the stares from other diners at nearby tables. She nodded her agreement, said a brief, 'Yes, truly delightful,' then took a sip of wine. Keeping her eyes lowered, she forced herself to concentrate on her food.

Cyril gave a soft low laugh, and Dottie risked a glance up, to look into his eyes which dared her to share the laughter. She didn't mind him laughing at her—he was so gentle in his teasing.

It was the fifth time in two weeks they had dined together. And she felt gloriously happy. They talked. They danced. They ate. They laughed. She felt they were so compatible, so divinely suited. It was heavenly.

They talked of his university days, of studies, of his

hopes for the future. She told him how her mother disapproved of everything she did and that her father didn't much care what she did so long as he was left alone. He talked of his ambitious determined father and his mother who urged him to think of his duty and stop wasting time and settle down.

'I know all children probably say this,' he said. 'But I really do feel that my parents were never young. They were certainly never impulsive or fun-loving.'

The waiter cleared away their empty dishes. Once alone again, Cyril leaned across and took Dottie's hand in his.

'I know I'm fearfully forward, but it seems to me that life is short and unpredictable, so I hope you won't judge me too harshly if I tell you that although according to my mother I'm a wastrel and a scoundrel, I am also acutely aware that there will come a time in the not-too-distant future when I will be ready to step up and take responsibility. And when I do, Dottie, *when I do*, I shall hope to have the love of a good woman to support me and keep my courage up through all the sensible decisions and responsible behaviour I shall have to exhibit.'

Dottie felt a tremble go through her whole body. She wanted to snatch her hand away but at the same time she wanted him to kiss it. His eyes looked into hers, and she knew her heart was in danger.

At that moment the waiter politely ahemmed beside them, and confections of meringue and cream were placed before them. The spell was broken, Cyril sat back in his seat, beaming at her, and she laughed again, only now realising that she had been holding her breath.

Later, they danced. He ordered champagne. What it was, Dottie thought, to order whatever one wished and not heed the cost. She talked about Christmas and her mother's plans for entertaining. She almost felt like weeping when he revealed he would be away from the day before Christmas Eve until the 6th of January. A sense of gloom filled her at the thought that all those days—a time meant for happiness and celebration—would have to be spent without Cyril. What would even be the point of getting out of bed each day, she thought.

'Don't fret,' he said, as he took her hand again, 'I'm not going for another week and a half!' And his hazel eyes met hers in a glance that warmed her through and through.

He took her home, and dared to kiss her before knocking on the door and delivering her to her mother.

Dottie had a hectic schedule of shows and private viewings to model for. By Friday evening, she was ready to fall asleep where she stood. Only the memory of her mid-week romantic dinner with Cyril Penterman kept her smiling through the critical comments, the stares, the envious, carping remarks from the women and the lustful glances and impertinent winks of their husbands and sons.

When she finally arrived home at almost ten-thirty on Friday evening, she wanted nothing more than to sink into her bed.

But at the Mandersons, a card party was still in full swing. 'At least I shan't have to go and get myself ready,' she thought as she entered the brightly lit hall. Her dress may have been plain, but it was a good cut and a flattering colour. And had cost her a deal more than she ought to have spent. Her hair and make-up were perfectly adequate for an intimate card party, if they were good enough for a modelling assignment. She hastened upstairs to put on some more comfortable shoes and to get rid of her hat and gloves, and returned less than five minutes later ready to smile until her face ached.

There were three tables set up in the drawing-room, with three games of bridge in progress. In the corner by the French windows, the gramophone was providing a suitable background entertainment, with her father doing duty with the recordings and the handle.

The perfect hostess's daughter, Dottie halted at each table to smile and greet the guests. At the first one sat the Honourable Cyril Penterman and his aunt Mrs Gerard. Cyril looked up and greeted her with a broad smile. Mrs Gerard beamed in delight, like a fond parent, and patted

Dottie's hand.

At the next table, the Honourable Peter St Clair St John was also in position, and he too required notice and admiration from her, but his crooked smile was more for his own achievements than any pleasure he felt in seeing her again, and it seemed her presence was forgotten almost immediately when his partner spoke to him.

She meandered on to the third table. And there was Sergeant William Hardy, his back to her, which possibly explained how she had failed to notice him sooner. He glanced up from his cards and subjected her to one of his peculiar, intense scrutinies, which had her blushing unbecomingly and left her feeling horribly aware of her heart pounding in her chest. Blast the man. Why was she so discomforted by him? Did she have a guilty conscience about something?

As the games ended and the points were totted up, her mother declared a break for coffee and sandwiches. A few guests took their departure after the refreshments, but unfortunately for Dottie neither the policeman nor the more tiresome of the two Honourables took their leave, so she was unable to pour all her admiration on Cyril as she would have liked.

And she had no opportunity for conversation with Cyril as her father had thoughtlessly monopolised him for the whole time. With a heavy heart she turned to Peter, who it appeared, required an interested pair of ears to listen to him talking about himself and all the wonderful thoughts that had gone through his mind over the course of the evening, and all the ingenious tricks he had won in his games.

Obligingly she took the seat next to him and mechanically uttered such responses at more or less the right time as would satisfy his ego. She could see William Hardy hovering uncertainly between two cliques of people, not included by either.

All at once she felt sorry for him, and a little exasperated. He was neither one thing nor the other. His job put him into almost the same class as the maid who had served him his coffee, yet his upbringing and background clearly suited him for the drawing-rooms of the country's great houses.

'Why didn't he become a barrister if he had to work for a living?' she asked Peter, cutting across his re-enactment of winning a particular trick. Surprised, he followed her look and saw William Hardy accepting another ham sandwich from the maid.

'Hardy? Usual story. Father overextended himself. Invested in the United States' share market, some relative—his father's sister, I think, married a Yank, lost it all in the Crash. Hardy had to leave Oxford and get a job, of all things. Father died a year or so ago, he'd had a stroke after the crash but lingered on, never recovered. Pneumonia got him in the end. Did you see my...?'

She interrupted him with an impatient shake of the head. 'Do you know much about the family? His mother and sister were here for Mother's party two weeks ago.'

'Sister—nice enough girl. Bit wishy-washy. Still very young, mind you. The mother's a broken woman by all accounts. There's a younger brother too, still at Repton. Presume the copper's salary pays for that. By the way did I tell you about my new car?'

With an inward sigh, Dottie resigned herself to listening to Peter's tedious story about his tedious car.

Mercifully only five minutes into the story—he was still describing the colour of his new toy—her mother clapped her hands to bring those still playing back to the tables. With some of the guests having left, one of the tables was taken away, and the card players now redistributed themselves about the two remaining tables. In a way, Dottie decided, it was a good thing that Cyril, Peter and Sergeant Hardy were all at the same table, that way she only had to look in one direction, and she could save herself a crick in the neck.

Mrs Manderson was kept busy for the next twenty minutes with saying goodbye to those who had wanted to leave early. As the clock struck midnight, Dottie thought longingly of her bed but knew her mother would be put out if she went up when they still had guests in the house. So she poured another cup of coffee and went to the French windows to look out into the garden. A capricious moon shone fitfully between fast-moving clouds. Now and again she could catch sight of an urn or a bay tree in the shadows of the garden.

'I'm dummy,' said a voice behind her and she turned with a smile of delight for Cyril Penterman on her lips.

'Perhaps you'd like some more coffee?' she suggested. He smirked at her.

'Perhaps I would.' And he took her cup from her saucer, and drank it down in one gulp, handing her back the empty cup. She giggled and her mother's head turned sharply in their direction. Dottie took a step back to put a little more distance between herself and Cyril. Her mother's stern expression relaxed slightly.

'Do you often have card parties?' he asked as if merely for something irreproachable to say.

'Not often, but once or twice during the winter,' she said. 'In the summer it's tennis parties, usually.'

'Oh do you play tennis? I see you don't care for cards.'

'Yes, I do play tennis. Not very well, though. Schoolgirl tennis.'

'Then I must hope to be invited. Although summer seems awfully far off at the moment.'

'Yes.'

'So now we've covered cards and sport, what about politics? Are you at all political, Miss Manderson?' he asked with a laugh.

'You usually call me Dottie. If you don't, I shall feel I have to call you the Honourable Cyril, and in my mind you're just plain Cyril.'

'Plain Cyril? Oh dear, how mortifying. If I'd known you thought so lowly of me, I wouldn't have bothered to wear my best suit. I'd have just wandered in wearing pyjamas and a smoking jacket.'

They laughed.

'No, I'm not especially political,' she replied.

'Your suffragist sisters will be very disappointed to hear

that. After all the effort they went to on your behalf.'

'No doubt, but you know it seems to me that until there is a change in politicians, there's not much point in changing the voters.'

He gave her a look of surprise and nodded as if in grudging admiration.

'Very cutting. And unfortunately true. Do you mind if I smoke?'

She shook her head. 'Of course not, almost everyone else is,' she said, looking round. But not, she noted, William Hardy. Who was watching them with his characteristic quiet intensity, she now saw. Cyril lit a cigarette. He offered one to her but she shook her head.

'No thank you, I don't.' And across the room William Hardy smiled and looked back down at his cards. Somehow she felt he had approved of her choice.

'To come back to your point about politicians, I hope to run for parliament the year after next. I do hope I can count on your support.' He leaned in close. Her mother, crossing the room, cleared her throat rather loudly. Dottie leapt back, and folded her arms across her chest.

'Oh we shall have to see about that when you announce your policies,' she said with an attempt at lightness.

'Well, I shall make champagne free to the poor, of course,' he laughed. Their conversation was interrupted by calls from his table. 'Sorry, duty calls,' he said and just briefly touched her hand before returning to his game.

'I've told you before, Dorothy, it is *essential* you check any impertinence in the early stages, or it could lead to trouble,' her mother murmured as she crossed the room to collect Dottie's cup and saucer.

'Yes, Mother,' she said dutifully.

'In any case, we already know you're wasting your time. His mother has made his choice for him,' Mrs Manderson continued in a quiet voice meant only for her daughter's ears.

'We don't know that for certain,' Dottie snapped.

Her glance automatically went to Cyril as he took his seat and picked up his cards. He felt her eyes on him and looked up to return her smile. Her heart seemed to experience a slight flutter. And then she found herself unable to resist a glance at William Hardy sitting opposite Cyril. He, too, looked back at her, an appraising look. Somehow, she felt he knew more than she did about her own feelings. She felt a slight twinge of discomfort, and made up her mind to ignore him whenever it was impossible to avoid him completely. And then, quite suddenly, he winked at her.

She was so astonished, she caught her breath and had to turn away and pretend to examine the garden again to disguise her laughter.

It was an odd evening. It was well after two o'clock before everyone had finally left, and Dottie was almost dropping from exhaustion. She had refused to allow her thoughts free rein until she could reach the quiet of her room. But by the time she crawled under the blankets, her mind was refusing to function, and in less than a minute she was sound asleep.

*

Chapter Twelve

The week before Christmas was a hectic social whirl for Dottie. On the Monday she dined out at the Ritz with Flora and George and another couple; on Tuesday she went to the theatre to see a wonderful detective play with Cyril, who afterwards took her to a late supper, and held her hand for an hour straight and murmured a mixture of jokes and stories and flattering comments about her eyes. During the day, she had shopping to do, presents to wrap, she wrote her Christmas cards and gave them to Janet to post and there were a couple of short, last-minute sessions to do for Mrs Carmichael.

On the Wednesday she was glad of a quiet evening at home, but then found herself under threat of interrogation by her mother and had to invent things she simply had to do upstairs.

On Thursday morning, Cyril called for her and took her shopping and for lunch. He was really so attentive, she thought, and when he invited her to supper at his parents' home that evening, she accepted without hesitation even though she knew her mother would be furious. At home, there was the predicted scene over the tea-things.

'I'm terribly sorry, Mother, I'm afraid it just slipped my

mind. I've known about it for a week, and I really thought I'd told you.'

'Dorothy! How could you! You know perfectly well I'm expecting Mrs Angkatell and her daughter, and the Moyers.'

'I really am so sorry, Mother, but I don't see how...'

'I'm quite certain Dottie told you on Tuesday at breakfast, dearest,' said Mr Manderson's voice from behind his newspaper. A hand reached around the page to obtain a sandwich.

'She most certainly did not,' snapped Dottie's mother, and then all at once, the wind went out of her sails and she said pettishly, 'Oh do as you wish, you always do. I'll go and tell Cook.'

Once her mother had left the room, Mr Manderson lowered his paper to exchange a smile with his daughter.

'Thank you,' she said softly, sitting on the arm of his chair.

'I don't think she fell for it anyway,' he replied. 'I assume you're well and truly smitten with this young fellow?'

'Yes, I'm afraid I am, Father.'

'Your mother seems to think his heart is promised elsewhere.'

'I thought so too at one point, but no it isn't. I'm beginning to think...' Then, hearing the angry footsteps returning, Dottie hurriedly got to her feet and ran upstairs, and her father retreated once more behind his paper, taking a lemon petit-fours with him.

Her mother was still in high dudgeon when Cyril arrived to collect Dottie at seven o'clock. Dottie had remained in her room until she saw him coming up the steps from the street, then she raced downstairs, threw open the door and called a hurried, 'I'm going, bye for now!' and grabbing Cyril by the arm she dragged him back out of the doorway and down the steps, leaving Janet to slam the front door behind them.

'What was that all about?' Cyril demanded, as they

drove off, Dottie turning back, laughing, to look at the house. She felt sure she could see her mother at the window. Briefly she explained.

'Then I'm afraid to disappoint you,' Cyril said and for a moment Dottie was worried what he might be going to say, but he just smiled and added, 'My parents are dining out unexpectedly, so you and I are going to have a nice dinner at the Royal instead.'

'Oh,' Dottie said. 'Well that's very nice.'

'You don't mind, do you?' he asked her anxiously. 'I know it's nowhere near as good as the Ritz, but...'

'It's absolutely fine, don't apologise.' She gave him a huge smile and he leaned back beside her, clasping her hand. The warm, happy feeling spread throughout her being and she decided that she wouldn't mind if they never made it to the Royal. Just to be here with him, driving through the streets of London, glittering with frost and festive lights, was all she could ask.

They lingered over the meal, and enjoyed their conversation. They always seemed to have so much to talk about, and he never failed to make her laugh. It was a heavenly evening, Dottie thought. The dessert was still disappointing. But forewarned was forearmed, and Dottie didn't mind so much having to make do with cheese and coffee.

When they arrived back at the Mandersons' front door, again, in spite of the cold, they lingered, his arms warm about her, his lips soft and warm on her cheek, her neck. He whispered sweet things that made her feel as though her heart would take wings and fly away. At last, however, he had to go. The hall clock struck midnight, just as loud outside as it was inside the hall itself. One last kiss. He cupped her face in his hands and kissed the tip of her nose. 'I'm leaving early in the morning, when I come back it will be a whole New Year! Have a lovely Christmas, Dottie dear, and think of me on Christmas morning.'

She waved and waved as he drove away, and then he was out of sight, and on the point of tears, she went into the house and closed the door. Her parents had already gone up, for which she was grateful. A shadow at the top of the stairs called out to her,

'Dorothy? Is that you? Do make sure the fire is banked before you come upstairs. It's really rather late you know. Goodnight.'

'Goodnight, Mother.' Dottie replied and was glad her voice sounded fairly steady.

By the fireside in the drawing-room, she wept a little then told herself she was being silly. In a couple of weeks she would have him back, and she could carry on falling in love with him. She sat and thought about that for a while.

A dreary tea-party in the Manderson's own home the day before Christmas Eve was useful for two things: one, Dottie and her parents received an invitation to dine from Mrs Gerard, which would, as Mrs Gerard herself confided to Dottie, give Dottie and Cyril the chance to see one another again. Mrs Gerard seemed rather excited about it, and kept patting Dottie's hand and arm. She was so clearly determined to make them a match that Dottie even wondered if she had arranged the dinner entirely with this in view.

Once the tea-party had broken up and everyone had gone home, Dottie ran upstairs to rest before getting ready for dinner. Flora and George were joining the Mandersons the next morning and staying until Boxing Day, and Flora was bringing her presents over to put under the tree that was standing in the hall. After lunch, Dottie and Flora would decorate the tree, as they had done since they were little girls.

Dottie thought back to Mrs Gerard's invitation. If only Cyril's mother was more like Mrs Gerard. But Dottie supposed she might warm to Mrs Penterman in time. Or rather the other way about. Perhaps there had been some misunderstanding? She didn't know what, but it seemed possible. Perhaps getting to know the Pentermans better would make them seem less daunting, less overbearing and disapproving. So long as Cyril didn't have one of those militarily-fearsome fathers, of course. Though even if he had, she told herself in the mirror with a pert upturn of her chin, there's nothing he could do to stop us getting married if Cyril really loved me.

Her impromptu use of the L-word pulled her up short. She was cross with herself for blushing, even in the privacy of her own bedroom, and brushed her hair vigorously to dissipate her annoyance. Her maid Janet had promised to bring her intelligence of Cyril gleaned from the servants' hall. Metaphorically, seeing as the Mandersons, like most people in the modern era of the 1930s, no longer possessed a servants' hall as such. After all they only had three full-time and two part-time staff, a fact much-lamented by her mother in her wistful reminiscences of 'before the war'.

But to Dottie's disappointment all Janet's intelligence amounted to was, 'Everyone says he's ever so nice, and we all agreed he is *the* most good-lookingest gentleman we've seen for ages.' All of which Dottie already knew. Oh how she longed for Christmas to be over so that he would be back by her side.

The other good thing to stem from the Mandersons' dullest of dull tea-parties was that in response to Dottie's vehement but whispered complaints about the tedium of it the next morning as they trimmed the tree, Flora had declared that she could certainly provide a much more entertaining tea than their mother, and that Dottie should be coming to that just as soon as she had settled a date with Cook.

For Dottie the most aggravating thing was that neither of these events could take place until after January the 6th, as that was when he would be returning home from his mysterious trip away. She wondered in an agony of despair when she would next see Cyril. Would he call for her the day he returned home? Or the next day? When?

Christmas Eve afternoon brought with it Mrs Manderson's Uncle Bernard and Mr Manderson's mother who could bear neither the sight of her daughter-in-law's uncle nor her daughter-in-law. They too, would be staying until Boxing Day tea-time, and almost immediately the tension in the house became rather more fraught. Dottie cleverly avoided any yuletide catastrophe by the simple expedient of getting everyone a little tipsy, constantly topping up their glasses of sherry, gin or mulled wine.

George ensured the fire remained well-stoked all the cold afternoon and evening, so that the heat and alcohol took their toll, and by half past six, apart from George and the two sisters, everyone was snoozing in their armchairs. George roasted a vast quantity of chestnuts, and he, Flora and Dottie sat by the fireside, chatting quietly and eating.

The old people retired once again to their chairs in the drawing-room after dinner, and promptly fell asleep. The fire crackled pleasantly, and even the young ones were drowsy. They sat on the floor by the fire all the evening. Dottie fetched some photo albums; she and Flora pored over them. George gazed fondly at his wife with even more of a besotted look than usual. It was almost bedtime before it dawned on Dottie that they were giving each other significant loving looks, and finally, snapping shut the last album, she said, 'What's going on? Why are you two even more soppy than usual?'

They demurred of course, but then with a nod from Flora, George stood in front of the fire, gently jingling his teaspoon against his coffee cup, waking up the oldies.

'Erm—sorry to disturb everyone when we're all having so much—erm...' He took in the bleary-eyed faces surveying him and he hesitated. Another nod from his wife and he continued, 'The thing is—erm—the thing is...'

And then Dottie realised what it was he was about to say. She turned to look with an open mouth and raised eyebrows at her sister who nodded, her eyes misty with happiness, her smile tremulous. They hugged. Dottie, still quite taken aback, nevertheless whispered congratulations and that she was very happy for them, ignoring the little selfish voice inside her head that wanted to wail, 'But this will change *everything*!'

Finally George was coming to the point, though slowly. 'I'm tremendously proud and pleased as punch to announce that Flora is—erm—well—she is expecting a baby. Seen the doc, everything proceeding according to—erm and n-new arrival should make an appearance about the beginning of J-July. So—erm...jolly good show, Flossie.' He floundered to a halt and took a hefty swig from his coffee cup, spluttering as he did so. He really was appalling when it came to making a speech, Dottie thought. She moved across to the drinks cabinet and began to pour everyone a glass of wine. She turned to catch his eye and mimed drinking. He got the idea.

'Oh yes, of course, so if you could all—erm—please do yes, raise your glasses to my beloved Flora and our happy news.'

The older ones cast about them for their spectacles and sat up straight, ready to toast the happy parents-in-waiting. Dottie heard her mother say, 'To Florence,' not 'To Flora', but it was done. The ladies crowded round Flora to kiss her and hug her, and for some reason that Dottie couldn't fathom, although she knew it was traditional, her father hurried away to get a box of special cigars for the men. There was a certain amount of embarrassed back-slapping and hand-shaking, as if George had performed some miraculous feat.

And on that happy note, the evening came to an end. Everyone was staying in the house, so Dottie and Flora went up together, both too tired to talk, and they hugged on the landing and once again Dottie said how happy she was, and they said goodnight.

In her room, Dottie hurriedly finished wrapping a few final presents, and an hour later, when the men all came upstairs, she tiptoed down with her packages and arranged them under the tree in the hall.

She wandered into the drawing-room and sat for a few moments in one of the chairs, thinking about the new baby and the changes that he or she would bring. Her mother would no doubt start knitting like mad, Dottie thought, and possibly Flora might try her hand at knitting too, not that she had ever shown much interest—or indeed ability—in the pursuit before. Dottie shook her head at the strange idea of her sister as a mother. It was hard for her to imagine Flora reminding little ones to brush their teeth or drink their milk. Once again Dottie felt that odd quirk of fear, and had to push it away. Her common sense admitted there would always be changes in life, but that Flora would always be her sister and nothing would come between them. She would simply have to remember that once the baby arrived, Flora wouldn't have the same amount of free time she had before.

Mechanically Dottie tidied the room, plumping cushions, straightening the antimacassars, picking up discarded newspapers, tipping the ash and cigar stubs into the fireplace. Doing so she remembered the cigarette-girl George had chatted to at the theatre. How she had said that Archie Dunne had asked her to alibi him so that he could spy on his wife.

What if Susan *was* expecting a baby? Perhaps they ought to try and find out. Dottie didn't want to do or say anything to Susan until she knew for sure but at the same time she felt a vague concern for the woman. What would Christmas be like for her, a new widow, if there was a baby on the way? But no, Dottie reminded herself, Susan had a family who could support her, and had her comfortable—perhaps comfortable was not the right word—but nice—or well, perhaps not nice either—but spacious, yes, Susan had her spacious home and at least one maid to help her. It certainly seemed unlikely that Susan would welcome any offers of help from Dottie.

But perhaps in a few days, once Christmas was over, Dottie should suggest either to her mother or to her sister that Susan or if not her then at least her sister Muriel should be invited to afternoon tea, or morning coffee or something, and so give Dottie the opportunity to find out a bit more about the situation and thus set her mind at rest.

She thought about the policeman William Hardy. Had he solved the mystery of Archie's murder? Was someone even now in custody and waiting trial? Nothing about the case had been reported in the newspapers for days. Did that mean the investigation was going well, or floundering? She might try and find out about that too. Perhaps he or his family could be invited to, oh, something, anything, so she could ask him a few subtle questions.

She was falling asleep. She'd better get back to bed. It wouldn't do to be found here still in her nightdress by the maid on Christmas morning. Besides which, the room was growing cold since the fire had gone out.

William Hardy sat in his armchair before the fire. He had taken off his jacket once his family had gone up to bed. He nursed a glass of brandy, not that he was in the habit of drinking brandy, not since his days at Oxford when his pocket had been rather deeper and his tastes rather more expensive. But he liked to take a glass now and then.

Truth be told, he was feeling somewhat morose. He felt a little sorry for himself and it was because things were not going well either in terms of the investigation, or in terms of a certain young lady who filled his thoughts and was, he knew, walking out with someone who could buy up everything William Hardy owned with the small change from his pocket.

He took a drink, and stared into the dying embers. He needed to find the murderer and close the case if things were going to go his way at work. Admittedly he had been promoted, but even so, he didn't want to be a lowly policeman all his life; that wouldn't suit his plans at all. And if he didn't look lively, that particular young lady would be making a match with that other gentleman, and Hardy would have missed his chance there too.

But how was he to move forward with either situation? He didn't know. And that was why he was still sitting there drinking brandy. How he wished Christmas was over and he could get back to going to peoples' homes with legitimate questions to ask.

*

Chapter Thirteen

The New Year of 1934 was greeted by revellers all over the world. In Britain, the Mandersons joined the Gascoignes and a host of others in welcoming in the New Year and bidding farewell to the old.

Dottie was glad not to be part of the receiving line. Her parents, and George's, along with George himself and a radiantly happy Flora stood ready in the vast front hall to welcome their guests as they arrived at the Gascoigne family seat, Ville Coign. By nine o'clock the house was brimming over and the noise level was shocking. Dottie lay aside the wrap she had carried downstairs, too warm to require it, and went in search of a long, cool drink.

If only Cyril could have been there! Dottie felt a little lost, knowing she had nothing remarkable to look forward to that evening beyond the pleasure of dancing with a lot of pleasant young men and celebrating the arrival of a new year.

In the wide ballroom, the members of the orchestra were tuning up their instruments, and having overheard their conversation as they did so, Dottie knew there would be at least one tango. But what was the point of a really intimate, powerful dance when you would have to stand up with some ordinary young fellow and know that it would mean absolutely nothing? She felt bored and bad-tempered.

The face of William Hardy sprang unbidden to her mind and she felt irritated with herself. Why did she keep thinking of him? Admittedly she had begun to see another, more human side of him, a side that had elicited her sympathy, but that had to be all. It was Cyril—wasn't it—whom she was falling for? Of whom she already had dared to entertain hopes?

A manservant glided up to her bearing a tray of drinks, and she took one, thanking him with a smile. When he continued on his rounds, she turned to look around her, drink in hand, taking the occasional sip. She daren't drink it too quickly, even if it was New Year. Mother would be furious if she got even slightly tipsy. Mother had ideas about the Proper Behaviour of a young woman at a New Year ball.

The house was filling up. People were beginning to assemble in the ballroom ready for the first dance, but she felt alone, and found she couldn't bear to be there. New Year's Eve was usually so full of hope and promise, she loved the excitement of it, yet tonight she was wishing it already over. She didn't want to stay in the ballroom, didn't want to see the dancing, didn't feel like dancing herself. She crossed the room as best she could, threading her way through the laughing and chattering couples and groups, and at last reached the door into the much cooler hall. She hesitated, then turned to her right and went along the hall to the library. She hoped it would be empty.

It wasn't, but there was only one other person in there: George's sister Diana was just carrying a radio from a table behind Mr Gascoigne's huge oak desk. Dottie hurried over to help her, glad for a moment to have something to do.

'Thanks Dottie, we really ought to have done this earlier, before everyone arrived, but it completely slipped my father's mind.'

'Putting it on that table in the front hall like last year?' Dottie enquired.

'Yes, Daddy loves to hear the midnight chimes from Big Ben. So we'll stick this in the hall, then at a couple of minutes to midnight, Overton will turn it on to warm it up, then he will signal to Daddy, and Daddy will signal to the orchestra to stop playing, and we can all have our champagne toasts and listen to the chimes.'

'It always give me a thrill to hear them—it's the one thing I think of when I think about New Year's Eve. Mother always says in her day they didn't have the chimes broadcast—well of course they didn't, there weren't any radios! But I love it. It gives me chills.'

'Me too,' Diana laughed. Dottie ran to hold the door wide open for her, and soon with lots of 'coming through' and 'excuse me please', they had the radio in position ready for the crucial time.

'To be honest,' Diana said, 'I'm rather dreading the whole thing since my engagement broke up. He'd been here for the last three New Year's Eves. This year, I don't much feel like dancing.'

'I don't suppose you do,' Dottie said, 'New Year's Eve always seems made especially for loving couples. As a single girl, I feel somewhat out of place.' She looked about her again now, already feeling a little lost.

'Tell you what, let's go up to my room. I mean, if you really do want to escape? I know it's not very exciting, but... And we could come down again for the chimes. We'll take some drinks up and look at magazines or something. That is, if you want to.'

'I do, I absolutely do!' Dottie said fervently. Diana led the way up the sweeping staircase, past all the ladies and gentlemen making their way down to the ballroom after leaving their evening wraps and greatcoats in the gallery.

'I know it's awfully boring of me, but I feel really done in at the moment. Work has been so hectic, and since Christmas Eve it's just been one social event after another. How I'd love to just get away for a while,' Dottie was saying as they went along the corridor.

'We've been fanatically busy. I've been coming down with a cold or something for the last couple of days and I'm sure it's just because of all the people we've been meeting and all the entertainments we've attended. Do you think we're already getting too old for socialising?'

She stood back to allow Dottie to precede her into the bedroom. Dottie glanced back and laughed.

'Oh I do hope not! I think it's just that we need a brief respite.'

'Well, you can tell me the latest fashion news from Mrs Carmichael's warehouse and we can talk about our plans for our Spring wardrobes. I love to think ahead to Spring. January is too dreary after the fuss of Christmas!'

They sprawled in armchairs beside the fire and for the first time in several days, Dottie felt as though she was actually starting to relax. She was even tempted to close her eyes for a few moments, but not only was she afraid of appearing rude, she was also fairly sure she would fall sound asleep. Perhaps Diana was right, and they were, after all, too old for merrymaking! She glanced around the room, appreciative of the soft greens and creams that gave the room a light but soothing feel.

'I do love the colours you've chosen for in here, it's such a peaceful room.'

Dottie noticed Diana had picked up a small embroidery frame and was already making a careful stitch in the centre of an unclear shape.

'Actually it was Mummy who chose the colours whilst I was away at finishing school the year before last. I must admit I was rather petulant and horrid about it. For some reason I had set my heart on crimson and gold. How ghastly that would have been! But one has these ridiculous ideas when one is young. I've grown up so much in the last two years! Luckily Mummy put her foot down—and she was right, as always.'

Dottie laughed. 'I was the same about a gown for my eighteenth birthday ball. I wanted peach taffeta, which of course I see now would have been rotten with my complexion, but at the time I made no end of a stink about it. I suppose our mothers always know best. Except when it comes to choosing a nice young man, of course.'

'Goodness, yes,' Diana laughed, and took another careful stitch, 'My mother's idea of what makes an eligible young man is rather different to mine—she only cares about his family background and how much money he's got. I want someone who will be my soulmate, the other half of my heart.' She laughed a little shakily and added, 'Hearing that out loud makes it sound so sentimental and childish.'

'No,' Dottie said, 'I know exactly what you mean. I suppose our mothers did marry for love, but I'm not completely...'

'It's hard to tell with my parents,' Diana said softly, 'I do wonder—well, I know I shouldn't say this—but I do wonder whether my mother married my father because of the Gascoigne name and the status. She often seems to detest the very sight of him.'

Dottie couldn't help but laugh. 'Oh I'm sorry, I know I shouldn't but, well that's exactly what I think about my parents. Father is so different to Mother, and of course, I can't believe that they were ever young and inconsequential like us.'

'Definitely not! Mine were born old,' Diana said with a laugh. She bent once more over her frame and made another tiny stitch. 'I do hope you don't mind me doing this, I find it so relaxing.'

'Not at all,' Dottie said, 'I wish I had your patience.'

'George and Flora seem very happy, though, don't they? I'm sure they married for love rather than mere economy.'

'Yes, they are blissfully happy,' Dottie said wistfully, 'I wish I could find a nice man like George.'

'I'm so excited about the coming baby!' Diana said, 'It will be the first in our family. Mother will be a bit too overbearing about it, I imagine, and will give poor Flora far too much useless advice.'

'Mothers tend to do that.'

'I think, don't you, that there is no greater gift a woman can give her husband than that of a child. It's a precious calling, to bear children for one's husband.' Diana said without looking up.

Dottie glanced at her, a little surprised, and murmured an embarrassed, 'Oh—er—yes, indeed.' Desperate for something to do Dottie picked up her glass and took a sip or two of champagne, and desperate for something to say, she said, 'I'm so sorry to hear about your engagement. No wonder this is a difficult time for you.'

'Thanks, but we weren't suited, I used to think that by sheer determination I could make it work. I didn't want to be one of those girls who gives up when things get difficult, but...well, in the end Alistair just wasn't the one for me, I suppose. Our Lord must have someone else out there just for me.'

'Hmm,' said Dottie. 'Let's hope he comes along soon!'

Looking about her again, she noticed a picture on the wall, and suddenly struck by it, got up to cross the room for a better look.

'Is that...?' she began, but what she saw answered the question. 'Why, isn't that Queen Esther? I've seen this same picture recently somewhere else.'

'Have you?' Diana set aside her needlework and came over to join her, and they stood side by side, staring at the woman in the gold cloak. 'I can't remember where it came from. Probably Mummy got it when she ordered the rest of the décor. It's rather charming in a way, I suppose. But of course it's just a print you know, not an actual painting. So there are probably thousands of them all over the country.' She glanced at Dottie. There was something alert in her look that seemed at odds with her casual words. 'Where did you see it?'

Dottie took a step away, and, giving herself a moment to think, returned to her seat, sat down and took a sip from her glass before replying. 'Oh I forget. Somewhere recently. Probably at a card party or something. We've been all over the place these last two weeks. I just vaguely recall someone commenting about it.'

Diana sat opposite her, and Dottie felt as though Diana's rather pale eyes were fixed rather too sharply on her face. She felt as though she couldn't breathe, she felt the air in the room had changed, and that she must be very careful what she said. Suddenly, strangely, she felt Diana was not Diana anymore. Which was ludicrous, of course. At last, and a little desperately, she made herself say, 'I don't recall the story of Esther—I'm afraid I never did pay attention in Sunday School.'

'We learned about her in RI—Religious Instruction—at my school,' Diana commented. She was holding her glass in front of her face, all Dottie could see were her eyes, but from the tone of her voice, Dottie's obvious discomfort amused her. 'She was a beautiful girl who caught the eye of King Ahasuerus and through her obedience earned his trust so that she was able to speak to him and save her people when they were in danger. I suppose Mummy thought that Queen Esther was an appropriate woman from history for me to emulate.'

'Yes,' Dottie said, and unsure what else to say, she added, 'What school was that you attended? Flora and I both went to Lady Margaret's.'

'Oh, I went to Blackheath, then Our Blessed Lady's college in York. Let me tell you, it's true what they say about nuns—they really can be very stern!' Diana smiled with her lips but her eyes were still on her, watching, waiting, and there was a long heavy silence that seemed to hang on the room like a pall. Now for the first time, Dottie became aware of the music issuing up from the ballroom beneath their feet, and the accompanying hubbub of voices and laughter. She began to say, 'Perhaps we should go back down,' but no sound came from her mouth. She swallowed hard, trying to moisten her throat for speech.

'Well, Queen Esther clearly inspired you, Dottie, just as she has me,' Diana said suddenly, her voice soft.

'What do you mean?' Dottie asked.

'Her lovely gold cloak, of course. I know you have one just like it. Several of my acquaintances have remarked on it.'

Dottie found herself blushing for some reason she didn't quite understand, as if she had been caught out in a lie. All she could do was nod.

'It is a gorgeous colour,' Diana continued, 'and I've also commissioned my dressmaker to make me a cloak up in that same colour. Great minds think alike, I daresay!'

'Indeed they do,' Dottie agreed mildly, proud to be able to keep her voice steady again. Diana got up and coming over, put her hand out to pull Dottie to her feet, her skin cool, her fingers bony and strong.

'Come on, let's go down. I think I'm ready to dance now.' And putting her arm through Dottie's, she guided her back down the stairs to the party. Dottie was aware of a profound relief flooding through her as they went into the company of other people.

It may have been an evening of revelry for some, but William Hardy was working. He had driven his mother, sister and younger brother to his married sister's home for a few days, then had returned to his desk at the police station, and had gone over and over the evidence he had before him.

By the medical report, it was clear they were looking for a special kind of knife, something rather out of the usual way. If it had been sharp enough, there was no doubt that the crime could have been committed by a woman, if she happened to catch Dunne off guard although she would have to deliver the blow with sufficient force to pierce the evening jacket, shirt and undershirt before reaching the flesh itself. Hardy wasn't sure. It could be done, it might be possible, but then again...

His superiors had wanted to know about the girl who had found the body. Nine times out of ten, they reminded him, the person who found the body was the killer. Here again, Hardy found himself at odds with his betters. He couldn't believe for a single moment that Dottie Manderson was the perpetrator of the act. If they had seen her white, shocked face as he had they would not doubt her. Useless to tell them that, of course, they would think him sentimental and a fool. And hadn't the wife already told them she believed he was having an affair?

That was what they would say to him, and he had to admit that from a certain point of view, it made sense. Even if she wasn't the killer, it seemed likely she was the mistress. And there was the letter D in the diary. Again, it was only his own delicacy, his refusal to think so ill of her, that prevented him from believing she was the type of girl to involve herself in such a scandalous situation. To himself, and himself alone, he acknowledged he had placed her upon a pedestal and would not believe anything bad of her.

He drifted off into a daydream about her eyes, her smile. He heard her voice as she sang the song to him, her voice soft and tremulous but melodic and very, very pretty. With a sigh he roused himself and saw from the clock that he had somehow lost ten minutes with such thoughts. He took up the pile of statements and began to read once more. Somewhere in the distance, he heard the sounds of cheering and laughter and the popping of champagnes corks. It was a new year.

*

Chapter Fourteen

At the end of the ball, Dottie had crowded into the gallery with her father to collect their outdoor things, leaving her mother, sister and George to say goodbye to George's parents and sister. Remembering what had happened previously, Dottie really hadn't wanted to put on her cloak without examining it first. But with the throng of guests all pressing about her, all wanting to get their things and leave, and because she didn't want to draw attention to herself, she had to be satisfied with a hasty surreptitious glance over its folds as she moved out of the way of everyone else. At the front door, seeing the frost glittering on the drive and his breath hanging in the air in front of him, her father had twitched the cloak from her fingers and draped it round her shoulders.

By the time they had reached George's car she had been pricked again and she had to sit very still in the back of the car next to her parents. Once they had let Mr and Mrs Manderson out at their home, and driven on to George and Flora's, Dottie contrived to wriggle out of the cloak, although it was too dark to see what had pricked her. She felt irritable and upset.

As she was getting out of the car, the streetlamp caused something to glint softly, and when Dottie put out her hand to see what it was, she found a dressmaker's pin on the floor of the car.

Indoors, George went off in search of Greeley, the Gascoignes' butler, and Flora and Dottie went into the dining-room, where Flora was able to spread the cloak out on the long table to examine it. She studied the fabric as Dottie began to tell her what had happened in Diana Gascoigne's bedroom.

'There!' said Flora. Looking to where Flora pointed, Dottie bent over the cloth and sure enough, there was a pulled thread, and next to it, two pairs of tiny holes.

'That's where the pin was,' Flora said, 'and another like it,' and Dottie had to agree.

'But why?' Dottie asked.

'It seems quite clear enough to me. Someone put a note on your cloak again just like last time, then for some reason, either the same person or another person took the note off again. They were in a hurry, which is why one of the pins got left behind. No doubt there were too many people coming and going in the gallery for them to risk being seen. Either that or it just got pulled off accidentally in the general muddle as everyone collected their things.'

'Or possibly someone just wanted me to get pricked by a pin?' Dottie said, but Flora shook her head.

'No, Darling, because if the aim was just to hurt you, they'd have put it higher up at the front, where you would hold the cloak as you put it on, or gather it around you against the cold. At least, that's what I would do.'

They looked at each other. After a moment, with reluctance, and somewhat fearful of sounding foolish, Dottie said, 'Do you think it could possibly be a warning?'

Flora gave her a straight look. 'I don't see how it can be anything else.'

'B-but why?'

'Well, it's clear from what has been said, and the little incidents that have occurred, that the cloak is being associated with that picture we've seen—all right—you've seen twice and I've seen once—of that Queen Esther character. Think about the wording of the note: *The Queen's colour*. Someone is upset with you because they think you oughtn't to wear this gold cloak. They think it's a colour that only the Queen should wear. Or her—what are they—followers, servants? And not just any Queen, either, but *the* Queen. For that person or persons, that means Queen Esther.'

'B-but why?' Dottie said again, this time sounding more confused than worried. At that moment George put his head around the door.

'Greeley says there are cakes, sandwiches and soup, cocoa and mulled wine in the drawing-room if you want them. I'm going straight to bed.'

'Greeley is a wonder! I adore him!' Flora said with a laugh.

'I'm not telling him that, he already thinks far too highly of his own opinion!' George said. 'He never used to go to this much trouble when I was a bachelor.'

'I don't want anything,' Dottie said, but Flora followed George out into the hall where Dottie could hear them slowly saying goodnight. She called out, 'I can still hear you from in here!'

She smiled as she heard George give a low laugh and there was a soft sound which she knew was him giving Flora a gentle slap on the bottom. Then Dottie heard the sound of him going upstairs. She sighed. She had to admit that Flora and George made being in love seem so easy. And so romantic.

Flora came back into the room, looking pink with embarrassment.

'Remind me never to stay in the house of newlyweds again,' Dottie said, rolling her eyes.

'We're not newlyweds anymore, we're an old married couple—once the first year is out of the way and the babies start to come along, well, it's the beginning of the end really.' Flora looked ruefully down at her waist, which as far as Dottie could tell was as flat as ever. 'I hope he still loves me when I'm fat and tired all the time.'

'Of course he will, he'll still be chasing you round the bedroom when you've got six of the little blighters.'

'Oh God,' Flora said, looking worried, 'I hope we shan't have six. Come on, let's go and get comfortable in the drawing-room. If you need me to use my brain, I need some food. I can't think on an empty stomach, and now that I'm...'

'I was wondering how long it would be before you said it!' Dottie smirked at her sister, and followed her into the room, mimicking her sister as she went, "Now that I'm eating for two!' Just remember that what you eat now is going to sit on your hips for the next fifty or sixty years.'

Flora, flomping down on the sofa, threw a cushion at her.

In spite of what Dottie had said, they both opted for sandwiches and mulled wine, kicked off their high-heeled shoes and curled up in opposite corners.

Ten minutes later, feeling pleasantly full and drowsy, and seeing the fire was dying down in the grate, Flora said, 'Let's go up. We can talk about this tomorrow.'

'Today, I think you mean,' Dottie corrected her. 'It's after three.'

Flora groaned. 'I do hope we don't get any visitors calling horribly early. And that includes the parents. They're joining us for lunch. I hope they realise that means they're not supposed to arrive until twelve o'clock at the earliest. Night-night Dot-Dot,' she said, in the manner of their nursery days, and she dropped a kiss on Dottie's hair, straightened and said, 'Don't forget George is bringing some of his pals back for dinner tomorrow—today rather—though they won't arrive until about half past six or seven o'clock.' She blew her sister another kiss and left the room.

Dottie decided she may as well go up too. She shivered in the hall. The New Year was only three hours old yet already the colder winter weather had begun to assert itself.

As she peeled off her stockings and balled them up, and pulled her dress up and over her head, leaving it in a bundle on the floor, she thought about her gold cloak and the reactions it had provoked.

It was clear. Someone—or possibly several people—hadn't liked her wearing it. The saleswoman at Liberty's had told them several others had bought the stuff, including Susan Dunne who also had the picture, and her friend the mysterious Mrs Penterman. The only Mrs Penterman amongst Dottie's acquaintance was Cyril's mother. And yet, for all her faults as a hostess and an overly watchful mother of an eligible bachelor, she had not seemed the type to pin warning notes on people's cloaks, or whisper enigmatic, possibly even threatening messages. Dottie certainly couldn't imagine Cyril's mother in a gold cloak of her own. So was there another Mrs Penterman?

What was it the unknown person at the Moyers' had said? *You wear your colour too boldly*, or words to that effect?

Dottie got into bed and reached to turn out the light. She tried to remember. Had Susan Dunne or Cyril's mother been anywhere near her when the voice had murmured in her ear? She shook her head. She just couldn't remember. But both women had been present at the Moyers' engagement ball although not at the Gascoignes' that evening.

What outer wear had Mrs Penterman worn to Muriel's engagement? Again, try as she might, Dottie just couldn't remember. She didn't know whether the Pentermans had arrived before or after the Mandersons but she felt sure that if she'd seen anyone wearing a gold cloak similar to her own, she would have noticed it at once. And probably would have remarked on the fact to the wearer.

But that murmured comment had seemed to say such bright colours shouldn't be worn in public. Yet what was the point of having such a lovely, and warm, cloak if not to wear it? If not to go out in public, when would one wear a cloak? After all, cloaks were designed exactly for those times when one went outside, surely?

Dottie gave it up. As sleep stole over her body and she

closed her eyes, she resolved to speak directly to Susan about the matter. No more wondering and beating about the bush. Besides, it was the only way to satisfy her own curiosity. She was fed up with being pricked by pins. Her last waking thought was, oh and Diana is also going to have one made. I must remember to tell...

'And why did they call me 'sister'?' Dottie asked herself the moment she awoke. She had dreamed all night of nothing but the intrigue that was going round in her mind, and it had caused her an uneasy sleep. It took a few moments for the dream to recede. She looked around for a moment, then remembered she had slept at Flora's home. She settled back under the covers. The Gascoignes' guest room was as much her own domain as her bedroom at home. She thought back to the message. She had only one sister—Flora. There was no possibility of her having anything to do with all this. It therefore didn't mean actual sisters, but metaphorical sisters. 'So where does that leave me?' She hugged the blankets about herself, shivering.

She smiled at Janet as the maid brought in her tea, and wished her a good morning. Dottie pulled herself up into a sitting position and received the tray across her lap. 'I thought you'd gone to visit your mother?'

Janet was hauling the curtains open and letting a half-hearted sun shine into the room. 'Happy New Year, Miss.'

'Happy New Year,' Dottie responded, surprised to recall that it was still only New Year's day.

'I was meant to be going to my mum's, Miss, but then I had a row with my young man. He was staring at some girl all the evening and I took him up about it. So then we had a row, then after that I didn't much feel like going to Hyde Park to see the New Year in—it all felt a bit flat. So then I stayed here instead of going to Mum's.'

'I know what you mean,' Dottie said. 'The ball last night at the Gascoignes' wasn't particularly vibrant either.'

'No handsome young man there who took your eye?' Janet was now unravelling the bundled stockings and placing them in the laundry bag. Next she held up the navy blue satin gown Dottie had left on the floor. 'Looks like...' Janet gave an expert's sniff, 'Oh yes, that's mulled wine all right, all over the front hip and down to the hem. I'll get it dealt with presently.'

'Don't bother,' Dottie told her. 'I don't like it any more. So what time did you get back here? Did they have a room ready for you?'

'Well, Miss, usually they gives me a cosy little room up the top at the back, the one with the lovely view of the park, but because I didn't give them no notice of coming, I had to share with Miss Flora's maid Cissie. Lord, how that girl can talk!'

Dottie chuckled. 'That's why Flora and Cissie get on so well. Did she tell you Flora's news?'

'Oh yes, Miss, ever so excited Cissie was, they all are. I was in the kitchen last night with Cook and Mr Greeley and well—in fact, we was all there—and we had our own little New Year's party, and we toasted Miss Flora and Mr George and their happy event. The coming baby was all Cook talked about all evening. Dead excited she is. There's nothing like a new baby, I always say,' she added sagaciously.

'Very true.'

Janet was about to leave, the navy gown over her arm, when Dottie said, 'Janet, you know my new cloak? The gold one? Have you seen any other ladies wearing one like it?'

'No Miss, I can't say as I have. Mind you, I haven't been away apart from to come here. But no one's been to the house in one anything like yours. Why, has there been a run on them or summat?'

'I'm not sure, but I'm beginning to think there may have been.'

'If that's the case, you'll like as not stop wearing it. I know you, Miss, you like to be a little bit apart from the crowd, don't you, Miss? But I say, it's a real becoming cloak on you, so don't rush into getting rid of it till you know for sure everyone's wearing the same one.'

'Hmm. You're right, Janet, as always. See you in a bit. I'll probably be going home tomorrow morning, Flora and George have got friends coming for dinner, so I'll stay the night and go home after breakfast. If you want to go back tonight, you can, if they need you. Otherwise just stay and keep Cissie and the Greeleys company. Perhaps get Mr Greeley to telephone home and ask if you're needed there, we don't want my mother on the warpath.'

'Yes, Miss, I will. Just ring for me if you need anything else, I'll be in the kitchen most of the time once I've done your bathroom and had a bit of a tidy up.' Like her mistress, Janet was also almost as home at the George Gascoignes' as she was at the Mandersons'. Both of us are so used to going back and forth, Dottie thought, and couldn't help wondering momentarily how the new arrival would affect her casually popping in and out of her brother-in-law's house as she had been used to doing.

She got up reluctantly and got herself ready to face the day—the first day of the year—she reminded herself. Next she went to find her sister.

Flora was looking very pale, Dottie was alarmed to see, and she rushed to her side, demanding to know what was wrong.

'I've been as sick as a dog since five o'clock this morning,' Flora told her. She looked really unlike herself. 'George is off somewhere doing something manly with his cronies and some guns, and they'll come back for dinner this evening. Oh Dottie, I didn't know it would start so soon. I feel ghastly. And Mother and Father will be here in an hour and a half.'

Dottie pulled a chair over to sit beside her, and put her arm about Flora's shoulders. 'Have you had any breakfast?'

Flora shook her head. 'I didn't think I could bear...'

'Nonsense,' Dottie said briskly. 'Everyone knows you have to take toast and sweet tea until at least the end of the third month. I'll go and see Cook. You should have sent Cissie to get it for you.'

'I'm afraid she's still changing my bed and airing out

the room,' Flora said ruefully.

Dottie looked at her and grimaced. 'Oh dear. Right ho, you stay put, I'll be right back.'

She was gone for five minutes and returned with Cook herself carrying the tray for Flora.

'Mrs Greeley insisted on coming to take a look at you,' Dottie explained.

'Ten children I've had, and they're all still alive, thank the good Lord,' said Cook almost before she entered the room. 'So if there's anything I know about, it's being in the family way.' Small and slender, she was as unlike a cook as Dottie could imagine. Which belied the seductive power of her rice pudding and sponge cakes. Cook set the tray down and took a good look at her young mistress. 'Hmm. Peaky, that's what you are. What you want, Madam, is a little bit o' toast, and some hot sweet tea, then back to bed with you.'

'But...' said Flora.

'No buts now. You do as you're told, Miss Flora,' Cook told her severely. Flora smiled. It had been over a year since anyone had called her Miss Flora. It was comforting. 'Now here's a little bit of toast with the crusts cut off. Just have a wee bit of butter on it and a drop of nice sharp jam, I've brought blackcurrant, but I can just as easy go and fetch you a pot of gooseberry or plum. And lots of sugar in your tea. Now, while you're—you know—you'll find it helps to have a little bit every so often rather than big meals. And get as much rest as you can. It'll soon pass and then you'll begin to bloom, you mark my words. You just ring if you need anything.'

'Thank you, I shall, and will you please tell Cissie how sorry...'

'Ah! Don't you go apologising to Cissie. She don't mind in the least. You've never been the slightest trouble. And when you goes back to bed, it'll all be spick and span in your room. And you just take yourself a nice rest and you'll be as right as ninepence. Now, stop worrying and take care of yourself. Call me if you need me, or send Miss Dottie down. Er—I'm guessing Mr and Mrs Manderson won't be joining us for lunch after all?'

'Oh Lord, I don't know. Dottie?'

'I'll telephone to them and say you're under the weather, and they can come in time for dinner. I expect Father will be glad of some time to read the paper in peace, anyhow. He had quite a few drinks last night.'

'Oh thank you,' Flora said gratefully. 'I don't feel up to Mother quite yet.'

And Cook, nodding her approval and saying, 'Well that's settled then,' bustled away leaving a tearful but happy and reassured Flora to nibble at her toast.

When Dottie came back from telephoning, she set herself the task of keeping Flora's teacup topped up and soon Flora admitted she was feeling a little better. She allowed herself to be persuaded to go back to her room, where her bed had indeed been remade, and the room was fresh and clean, a scent of lavender hanging on the January air. Cissie hovered, 'just in case', but Flora thanked her and allowed her to return to the kitchen, adding,

'Perhaps you wouldn't mind waking me at four o'clock if I'm not up before then? Thank goodness the men won't be back until seven. And Mr and Mrs Manderson will now also be arriving for dinner.'

Flora lay back under the covers and Dottie could see she was really going to go to sleep. She had hoped to tell Flora about her dream, but it would have to wait. She kissed Flora and went back downstairs.

She went into the little library that was a pale imitation of her father's but nonetheless a comfortable room. She sat at the desk, pulled out pen, ink and paper, and wrote down everything she could recall of her dream, just in case she had forgotten it by the time she had the opportunity of telling her sister all about it. Dottie wrote: 'In my dream I was wearing my cloak and I was walking in a garden. I didn't recognise where I was, but somehow I knew it was the home of the Pentermans.

'It had been sunny, but suddenly the sun was gone and it had turned to deepest night. The trees and shrubs pressed in all about me, and I heard strange calls and slitherings and rustlings as if I was in a jungle. I felt frightened and began to really push my way through the vegetation, certain that I couldn't afford to lose sight of the others, though I don't know who the others were or where they had gone. They were ahead of me somewhere, that was all I knew.

'I hurried on and had to keep freeing my cloak from thorns and branches that it got snagged on and which pricked me and scratched me. Ahead of me stood a tree on the edge of a clearing. I hid myself behind the tree and peered out. I could see a fire burning, and there was an altar, and around the altar and the fire were a dozen or more shadowy figures, all dressed in cloaks just like mine. They were chanting softly, and I could tell from their voices that they were all women. But I couldn't see their faces because their hoods were pulled right up over their heads, so that their faces were hidden in shadow.

'Then, I began to feel terribly afraid, and the sound of my heartbeat was so loud it made them all turn around and they began to come towards me. But instead of running, I just stayed where I was, rooted to the spot, unable to move. I was frozen with fear. I held up my arms in front of my face to try to ward them off, but I knew I couldn't escape.

'The first one, the one who I thought seemed to be in charge, came up to me with her hand stretched out and as she touched me, her hood fell back and in the firelight I could see her face. It was Susan Dunne. And she began to sing the song that Archie had sung, then when she stopped, she drew out a dagger from under her cloak and plunged it into my chest, saying, 'How dare you wear the colour of the daughters of the Queen!"

Dottie stopped writing and rubbed her aching wrist. Yes, that was more or less everything she could remember, except the fact that, when Susan had said those words, Dottie had fallen to the ground, and it was then that she had woken up. It all sounded so melodramatic and silly now that she was thinking about it in the cold light of day, but she couldn't forget that when she had first woken from the dream, she had been shaking with fear.

*

Chapter Fifteen

Flora slept soundly until Cissie woke her at four o'clock, and came down to join Dottie for afternoon tea, still wearing her nightgown and negligee, and with a pair of George's socks on her feet instead of her usual satin mules.

'I'll get dressed in a bit,' she said, 'but right now I'm desperate for a cuppa.'

Dottie approved the return of colour to Flora's cheeks, and the absence of the bags under her eyes. She looked young and pretty, and completely herself again.

'What have you been doing with yourself all afternoon?' Flora asked.

'Ah! I'm glad you asked. I had a rather horrid dream last night so I went into the library and sat down in a very business-like way, and I wrote it all down in case I forgot it, and now I want you to read it, if you feel up to doing that?'

'I feel fabulous, actually,' Flora said, and she certainly looked it. Dottie told her so, then went to collect her sheet of paper from her room.

When she came back, they spent half an hour just

enjoying their tea. Finally, Flora declared herself ready, and piled her plate, cup and saucer back on the tray and held out her hand. Dottie passed her the page, saying, 'Tell me what you make of that.'

'Oh gosh, there's enough of it! Both sides!'

'Sorry, there seemed to be so much to say. It's not just about the dream but my feelings about it, and about the other things that have happened.'

On the mantelpiece, the clock that had been a wedding present from one of George's hundreds of aunts ticked loudly and drowned the silence as Flora sat reading. Dottie could hardly contain her impatience when Flora went back to the beginning and read the whole thing through a second time. At last she handed the page back to Dottie, and Dottie practically snatched it from her, demanding, 'Well?'

Flora raised a delicate brow.

'I think you're absolutely right.'

Dottie was momentarily confused. That was not what she had been expecting. Flora explained. 'I've been thinking of what we said last night about why anyone has a cloak. And the fact that you've been wearing yours has seemed to upset at least one person, and possibly two or three people.'

'And?'

'I think you're right. The only explanation it can possibly be is that there is some kind of peculiar sect or secret society whose members wear a gold cloak as a sign of their—what you may call it—belonging.'

'Allegiance,' supplied Dottie, 'or affiliation. Membership.'

'Exactly. It seems to me that's the only way any of this makes sense.'

'But a sect?' Dottie repeated, shaking her head, 'Or a secret society? It's all a bit...don't you think? And one for women?'

'Why not? Women have had the vote since I was little. Perhaps some women are now ready to branch out into more—esoterical—um, thingies.'

'How beautifully you express it,' Dottie laughed. 'I suppose there are enough things that are for men only. Cyril was saying the other day that one of his clubs now admits women members. Apparently half the men have resigned their memberships in protest already. And Cyril said, what's to stop some clubs from being exclusively for women? Cyril said he thinks women should have the same advantages as men.'

'Oh Cyril said that, did he?'

'What do you mean? Why shouldn't he?'

'Oh no reason. Apart from the fact that you go all pink and soft and fluttery when you talk about him—or even just think about him.'

'I do not!' Dottie said, and promptly demonstrated that she was lying by going extremely pink. 'I just realised that the assistant at Liberty's told us that his mother was one of the women who bought the gold fabric, that's all. Or at least, said a Mrs Penterman bought some of the fabric. It might not be the same person. And, I forgot to tell you, George's sister Diana is planning to have one made up, she told me. And she said some very odd things about wifely duties. At least, it was more the way she said it.'

'Hmm,' Flora murmured, deep in thought. She stared into space for a moment then said, 'Perhaps we should call on Mrs Penterman. Have you met her?'

'Only briefly. Not enough to say that I know her, more like seen the side of her face across a room. I don't think she likes me.'

'Ah the fateful tea party! I'd forgotten about that. I wonder if we could persuade Mother to help out with her?'

'I'm sure she would,' Dottie said, 'so long as she doesn't know anything about the cloak thing. She'll be happy just believing that she is forging bonds for the future. Though I should mention that she was more than a bit put out over the way Mrs Penterman received us at her afternoon tea. Mother thinks Mrs Penterman wants someone else for Cyril, and will make him take her instead of me.'

Flora raised an eyebrow at this, and looking at Dottie

said, 'I hadn't realised things had progressed so well between you and Cyril.'

'We've dined a few times, and danced, of course. He's been to us for cards, and of course dinner and afternoon tea. And we've had lots of long talks about the future. He said,' she faltered, then went on with a stronger voice, 'Don't tell Mother, but he said his parents wanted him to settle down and get married and that he had come to realise that was just what he wanted to do. He said we should have a serious talk when he comes back from his Christmas break on Saturday. He-He kissed me.'

'My, my!' Flora said and came to hug her sister. 'I'm very happy for you, Darling, he's a delightful chap, and I'm sure you'll both be very happy. You will tell me, won't you, the minute he proposes?'

'Of course,' Dottie said. 'I don't think we're anywhere near *that* yet!' she said, but inside she was thinking, he's going to propose next time we see each other. This time next week, we'll be engaged. She still felt flustered and embarrassed, but it was rather a relief to talk about it even a little. She nibbled at another petit-fours, and poured herself some more tea. 'And now, coming back to business, how about another visit to Susan Dunne?'

'She didn't exactly welcome us with open arms last time,' Flora pointed out.

'True, but I'm planning a more direct attack. This time I shall simply say, tell me about the Esther thing and what it's all about. Perhaps I could pretend I want to join?'

'Do you really think she'll tell you anything? Or even admit there is anything to tell?' Flora laughed. The clock struck the quarter and Flora, shocked, leapt to her feet.

'Oh for goodness' sake! A quarter past five! George will be arriving home at seven with his pals!'

And she leapt to her feet and hurried out into the hall. Almost immediately Dottie heard her running up the stairs and reflected that Flora had certainly made a good recovery from her bout of sickness that morning.

Dottie was seated between George's friends Charles and

Alistair, the doctor who'd assisted Archie Dunne on that fateful night a month earlier. She decided that Flora must have planned the table that way to maximise Dottie's enjoyment of the evening, for the two young men were highly entertaining, and kept her amused throughout the meal, so much so that she hardly had a moment to spare for conversing with anyone else.

Glancing across the table to where Flora was laughing at something the gentleman on her left had said, Dottie felt a huge sense of relief to see her looking so well, and so like her normal self again.

During a lull in the conversation, whilst Alistair was exchanging a comment with the lady on the other side of him, Charles turned to Dottie and with a serious look, asked if she had quite recovered from 'that dreadful business' back at the end of November. She had long suspected him of being fond of her, but although she enjoyed his company, she found it difficult to view him as anything more than a kind of unofficial cousin. She had known both him and Alistair for years, although not as intimately as Flora and George.

Coming back to his question, she told him she thought she was quite recovered, but that she would dearly love to know whether anyone had been arrested for the crime.

'That's the awful thing about it,' she said. 'The police came round and asked lots of questions, then that's practically the last one hears of it unless there's something in the newspaper.'

'Well, that Hardy chap still seems to be on the case,' Charles said. 'He spoke to both of us again just last week. That must mean that things have ground to a halt and he's gone back to the beginning of the case to try to find some clue that's got overlooked. Like they do in detective stories.'

Dottie nodded in agreement, biting her lip. 'Do you know him at all?' she asked.

'What Hardy? Yes. Not as well as we used to, of course, not since that business with his father. Before that we used to see each other all the time. Good chap. Quiet. Very sharp though, never misses a trick. No doubt perfect as a detective, don't you know.'

Alistair had returned to the conversation by now, and he nodded, and said, 'Shame about his engagement. He was madly in love with some girl who, as soon as the money dried up, wasn't seen for dust. Left the fellow flat less than a month before the wedding. That couldn't have helped the financial situation, all that money spent and everything cancelled at the last moment.'

'How awful,' Dottie said. 'Poor Sergeant Hardy!' A uniformed arm leaned across and removed her plate. She smiled up at Greeley and thanked him, adding softly, 'Tell Mrs Greeley that was truly divine. I don't know how she does it.'

Greeley nodded and leaned closer to whisper to her, avoiding the notice of the other guests, 'I'll tell her you said so, Miss Dottie. To tell the truth she was a bit worried how it would turn out, she hadn't tried that recipe before, but the fishmonger let her down at the last minute.' They exchanged a conspiratorial smile, then he moved on.

'What about Archie Dunne? Did you know him too?' she continued, turning back to Charles and Alistair.

'Sadly no. He was a couple of years below us at Oxford. Of course one knew *of* him. His reputation.'

'His reputation?'

'Terrible philanderer. Made Henry VIII look quite the monk.'

Dottie thought about this, then on impulse, she revealed to Charles and Alistair the information George had gleaned from the cigarette girl at the theatre.

Alistair laughed. 'What rot!'

Dottie was somewhat taken aback. 'What makes you say that?'

'First of all, he'd ever be concerned about anything Susan got up to. She has always been more than a little odd, and frankly he could hardly bear to be in her company for more than half an hour, if the gossip at the club is anything to go by.'

'Yes, and also,' Charles chipped in. 'That just sounds

like something out of a play or the music hall. Pretend to be his girlfriend so he could follow his wife? No one would fall for that rubbish for a moment. Mark my words, that young lady was pulling old George's leg.'

He seemed so certain, and with a full stomach and in such genial company, Dottie found herself admitting that he was right, it didn't sound at all likely now she thought about it.

'So had he a special interest in any particular young lady at the time of his death, according to the talk at the club?' she asked.

'I was afraid you might ask that,' Charles said, and for the first time he looked uncomfortable. He delayed the moment of revelation by taking a long drink of his wine, then glanced across the table to where George and Flora were laughing with their guests. For what seemed like an hour, Dottie couldn't breathe. Then she managed to tear her eyes away and looked back at Charles with a look of concern.

'You can't mean...?'

'What? No, no! Heaven forbid!' he said hastily, and Dottie's shoulders slumped in relief. 'No, not a bit of it, sorry to make you think...' He took another drink. 'Though I hardly like to say.' He exchanged a look with Alistair who nodded. 'It is a little close to home—but certainly not as close as *that*.'

Dottie fixed him with a look and said firmly, 'Just tell me, Charles.'

Another look passed between the two men then Charles said hastily, 'Look, I don't say there's anything in it, it's just what chaps are saying, what everyone is saying.'

'And?' prompted Dottie.

'Well, the word is that Archie Dunne had taken up with Diana Gascoigne.'

She grabbed his arm. She whispered, 'Diana Gascoigne? George's sister?' He nodded ruefully.

That gave her cause to think. And as the next course was served, and the servants were coming and going and guests were exclaiming excitedly over their plates and laughing and chatting, she thought furiously.

'Look, I'm sorry,' Charles was saying, clearly feeling he needed to make amends. 'Perhaps I oughtn't to have said anything. I didn't want to upset you. Y-you won't say anything to old George?'

'No, it's quite all right, Charles. Don't worry about that.'

'It's what I've heard, that's all. Eh, Alistair, that's what everyone's saying? Archie Dunne and Diana?'

'Oh rather,' Alistair said, dipping his head in the characteristic manner that made him seem much older than he really was but was also very doctorly, Dottie thought. 'Yes, that's why I for one was so astonished when she went and announced her engagement to that other fellow, that Jeremy Wotsiname. Because everyone knew she and Archie... In fact, I'd been expecting the chap to leave Susan, he was reported to be so besotted with young Diana. I did hear that he went round to the Gascoignes' to have it out with Diana, but her father saw him off, threatened him with a horsewhip if he dared to show his face again.'

'That sounds like a lot more than just gossip, sounds as though it could be genuine,' Dottie said, thinking aloud. They looked at her in concern.

'You won't say anything, will you?' Charles said again, with a worried glance down the table. 'Wouldn't want poor old George to know I've been bad-mouthing his little sister.'

*

Chapter Sixteen

Inspector Hardy took the newly-promoted Detective Constable Frank Maple with him when he went to Archie Dunne's flat. They travelled by mini-cab from the police station and got out a little along the road from Richmond Villas, the modern block where Dunne's flat was located.

'This explains where he was going, too, the night he was killed. This road leads off Mortlake Gardens,' Hardy remarked. 'Clearly he was on his way here that night.'

As they walked the remaining few yards, in spite of the miserable weather Hardy formed the opinion it was a pleasant area. Almost immediately Maple said exactly that, adding, 'And it looks a sight better kept than Dunne's proper home too.'

Hardy paused to fish the key out of his jacket pocket, still in a small envelope in case he should lose it or mistake it for his own. 'Just what I thought myself,' he said. 'And you'd think Mrs Dunne would be happier in a modern flat rather than that dark, scruffy place.'

'Women don't usually like dark places,' Maple said. 'Dark places are often damp and that brings in the insects, earwigs, spiders and whatnot; women don't like those.'

'I bow to your experience in that,' Hardy said with a laugh. The outside door was open when he turned the handle, and just as well as the latch-key wouldn't have fitted that lock. They went into a dim hallway, with stairs going off to the right and ahead of them, a front door with a number 2 in the middle of it, and to the left, a door bearing the number 1.

'I presume flat 4 is on the next floor,' Hardy said, and he moved across the black and white tiles, so like those in the entrance of the house where he and his family were currently living, and he started up the stairs.

Sure enough flat 4 was the one facing them across the hall as they reached the landing. Here the floor tiles had given way to a cheap but clean dark green carpet; light streamed in at a window and lit a somewhat dusty but otherwise healthy-looking aspidistra in an enormous painted clay pot. The landing's painted walls were dull but clean, and once again, Hardy was struck by the thought that if the quality of the furnishings and decorations were not of the highest standard, the place was, at least, quite clean and reasonably well-maintained.

Maple was about to ring the doorbell of flat 4, but Hardy stopped him and slipped the key into the keyhole and turned the door handle. The door opened with a slight creak and from within, Hardy heard a muffled curse and voice of a frightened-sounding young woman called out, 'Who's there?'

The inner hall of the flat was dark, and heading in the direction of the voice, Hardy collided with a small, fair-haired woman in a negligée.

'If it's about the rent, I told you...oh!' she said. 'You're not the landlord.'

'No, Miss. We're the police,' Hardy told her. 'Who are you?'

'Erm...' Clearly she was debating whether to make up an alias or to tell the truth.

'I don't want to arrest you for hindering a police investigation, but I shall if I have to,' he warned her. Maple moved forward, his hand going to his pocket as if reaching for handcuffs.

She exhaled heavily, her shoulders sagging. She turned and headed back into the room, saying over her shoulder, 'Oh very well. I'm Diana Gascoigne. You'd better come in.'

So here was 'D', Hardy thought triumphantly, and hard on that a soft voice told him he'd known all along that Dottie Manderson couldn't have been the mistress of Archie Dunne.

The room was sparingly furnished but with some nice pieces. The view from the window was of a small private park such as those scattered all over London, for the exclusive use of residents of the street or cul-de-sac. A soft, gentle snow had begun to fall.

'So now you know,' Miss Gascoigne said with a hint of defiance, 'I'm the 'other woman'. Have you been looking for me?'

'Yes, we have,' Hardy told her, and he took a seat on the settee opposite her, and a little uncertainly, Maple sat next to him and got out his little notebook and neatly sharpened pencil.

'I think you'd better give me an alibi for the night Archie Dunne was killed,' Hardy said.

She lit a cigarette with shaking hands, waving the match to extinguish the flame and flinging it into the ashtray on the arm of her chair. Her voice trembled as she spoke.

'Well, I was here, wasn't I? Like an idiot I just sat here waiting for the man who never came, and wondering why he was so late.' Her voice broke on the last word and she took a drag of her cigarette. 'I can't prove it. No one else knew, or saw me here. I have my own key, of course, so I can come and go as I please. I'd been here most of the afternoon. I'd cooked. Can you believe it? Me! Cooking a meal for my Lord and Master like some good little wife. If you'd told me a year ago... But no, to answer your inevitable next question, no one saw me.'

There was a long silence. Hardy watched her, waiting for something more. At last, the silence too much, she burst out, 'Well surely you don't think it was me? I've lost—well, everything, that's all. I've only lost everything—my future with the man I loved, that I worshipped, even. Why would I...? Whoever did this, they've destroyed my life, taken everything,' she repeated, her voice dying away.

'Were you aware that he had spent the night with another woman?' Hardy asked, watching her face carefully. But she was neither surprised nor upset by the news.

'That girl from the theatre? Oh yes, he told me about her. But I wasn't his keeper, you know. I knew there were—would always be—other women. But he loved me, I knew that. He would always come back to me. He was going to divorce Susan and marry me as soon as he was free. I didn't mind sharing him, even with Susan, not really. I wouldn't have minded if he never married me, it was only because of the baby. He said he didn't want the child to be illegitimate. He couldn't give me an engagement ring, that would have been noticed. But he gave me a brooch, partly as a gift because of the baby and partly as a birthday present. It's in the bedroom on the dressing table. You can check if you like.'

Hardy nodded to Maple who left the room, returning almost immediately with a small jewellery box. The brooch was there. Hardy saw immediately that it fitted the description from the jeweller's ledger, and was certainly a match with the other items he had brought away with him. If he'd had any doubts, her next words would have clinched it.

'He'd just had the other bits of the set cleaned for me, for my birthday as well. They've been in his family for donkey's years. But he hadn't given me the other bits, they will still be at the jeweller's if you want to check. I think I have the name of the chap here somewhere.'

'Don't trouble about it, I already know about the jewellery,' Hardy told her. 'And the baby, is it his?'

'Well obviously it's Archie's! I mean, what do you take me for? No, don't answer that. I know what you must think of me.'

'I'm sorry, Miss Gascoigne, but I had to ask, you know.

I don't doubt your word in the slightest. When is the baby due?'

'Not until June. He—Archie—was so excited. Every time he saw me, he'd stroke my stomach and say, 'how's my little chap?' We used to joke, I'd say why did he think it was a boy, that I was sure it was a girl, and that I was going to call it Henrietta, after my great-aunt, just to tease him...' She bit her lip, and sighed again, and shielded her eyes with her hand. 'What am I going to do?' she asked, scarcely above a breath. 'I suppose it's inevitable all this will come out.'

'I don't think even the police can cover up a baby,' Hardy said. 'I'm very sorry. I'll do what I can, of course, But I'm sure that Mr Dunne's family, and your own, will help you.'

'Oh Mummy and Daddy will hit the roof, but they will stand by me, I don't doubt that. I expect I'll mysteriously develop pneumonia and be sent off to some place miles away at the seaside for six months or so, then come back looking quite marvellous, and get on with my life, whilst some total stranger...' She bit her lip, and a tear rolled down her cheek. She looked at him. 'Please don't say anything official, not until I've told them. I'm begging you. Let me tell them first in my own way. I couldn't bear for them to find out from a policeman.'

Hardy promised he would give her time, adding, 'I don't believe I'll need to speak to your parents about this, in any case, Miss Gascoigne.'

He got to his feet. He held out his hand to her. She shook it, a little surprised, and with the air of one sealing a pact.

'Well good day, Miss Gascoigne, thank you for your assistance. If there's anything you need, anything at all, please don't hesitate to ask. Take care of yourself. We'll see ourselves out.'

The two policemen walked to the corner of the street and in Mortlake Gardens, hailed a cab. As it drove away, Maple said, 'Phew, what a turn up! D'you reckon she's telling the truth?'

'Yes,' Hardy said, 'I do.'

It was fortunate that Flora was not the sort of woman to be offended by gossip of a scurrilous nature about people who were part of her wider family. It was the day after the dinner party, and Dottie had told her what Alistair and Charles had said about Diana.

'Don't let George hear about it, though. You know how protective he is of his family honour,' she said, and indeed Dottie did. She promised to keep what she'd been told to herself, but making the most of George being out for the day, she felt no compunction about asking Flora what she made of it.

'I'd say it sounds exactly like the sort of thing Diana would do, to get involved with a married man. Her family proudly hail her as a 'free thinker', but I've always thought she was an immodest little madam. As Cook would say, she's no better than she should be. And she does have quite the reputation, I understand, though she's only, what, eighteen? Nineteen?'

'Nineteen in March,' Dottie confirmed. 'So only a year younger than me. I must admit I'm a bit shocked, but it does fit in quite nicely with our little mystery. It certainly makes me wonder if she was with Archie Dunne that night. Because now I've had the chance to think about it a bit more, about what that cigarette girl told George, you know Alistair was right, it does sound remarkably idiotic. Talk about a tall tale. Who would do anything like that? Go up to a girl he didn't even know and persuade her to back him up if anyone asked why he'd been out all evening?'

'Yes, I'm afraid we swallowed a big fat lie there. At the time, it just didn't occur to me to doubt her story.'

'I bet if we'd spoken to her, we'd have known immediately that she wasn't telling the truth. George is too gullible by half. It's because he's so jolly decent, he doesn't have our nasty suspicious minds,' Dottie added, and her sister nodded ruefully. Dottie got up. 'Well, thank you for the tea. I've got to dash, I told Mother I'd only be an hour, and I've still got to buy all the things she asked for. You will be there at the tea tomorrow?'

'Yes, I'm sure I shall. I'm feeling so much better now I'm taking Cook's advice and getting up slowly in the mornings, and having lots of sweet tea and toast. I shall weigh a ton by the time this baby arrives, and the sugar will probably rot all my teeth—but at least I shan't be sick in the mornings. Certainly by afternoon I'm fine.'

Dottie kissed her goodbye and hurried out. She quickly completed the purchases for her mother then took the opportunity to pay a flying visit to Liberty's. It was a huge relief to find the same woman at the sales counter.

'I see that gold cloth is all gone,' Dottie said to her. The assistant smiled.

'Yes indeed, Madam. Very popular it was, although we don't seem to be able to get anymore. Were you wanting a bit extra?'

Dottie reassured her on that score. Then she asked, 'Was all the fabric bought by ladies to make up cloaks, do you know? Only I've had a number of comments about mine.'

'Well I'm only guessing about the cloaks, as one or two of them bought the patterns too, but I don't know if that's what they were all using it for. Some said they hadn't made up their minds, but that the stuff seemed too nice to pass up. Mind you, most of the ladies sent their maids to buy the stuff, so the girls mightn't have known how it was to be made up. In fact, yes, I think most said they hadn't decided what they were going to do with the material. I think it was me said about the cloak and how warm and comfortable it would be for going out in this damp weather.'

'Yes, it was lovely,' Dottie said. 'Actually, it's getting a bit embarrassing. So many ladies I know now have these cloaks, my sister's husband says we all look like witches from the same coven. But you know what men are like!'

The assistant smiled politely. Then she said, 'Well Mrs Dunne is a very religious lady, so no one could ever think she would be involved in anything like that devil worship, or anything.'

'I should hope not,' Dottie said fervently. 'And of course her friend Mrs Penterman had some of the stuff too, and I saw her at both the Moyers and the Gascoignes, so it was a little awkward.'

'Yes, now I think of it, Mrs Penterman was with Mrs Dunne and they both had some of the stuff at the same time. Very pleased they were, and said it was exactly what they were looking for. Then Mrs Dunne's maid came in for another length of it, and I could only think that Mrs Dunne had decided to make herself a second cloak, or perhaps make one as a present for someone else. Oh, but, excepting the maid paid for it herself in cash, it was not to be put on Mrs Dunne's account. I thought that was a bit strange.

'Then what should happen the next day but that Mrs Penterman's maid came in for two more lengths. Two. Again, perhaps she thought they would make nice Christmas presents for someone she knew. I do always say that a good bit of colour about you is what you want to get you through these dreary winter months.'

'Oh certainly, you're quite right about that!' Dottie agreed heartily. 'Um, perhaps they were going to make something else out of the fabric.'

'Yes, perhaps.'

'And who had the last cuts of the fabric?' Dottie asked, 'I do hope it wasn't anyone else I'm likely to bump into.'

'One was a smart young piece, not the right class of girl at all. At first I thought she must be another maid, but she wasn't the kind of girl you'd have as a maid, I'm fairly sure. No, she held it up to herself in front of the mirror and said, 'how well it suits me, I must have some', and I thought, yes my girl but when will you ever go anywhere that needs something like that? And the other woman was a maid to Mrs Hambrook, as you might not know as she comes from out of town, somewhere in Essex, I forget where. And it was her had the last of it. Shame. It was lovely stuff; it was that good it practically sold itself.'

After a little more small-talk, Dottie thanked the

assistant and said goodbye. She had quite a bit to tell
Flora. But before that she'd need to find out who this Mrs
Hambrook was.

Another dreary tea on another dreary afternoon, Dottie
thought. Thank goodness Cyril would be coming back to
town in a few more days. She needed a bit of livening up.
If only it were Spring and the sun shining... She came
downstairs in response to hearing the arrivals in the hall
below. Her mother sent her an exasperated look before
directing a bright hostess smile at her guests. The weather
had taken a turn for the worst in the last twenty-four
hours and everyone was swathed in layers against the
driving rain that was washing away the thin layer of snow.
Hats and hair-dos tended towards more robust, practical
styles, employing a great many pins, rather than anything
too fussy; wisps and tendrils were definitely out.

Dottie made herself useful guiding various older ladies
into the drawing-room and getting them comfortable by
the fire, all the while convinced her mother must have
invited only people over the age of seventy to tea.

By the time tea was brought in, everyone had arrived,
sat down and got to know those around them, although at
least half were stalwarts of the Mandersons's teas. Dottie
had made herself pleasant to everyone except Minerva
Penterman whom she still found frankly terrifying. Tall
and fair like her son, Mrs Penterman nevertheless seemed
to possess none of Cyril's easy charm or general air of
good-naturedness. She had a deep vertical line between
her carefully shaped eyebrows and a small straight mouth,
both of which gave her the air of one who is permanently
displeased about something. Added to that, she had the
habit, terribly old-fashioned in Dottie's view, of peering at
everyone she addressed through a lorgnette. Dottie felt
rather like a specimen under a microscope.

So it was a huge relief when Mrs Gerard finally arrived.
Mrs Gerard spent a few minutes in enquiring after the
health and happiness of the Penterman household, which
couldn't be helped, Dottie supposed, as after all she was

the sister of the Honourable Mr Penterman, then Mrs Gerard made her way to a chair by Dottie's side, where she remained for the rest of the afternoon.

It was some time before Dottie felt the surrounding chatter was loud enough for her to risk saying, 'Mrs Gerard, do you by any chance know a Mrs Hambrook?'

'Euphemia Hambrook, do you mean? Or Angelica Hambrook?'

Dottie had to admit she didn't know. She was reluctant to tell Mrs Gerard everything about—well—everything. She didn't want to talk about the cloak, the mysterious and unpleasant notes, or how she felt they were somehow connected to the pictures of Queen Esther and the death of Archie Dunne. Because here in the drawing-room with the hubbub of chattering ladies about her and the occasional clink of cup upon saucer, it all seemed suddenly too childish, too impossible. And her so-called *evidence* seemed thin and unconvincing.

So she settled for vaguely commenting that she'd heard the name recently but couldn't place the lady in question, beyond the fact that she lived somewhere in Essex.

'Oh yes, dear, that would be Effie,' Mrs Gerard said immediately. 'They live out near Southend, for her chest you know. She was fifty last year, and heaven knows she's been at death's door since she got pneumonia at school when we were eleven.'

'A nice lady?' Dottie hazarded.

'A bit eccentric, but yes, I count Effie as a good friend.' Mrs Gerard narrowed her eyes and looked at Dottie with suspicion. 'Why? What have you heard?'

Dottie looked at her in surprise. 'Why, nothing. What have *you* heard?' She was a little surprised at her own boldness, and knew if her mother had heard her she would have reproved her.

But Mrs Gerard appeared to be mollified. She sat back and took a bite of a sandwich on her plate, then lay the sandwich on the plate once again.

Dottie leaned forward. 'Was Archie Dunne really carrying on with Diana?' she hissed. Mrs Gerard coughed on her sandwich and took a minute to recover herself, by which time every eye in the room was on them.

'Good Lord, Dottie!' Mrs Gerard exclaimed, but softly, 'I think—ahem, you'd—ahem ahem—better come and see me Friday, if that's the sort of thing you want to know.' Mrs Gerard took a couple of great gulps of her tea and then added, 'Come at about eleven o'clock, stay for lunch. That suit you?'

Dottie beamed at her and said that it suited very well. At last, she thought, I shall get some proper answers to the questions buzzing round my brain. And—I'll have something to do other than just sitting about the house waiting for Cyril to come home from—wherever it is he's been. Only now did she realise he hadn't said where he was going—and she reminded herself not to get her hopes up too much, in case he wasn't able to see her the same day he returned home.

*

Chapter Seventeen

'I wonder where he was going?' Dottie said suddenly the following afternoon, which was Thursday. Flora glanced up from her magazine. They had been idling the time away, neither of them much interested in doing anything.

'Who, darling?'

'Archie Dunne. It's just come to me. I don't know why I haven't thought of it before. I mean, he was obviously on his way somewhere when he was attacked. But where?'

Flora set aside the magazine and gazed at Dottie, her eyes with the far-off, lovely wistful look they got when she was thinking deeply about something. After a moment she said, 'How odd. You know, until you said that, I'd never given it a thought either. But you're right—where *was* he going? Obviously not home because the Dunne's house is nowhere near here.'

'You know, there are so many points I'd like to discuss with that—um—policeman fellow,' Dottie said casually as if she couldn't quite recall his name. 'It's a shame one can't just stroll into Scotland Yard, or wherever it is, and ask that they sit down with you and explain a few things. You know, take you through everything they've found out and show you all their evidence.'

'Hmm, yes, I can't think why they don't. Perhaps you ought to suggest it?' Flora said with a laugh. 'Now what about popping round to see Susan tomorrow? I doubt she'll encourage us to stay long, if she even lets us in the house at all after last time, but I feel we've got to at least try.'

'Good idea. I'm having lunch with Mrs Gerard tomorrow, but before then I've got a quick thing at Carmichaels, so can we either go fairly early in the morning before I go to Carmichael's, or when I've finished at Mrs Gerard's, just before dinner?'

'All right. Um, well mornings aren't too good for me at the moment, so let's pop in to see her at about half past five. No one dines before seven o'clock so that should be all right.'

'What if her maid says she won't see us as she's dressing?'

'We'll invite ourselves in and wait until she can't stand it any longer and gives in. We'll make it clear we just want a quick word,' Flora said.

They heard the sound of the front door opening and closing.

'Ah, my Lord and Master arrives!' Flora said, and waited expectantly for George to come into the room.

He did. Under his arm he carried a newspaper which he held out to Dottie, who took it, confused, and noticed that Flora was looking at him with concern at his grave expression.

'What is it, Darling?' Flora asked. Dottie heard fear in her voice. She knows his every mood, Dottie thought. Then she too wondered.

'Is something the matter?' she asked. George bent to kiss his wife hello, then turned back to Dottie.

'Dottie, dear, I've just come from my club. I'm afraid— Dottie, I'm most awfully sorry. Something's happened. Something that will affect you. Or rather, that will matter to you.'

'Darling, I do wish you'd just come out with it and tell

us what's wrong,' Flora said. 'You're scaring me.'

He reached out a hand to her. 'It's nothing to be scared of. Just...'

He looked at Dottie who was already feeling upset even though she still had no idea why. George took the paper, opened it to a particular page, and handing it back to her, repeated the words, 'I'm so sorry, my dear.'

Slowly, unable to quite understand at first, Dottie read the headline. She read it out loud, was halfway through reading it before it made sense to her. As soon as she saw his name, she felt a thrill of excitement, but then it was gone and she felt cold to the core.

'The Honourable Cyril Penterman today with his—new bride, the former Miss Anabella Wiseman of the New York Wisemans, attending a banquet in their honour at Pentulloch Castle. The b-bride and groom, who m-married on the last day of December, will journey to their secret h-honeymoon destination tomorrow. The bride was wearing a silk costume in palest pink, made by...'

Dottie dropped the paper onto the floor and turned to stare at the fire. She was dimly aware of a gasping cry from Flora and of her saying something, of an arm around her own shoulders but she couldn't really comprehend what was going on. Her mind was taken up with calculations whilst her memory replayed of every word, every look, his laugh, his voice, his smile.

Gradually it dawned on her, firstly that Cyril had married someone else, and secondly that her face was wet, and that thirdly and finally, she wanted to go home and go to bed.

Flora alternated between two states, tears and rage. George too, was coldly angry. The white, shocked look on his sister-in-law's face worried him, and he felt a paternal urge to see her bundled up in a warm blanket and fed beef tea. Dottie pushed them both away.

'I want to go home. I need—I need to go home. Now, please, if at all possible. I'm sorry to be a nuisance, but really, I think I need to just...'

George drove her, Flora sat in the back holding her hand and when they got to the Mandersons' it was clear the news had already arrived there.

Their mother said nothing, though, merely asked Flora to help her get Dottie upstairs. George went in search of his father-in-law.

Dottie sat on the edge of her bed like a doll, being undressed, dressed in her nightgown and covered. A hot water bottle was placed at her feet, and the light was turned out. The room was lit only by the glow of the fire, the flames licking softly at a new log.

'Why am I so upset?' she murmured in surprise, 'It's not as if he promised me anything...' But she couldn't seem to pull herself together.

Janet came in with a glass of warm milk with a tot of brandy in it, but Dottie only took a sip then pushed it away with a grimace. She turned over and lay facing the wall.

Flora, her mother and Janet all exchanged uncertain looks, then filed out, leaving the door slightly ajar. In the hall, Janet promised to check on Dottie every half hour in case she needed anything.

When Dottie got up the following morning, she knew she looked far from her best. She'd hardly slept, the newspaper headline had simply gone round and round in her mind, banishing sleep, even though it would have been bliss for her to escape her thoughts if only for a few hours.

With his new bride.

After she had washed and dressed, she did her hair and made up her ashen face with more than the usual care. She had decided to adopt her mother's strategy for coping with a crisis: head up, shoulders back and smile.

Her parents were surprised to see her at the breakfast table before them, drinking her morning tea as usual and giving every appearance of eating a slice of toast.

'Dottie, dear,' her mother said in an uncharacteristic rush of maternal devotion. 'Are you sure you're quite all right? I expected you to stay in bed this morning.'

'I'm perfectly well, thank you, Mother. I'm a little tired, that's all. I have a few things to do in town this morning after I've been to Mrs Carmichael's, is there anything you need?'

Her mother, robbed of speech by surprise, could only shake her head. Dottie continued, 'And then I'm invited to Mrs Gerard's for lunch, so I shan't be back until three or four o'clock, I shouldn't think. Do we have anyone coming to dinner this evening?'

Again her mother simply shook her head. Who was this calm, composed stranger in the appearance of her youngest, most emotional, most volatile daughter?

'I'm glad about that, I feel a bit done in, so it will be very nice to have a quiet evening. Right. I'm off, see you later.' *The bride and groom will journey to their secret honeymoon destination.* She got up from the table, kissed her mother's cheek, then her father's, and left the room, grabbing her coat and hat from the hall stand, and almost immediately Mr and Mrs Manderson heard the front door bang behind her and the sound of her heels clattering down the steps and receding into the distance.

Mrs Manderson looked at her husband, for once unable to give full expression to her emotions. 'Well!' was all she could manage.

He nodded, gave her a peck on the cheek before sitting down and taking up his morning newspaper. 'My thoughts exactly, dearest.'

Dottie had been summoned to Carmichael's for a quick fitting of some new dress bodices, and this accomplished, she was free for an hour before she needed to go to Mrs Gerard's. She wanted to sit quietly somewhere, and she wanted some tea. She didn't want to see anyone or talk to anyone. She just needed some time. She made her way to the Lyon's Corner House, even thought it was a fifteen-minute walk in the wrong direction for Mrs Gerard's house.

She found a table in a corner away from the door, and

having given her order, sat back to examine her thoughts and feelings, the chatter of the other customers providing a comfortable background.

At a nearby table, a young man surreptitiously reached across the table and took the hand of the young lady with him. After a quick look round, and failing to spot Dottie's stare, he kissed her fingertips and they smiled at one another. *The Honourable Cyril Penterman today with his new bride.* Tears prickled the back of Dottie's eyes and she turned away. It would never do to disgrace herself in such a public place. She rummaged through her handbag for her diary and pulled the tiny pencil out of its spine, ready to make a list of some sort should she feel she was becoming emotional. She watched a couple of comfortable matrons discussing a knitting pattern for an infant's jacket. I must buy some wool, Dottie thought, Flora's baby will need some jackets. And vests, and goodness knows what else. A shawl, she thought, a shawl would be a definite essential, and so easy to make, no awkward shaping of armholes. She made a note in her diary to buy wool. And possibly a book of patterns for a baby's layette. She amended her note to read 'yellow wool' as they didn't know whether Flora's baby would be a boy or a girl.

By and by with these prosaic thoughts, her emotional state was calmed again. She sipped her tea and ate the fruit bun she had ordered, and very soon she felt a bit better.

She was almost late getting to Mrs Gerard's, having forgotten that by going to the tearoom she had added quite a bit extra onto her journey. Mrs Gerard, always so kind, so untroubled by rules and regulations, was not put out in the least by Dottie arriving at ten minutes past eleven, but merely remarked how damp it was and ushered her into the little sitting-room she favoured for small tête-a-têtes.

The maid, carrying away Dottie's coat and hat, returned after a short time with a tray to serve them coffee. Then with a bob and a smile she left the room. Mrs Gerard turned to Dottie, and without any prevarication, came to the point.

'Well, dear, so I see Cyril has done the dirty on you and married that American girl. I can only say, I hope she can keep him. And of course, how sorry I am, my dear. As you know, I had hoped...'

'So had I,' Dottie said mournfully, and as tears threatened again, she said crossly, 'I wouldn't have minded half as much if he'd been honest with me. He really made me think...' She sighed.

'Men!' said Mrs Gerard. 'I'm afraid they're often a lot more trouble than they are worth. As I said, I'm truly sorry, dear, nothing would have given me greater pleasure. It was the greatest shock to open the newspaper yesterday and see...well, you know what. Even I was excluded from the family secret, you see.'

'Yes. Do you know this—his wife?' Dottie asked. 'I've seen her at Mrs Penterman's tea and she came to our ball, but I've never spoken to her. Is she a nice woman?'

'Oh she's lovely. A very sweet girl actually, and of course, fabulously wealthy. No, sadly I can't find anything about her to disapprove, and you may be sure she knows nothing of you, it's nothing personal on her side. I feel sure this was all his mother's idea. I can only hope he's worthy of her. Oh he's very charming, of course, and as a nephew he is a delight, but as a husband... Between you and I, Dottie, I'm beginning to wonder if Cyril's not something of a bounder, as we used to say in my youth. Things are beginning to reach my ears. Well, time will tell, I suppose. We may yet come to feel that you've had a fortunate escape. Now, what was it you really wanted to talk to me about?'

It was a relief to change the subject, and Dottie had decided to be completely open. She told Mrs Gerard all about the cloak, and the message attached to it by an unknown hand at the Moyers'. And the murmured comments and the pictures.

'Actually,' Dottie concluded, 'I was wondering if you had seen anyone wearing anything similar, or had heard of anyone talking about a gold cloak?'

'But that's not what you asked me the other evening?'

'Oh no. No, I also wanted to know if you had heard any gossip about Archie Dunne and my brother-in-law George's sister Diana. Someone told me that it was well-known, that there was...' she sought for the appropriate word, 'an involvement there. And I was just wondering if it was true. I know I've got no business asking such a thing, but...well I don't feel I can ask George, or Diana herself for that matter.'

'Hmm. You've had a busy time of it lately. Finding men dying in the street, upsetting widows, getting into trouble with your lovely gold cloak, listening to gossip, losing potential suitors.'

It was all said quite without malice, and Dottie could hardly pretend it wasn't all true. She said nothing, and Mrs Gerard hesitated, then added, with a gentle smile, 'No wonder you look worn out. I don't suppose you felt much like sleeping last night.'

'No.'

Mrs Gerard set down her cup and leaned back in her chair. She seemed to be thinking. Finally, she said, 'Yes, I believe I have heard some gossip about Archie and Diana. I think it is probably common knowledge. By the time these things reach my ears, everyone else has usually already heard. In this case, everyone except her own family, I should imagine. I don't know how they contrived to meet one another. No doubt some arrangement had been made. It's all very sordid. He was more than ten years older than her, not to mention a married man. A nice fellow, as a matter of fact, though a natural philanderer. Anything in a skirt, as they say. I should think she's very upset, and his death is likely to complicate matters as the families socialise quite a bit with one another, so Diana and Susan necessarily must be running into each other on a regular basis. But I suppose in time it will all be forgotten. At least, I hope so. One hopes these foolish childish obsessions will wear out in time, and that Diana will settle down into a good marriage. Susan was a fool to have married him, but he was such a charmer, and of course, her family have pots of money, whereas his were...'

'The familiar old story,' Dottie remarked sagely.

Mrs Gerard nodded. 'Indeed.'

'I wish I knew who'd killed Archie, though, and why,' Dottie said. 'It would be awful to think he was killed by someone he knew.'

'Better than an opportunistic crime merely after his pocketbook, committed by a stranger who will kill again and again.'

Dottie shivered and looked alarmed. 'I hadn't thought of that.'

'I should think it was either a jealous husband or an angry father, myself.'

They sat quietly for a moment. Then Mrs Gerard asked if Dottie would like more coffee. Dottie declined. Mrs Gerard then invited Dottie to take a tour of the house, and as they went, the change of subject soothed her and she found herself genuinely interested in the beautiful old house. What George and Flora's modern home lost in character and charm, it made up for in comfort and convenience. Mrs Gerard's home was four hundred and fifty years old and was large, sprawling and cost the earth to heat and light its long corridors and dark rooms, but charm it possessed in abundance.

'There's even a priest-hole,' Mrs Gerard told Dottie, leading her to what had once been an upstairs parlour, and she smiled in delight at Dottie's childlike enjoyment as the panel moved, revealing the place. 'It was in frequent use during the civil war, I understand. Our family were of Catholic origin and our history dates back to the days of the Conqueror. There is another, smaller one in the servants' hall in the back of the house downstairs.'

By the time they had meandered all over the house, neglecting neither attics, cellars nor priest-holes, lunch was served, and so they moved into the dining-room where the forbidding countenances of many generations glowered down upon them and made Dottie feel an urge to hurry her meal.

'A grim lot, aren't they? You might not think it to look at them, but they involved themselves in enough scandal to disgrace or offend half the top families in the country. To my mind that makes them seem a bit more human and a bit less daunting. And so I don't mind them glaring at me while I eat my lunch. But they can be a bit much for outsiders to take. And those two on the end lost their heads. Literally, during Elizabeth's reign.'

'Our family portraits are in the library,' Dottie said, 'I don't think any of them were executed though. They're so grimed up it's hard to tell what they even look like.'

'Best way,' Mrs Gerard agreed. 'Tell me about your work at Carmichael's. You must meet a lot of people.'

'Yes, but not always nice people,' Dottie said ruefully. The remainder of the meal passed with her recalling various incidents and examples of bad behaviour on the part of 'top' families, as Mrs Gerard was pleased to call them. They lingered for some time after the meal was over before moving into the drawing-room, whose windows faced west and often allowed a view of a lovely sunset, although with the current grey skies and drizzle, it seemed unlikely this evening's sunset would be a glorious one. They talked easily on fashion and literature, and travel.

'I'm going away next week. Always try to get away for January and part of February. Tunisia, this time; sometimes I go to Morocco or Egypt, it depends on what suits me at the time. So I shan't see you for a while. I hope you'll take care of yourself, and no doubt you're far too sensible to pine for a young so-and-so like my nephew appears to be. Once again, I'm so very sorry, but you may yet feel that things turned out for the best.'

'Possibly,' Dottie said, wondering if it was time to leave. But Mrs Gerard said, 'Let me just ring for tea, and then you can tell me about that cloak business again.'

The same maid who had served them before came now with a tea tray. Clearly Mrs Gerard did not keep a large staff. It wasn't truly time for a full afternoon tea, and so there were no accompaniments to their drink, for which

Dottie was grateful as she was still full from her lunch. But the hot drink was welcome.

She briefly summarised the business with the cloak. She had left out many details, uncertain how much she wanted Mrs Gerard to know.

'It sounds rather fishy,' Mrs Gerard said. 'Go back to Liberty's and ask the girl how many customers bought the cloth and what they said they were going to do with it.'

'I've done that,' Dottie admitted.

Mrs Gerard gave her an appraising look. 'Kept that bit back, didn't you? Which makes me wonder what else you're not telling me.'

There was a moment's silence. Dottie, feeling like a traitor, was about to reveal all when Mrs Gerard said, 'So who did the shop girl tell you had bought the stuff?'

Dottie told her.

Mrs Gerard nodded. 'Odd that the girl who works for Susan Dunne bought some more of the cloth. Think she wanted to make herself a copy of her mistress's? If she had bought it on Susan's orders, she wouldn't have paid cash, she would have put it on their account.'

'That's what I thought.'

'That picture's an odd thing too. You say it was exactly the same picture in both houses?'

'Yes, even the frames were alike. Though they were prints rather than paintings, just copies.'

'Hmm. Wonder where they got them from. You might find out. Though whether that would tell you anything, I don't know. Perhaps do a spot of research on this Queen.'

'What about the messages?' Dottie asked.

Mrs Gerard was attentive. 'Messages? I thought there was only one?'

Dottie, blushing and annoyed with herself, told Mrs Gerard about finding the pin the second time, although with no message attached, and about the whispered message at the Moyers'.

Mrs Gerard was deep in thought. The clock on the mantelpiece chimed once for half past three, and again Dottie wondered if she ought to go. Mrs Gerard said,

'Clearly there is something strange going on. It doesn't seem likely this fabric has been purchased for what one might term 'normal use'. If it had been, we would have seen people wearing it, and you wouldn't have had those messages. So it's a secret and something to be protected and hidden. We need to know more.'

'Flora and I are planning another visit to Susan Dunne this evening. I'm hoping she will be able to tell us something, so long as she agrees to see us of course. She got rather agitated last time and ordered us out. And of course, I don't really know her apart from through Muriel.'

'Then perhaps go to see Muriel, or ask her to invite Susan and you to her home?' Mrs Gerard said. She stood up. 'I do hate to be rude, dear, and it has been so lovely to see you. But I need to have my nap before dinner. Do take care, dear, and I'll see you when I get home again after my trip.' She gripped Dottie's arm in a strong clasp that contrived to convey strong emotion.

Dottie kissed Mrs Gerard on the cheek. From nowhere the maid reappeared with her coat and hat, and Dottie departed.

Upon reaching home, and reassuring her parents that she was perfectly well, she immediately went to telephone to Flora. Flora's maid Cissie answered and whilst Dottie waited for Cissie to find her mistress and bring her to the phone, Dottie leaned against the wall and closed her eyes. How she wished this day was over. Yet there was still an evening with her parents to get through.

'Hello? Dottie?' Flora sounded anxious, Dottie thought.

'It's me,' Dottie said, and realised her voice sounded low and dispirited. She made an effort to inject a little life into it. 'I hope you don't mind, but I'm so tired, I don't think I can face going out to see Susan Dunne. Can we go tomorrow instead?'

'Of course we can. Are you all right? You sound awfully tired. How was lunch at Mrs Gerard's?'

'It was very nice, I had a lovely time. But look, I really am so tired. I'll tell you all about it tomorrow. What time?'

'After lunch, say about two o'clock.'

That's fine. I must go, see you tomorrow.'

After saying goodbye and hanging up the receiver, Dottie decided that she would follow Mrs Gerard's example and she too went for a nap before dinner. What a relief she didn't have to go out again! And she felt doubly relieved that now she could just put her head on her pillow and let everything go.

*

Chapter Eighteen

After her nap and a quiet dinner with her parents, Dottie was feeling much more herself, and vaguely restless, she went into the library, curled up in a comfy elderly leather armchair and telephoned to her sister. Flora immediately bombarded her with questions about how she was feeling and what she was going to do.

'Do?' Dottie laughed bitterly. 'What do you mean? There's nothing to 'do' about Cyril Penterman except forget him. It's not as though we were engaged. Life goes on exactly as it did before I met him. Honestly Flora, you're as bad as the parents. They've been watching me like hawks all through dinner, and talking to me in hushed tones as if I were on my deathbed. It's driving me round the bend. I was hoping for some good old-fashioned common sense from you.'

At the other end of the line, Flora rolled her eyes at her husband and hastily apologised. Dottie said, 'Listen Flora, I want to go and see Susan. Shall we go tonight or...'

'Tonight?' her sister protested. 'But...'

'Oh very well, we'll go early tomorrow. She's fairly likely to be at home first thing in the morning.'

Again Flora protested. 'You know I don't do early mornings at the moment.'

'Well, it's either tonight or tomorrow morning—you choose.'

'But...'

'Let's make it tonight. It's only a quarter past eight; if you leave now, you can be here in five minutes. We would be at Susan's by a quarter to nine, possibly a little earlier. That's a perfectly acceptable time to arrive on someone's doorstep for coffee.'

'I need to change first,' Flora said, sounding slightly put out, 'Now it's no use complaining. If you want me to come—or should I say—if you want me to take you, you'll have to give me a few minutes to sort myself out. I'm not fit to be seen.' She put down the phone to put an end to any arguments. She huffed at her husband in annoyance and grumbled all the way upstairs to her dressing room where she flung open all the doors of her wardrobes and stared petulantly at her outfits.

George ambled in and kissed her on the neck, then asked if she wanted him to drive them, but she said no, she would drive. And after a few more minutes of deliberating, she selected some clothing and got ready.

It was a quarter past nine by the time they arrived at Susan Dunne's doorstep, the weather was horrid and both Flora and Dottie were in bad moods with one another. Flora parked right outside the house and they hurried up the steps and pounded on the door, squeezing together to keep under the porch roof and out of the rain.

Inside the house, there were lights were on, but for several minutes no one responded to their knock. Dottie saw one of the upstairs curtains twitch but couldn't tell if it was Susan who looked out, or if she'd sent her maid. She couldn't even tell if the person had glanced down to the front door and seen them huddled there, or only glanced at the road, which was deserted apart from Flora's car parked at the kerb, and another car a few doors down.

Flora knocked again 'just in case', as she said, though

there was no earthly chance that their first knock had gone unheard, Mrs Dunne's knocker was a heavy old-fashioned brass affair with a rap like the Day of Judgement. Again they waited.

Finally, they heard the sound of footsteps clattering along the hall. Dottie expected to see Susan herself opening the door, as the footsteps had sounded like those of someone wearing heeled outdoor shoes, but when the door was opened it was by the pretty young maid, Leonora. She held the door with her shoulder, only half-open. She wore a worried expression.

'Is everything...?' began Flora, but Leonora cut across her:

'I'm terribly sorry, Madam, but I'm afraid Mrs Dunne isn't able to receive visitors this evening. Erm—I'm afraid she's not very well.' This last bit was added in a near-whisper.

'Perhaps we can help?' Dottie suggested, and put a hand on the door to push it wider.

Leonora braced the door, and said firmly, '*No, Madam, if you please.* I can't let you in, I'm afraid. Mrs Dunne can't see anyone this evening. If you'd like to leave a card or message? Then good evening, ladies.'

And she shut the door with a bang. They heard the sound of the key being turned in the lock and bolts being drawn across at both the top and the bottom.

Flora and Dottie exchanged a look, then shrugged their shoulders. Clearly they had no choice but to leave, and without another word, they hurried down the steps and got into the car.

'Look,' Dottie said. 'Someone's looking out of the window upstairs.' Flora leaned across to see.

'Well, that must be Susan, Leonora couldn't have got all the way up there so soon. I wonder if she really is ill or if that was just an excuse to get rid of us.'

'Oh definitely a ruse, I should say,' said Dottie. 'Although, if she *is* expecting a baby, I suppose she might not be feeling too well.'

'Hmm. *If* she is expecting a baby. Well, she didn't let us

in, and we can't sit here all night. Do you want to go home or come back to ours?'

At that moment a loud rapping sound on the driver's window beside Flora made both of them jump with fright. A figure in a hat and greatcoat stood there. It took several seconds for them to realise it was the policeman, William Hardy. Flora pulled her window down a little, not wanting to let in too much rain.

'Yes, Sergeant, can I help you?'

'I just wondered why you were calling on Mrs Dunne this evening?'

Flora and Dottie looked at one another, mildly irritated.

'We wanted to make sure she was all right,' Dottie said, leaning across to speak to him. Further than that she was not prepared to explain.

'Would you follow me, please? I'd like to speak with you both, but this isn't the place.'

And he was gone. Again Flora and Dottie exchanged a look, this time of puzzlement. Dottie peered out through the streaming rain. Did he want them to get out of the car? Presently a car pulled alongside theirs, and they could see he was in the driver's seat. He signalled to them to follow him. Flora nodded and mimed 'all right,' and pressed the self-starter. They followed him all the way back to the police station, carefully observing all speed limits.

'I do hope we're not in any trouble,' Flora said, 'I don't think George will be very happy if he has to come down to the police station to pay a fine for us.'

'And you think Mother will be any happier?'

They parked the car and went up the steps to find Hardy waiting for them just inside the door.

'Follow me, please,' he said and turning, set off down a long corridor.

'I don't think this is the prison, so that's something,' Dottie whispered to Flora.

'No, he's taking us to a torture chamber in the basement, I expect. I bet they split us up and try to get us to put all the blame on the other.'

'The blame for what?' Dottie hissed, 'We haven't done anything.'

'Try telling him that. If my baby is born in prison, I shall never speak to you again.'

They almost cannoned into him as he paused to open a door and stood back to allow them to go through first. Dottie blushed; from the angry look in his eye, he had certainly heard their comments. As she followed Flora through, he said, 'Actually I do most of my interrogating in my office. We don't have a special torture chamber for that anymore. This way, Mrs Gascoigne.'

'Oh, you have your own office, do you, Sergeant? How jolly pleasant,' Dottie said tartly, and thought, oh dear, I sound just like Mother.

He led them inside, cleared boxes and books off two chairs, set them opposite his own on the other side of the desk, and with a wave of his hand, he invited them to sit.

No sooner had Dottie thought to herself, he's definitely not in a very good mood in spite of his politeness, than he banged his hand down hard on the desk-top and absolutely yelled at them:

'What the hell do you think you were doing, going to Susan Dunne's house this evening?'

Both women blinked in surprise. Dottie, who had been admiring the breadth of his shoulders, jolted and bit through her lip and couldn't find a handkerchief to staunch the ensuing flow of blood. With a look of exasperation, Hardy handed her his own. The simple human gesture sadly undermined the authority he had been trying to exert over them. Intuiting this, he sat down and leaned back in his seat, regarding them and wondering how to gain back his brief advantage.

Dottie's lip was not seriously injured. She put his handkerchief in her handbag, promising to have it laundered and returned to him. He was tempted to shout 'Damn the handkerchief!' but suspected that would work about as well as his thump on the desk. Therefore, it was through gritted teeth that he asked in a more normal voice, 'May I ask the purpose of your visit to Susan Dunne this evening?'

With some asperity, Flora said, 'We were simply calling on a friend, to condole and support.'

'Susan Dunne is no friend of yours,' Hardy said with astonishing certainty. He watched them exchange a look. 'Let's assume that you were calling on her out of sheer nosiness. No doubt you'd planned to ask her a few questions about her late husband.'

Flora shook her head but Dottie leaned forward, and fixing her rather lovely eyes on him, said, 'How did you know?' Her lips were red, her cheeks pale. Her dark pretty hair curled softly about her ears and neck. That rat Cyril Penterman's loss was the rest of the world's gain, William Hardy thought. Aloud he said rather haughtily, 'It's my business to know these things, Madam.'

Incredibly, she seemed stung by being called Madam; he saw the flash of hurt in her eyes. He hastily softened his approach. 'Miss Manderson, please just tell me what is going on. I have my reasons for being aware if Susan Dunne receives visitors.'

'Ooh, are you watching the house? Do you suspect her of killing her husband?' Flora asked, while Dottie added, 'Have you seen any sign of a gold-coloured cloak? Possibly two?'

He looked from one woman to the other and back again, and a distinct sense of being out of his depth crept over him. He recalled some wise words spoken to him once by his uncle, and accordingly got to his feet. 'Excuse me a moment, ladies.' He went out of the office, returning almost immediately. 'Sorry about that. I thought I'd order some tea. I suspect we're going to be here a while, and no doubt you'd welcome a cup, I know I should.'

The tea came, and Flora did the honours and as she did so, Dottie looked around the office. Everywhere was piled with boxes, books and manila folders of papers.

'Are you moving in or moving out?' she asked.

'In,' he said.

'I didn't realise sergeants got their own offices.'

'They don't,' he said. 'I've just received my promotion to

Inspector.'

And she smiled. He thought the sight of it worth a dozen promotions.

'Congratulations!' she said, and her voice was warm with genuine pleasure for him. 'I'm sure it's richly deserved. I expect your mother is rightly very proud.'

'She was extremely pleased, yes. Um—thank you.'

There was a moment's silence then Flora handed him his tea, milk, no sugar, Dottie noted, and then there was a general air of their original conversation resuming.

Dottie said, 'You're quite right, of course. We're not friends of Susan Dunne's. In fact, we're barely acquaintances. And she refused to see us this evening. The maid said she was unwell, but we're almost certain that was an excuse to avoid us.'

'Surely not,' he murmured. She glared at him.

'We saw someone watching us from an upstairs window,' Flora added. 'And it couldn't have been Leonora the maid as she'd just closed the door on us. And locked and bolted it.'

'Right on us!' Dottie agreed.

'And did you have any particular reason for your visit, other than...'

'Sheer nosiness?' Dottie asked. 'No, we didn't, you were quite right about that too. I mean, I think we already knew it wasn't terribly likely she'd see us. She has gone rather out of her way to avoid us. But we thought we had to try. We just wanted to ask her about the cloak, and the picture, and what it all meant, that's all.'

'What is this about a cloak? And what picture?'

So Dottie told him all about seeing the picture the first time they'd gone to the Dunnes' house, about the idea to look for the fabric, about what the saleswoman at Liberty's had told them, and that led to her telling him about the note pinned to her cloak, about the empty pin that indicated a second note, the whispered comment, the second picture in George's sister Diana's room. Lastly she said, 'Did you know Archie Dunne was having an illicit love affair with Diana Gascoigne?'

Flora protested but Hardy nodded and said, 'Yes. That's where he was going on the night he was killed. There is a flat not far from Mr and Mrs Gascoigne's home. She was believed to be staying with friends but in fact she was spending the night with him at this flat he was renting for that purpose. They had met there regularly for some time.'

'The little minx!' Flora said to Dottie, outraged. 'I told you, the morals of an alley cat.'

William Hardy, Detective Inspector, hid a smile, then got to his feet. 'Well thank you for coming in this evening, ladies, I won't keep you any longer. It's getting late.'

Disconcerted, they quickly gathered their things and followed him back to the door which led past the front desk and out onto the street. He saw them into Flora's car, then waved them off and went back inside.

Only as they reached Flora's home did Dottie suddenly say, 'But he didn't tell us anything! He got everything he wanted out of us, but apart from explaining where Archie Dunne was going that night, he told us nothing. We're still none the wiser.'

'Dottie dear, he's the police,' said her sister with great patience, as she opened the front door. 'The way things work is, people give the police information, and the police solve crimes. They don't give *us* information. That way, it's the police who do the detecting and we mere citizens stay safely at home out of the way and don't go around annoying detective inspectors.'

'Well—blast it!' Dottie said, frustrated. 'I'm staying the night by the way. Can I phone Mother and let her know?'

'Of course. Cocoa?'

'No. Wine.'

'Very well.'

*

Chapter Nineteen

'I want to speak to that cigarette girl at the theatre,' Dottie announced at breakfast.

George peered at her over his newspaper. 'Why?' he asked.

'Well, to begin with, I think you were all too susceptible to her charms, and we now know a little more about the situation, and I've thought of a few more things I want to ask.'

'I see,' he said and retreated behind his paper once more.

'He's getting very like Father,' Dottie commented. The newspaper appeared to be listening intently. 'Have you noticed how men always use a very large newspaper as a sort of shield between themselves and their womenfolk?'

'Yes,' said Flora, 'Sometimes it can be useful though. For example, I can pull faces at him like this, and he doesn't know anything about it.'

The newspaper dropped again and George sent her a half-annoyed, half-laughing look. She blew him a kiss and he returned to his news and she returned to her toast and sweet tea.

'Fortunately, as it's Saturday, there'll be a matinee showing, so we should be able to collar this girl. What was her name, George?'

'Valerie,' said the newspaper.

'Thank you, Dearest.' Flora said and put her tongue out at him.

'I saw that,' said the newspaper.

They managed to squeeze in a little shopping before making their way to the theatre. Dottie bought a large amount of wool in a number of soft shades, as she had planned to begin work on, variously, a shawl, bootees, and two matinee jackets. That would be her contribution to the baby preparations, and she felt quite excited to be making a start. Flora, of course, would be hopeless at knitting, Dottie thought, but she was unable to prevent her from also buying some wool and knitting needles.

'After all, I've got almost six months until the baby comes,' Flora said, 'so that gives me plenty of time to learn how to knit. I shall be quite the needlewoman by the time little Bonzo arrives.'

'You'd better start practising a school jumper. You'll need at least five years. And Bonzo? What on earth is George thinking?'

'Well, I've got to call it something, and I can't keep saying 'it' all the time. Obviously one doesn't have the faintest idea if one is having a boy or a girl, though Cook says it's definitely a girl, apparently I'm 'carrying all front', whatever that means, and that's ridiculous anyway as my tummy is still as flat as a pancake. But at the same time, Mrs Owens at the Ladies' Institute says I am most definitely expecting a little boy, as I'm all hips. I hate that woman, how dare she!' Flora bundled her wool and needles into her basket, adding, 'I do hope it's a boy, George will be so thrilled. We must try to find a name we both like. Hopefully Bonzo is just a sort of stop-gap measure.'

Dottie shook her head in a pitying manner. 'It sounds

like a dog's name. You could choose one of those names that is suitable for a boy or a girl—Hilary or Leslie, or Kim. You know...'

'I hate all of those. We'll probably have to call it George if it is a boy—poor little beggar—and if it's a girl, well no doubt we'll think of something dainty and feminine. But absolutely not Diana.'

'Or Susan,' Dottie said.

'Definitely not Susan,' Flora agreed.

They were on their way to the theatre now. They weren't able to park right outside, but had to walk back from a parking spot further along the road. On the way, Dottie suddenly grabbed her sister's arm.

'How are we going to get in to see this Valerie girl? Surely we won't have to actually pay for matinee tickets?'

Flora looked at her in dismay. 'Much as I enjoyed the show the first four times, I really don't think I want to sit through it again.'

'Me either.'

But they had to pay the full entrance fee; the elderly woman in the box office informed them tartly that it was 'no ticket, no entrance'.

'In which case we may as well have a box,' Flora said, waving the exorbitant cost aside. 'Does the cigarette girl still come along during the Matinee?'

'Yes, ma'am.'

'And is it still Valerie? She knows which ones I like,' Flora added to divert suspicion, not that there was any suspicion.

'Yes, ma'am,' repeated the woman in a bored voice. Her only concern was that they should move along and not hold up her queue.

So they spread themselves out in the box and got ready for the show. 'We might as well be comfortable,' Flora said. 'Then as soon as we've seen this Valerie character, we can leave, unless you especially want to stay to see the rest of the show?'

'I never thought I'd say this about poor Fred Astaire, but I'd be perfectly happy to never see him again,' Dottie said. 'He may be a fabulous dancer, but that high-pitched singing voice of his gets rather on one's nerves after seeing the thing six times. How I long for a nice baritone.' She pulled off her gloves one finger at a time and lay them on top of the pile which was her coat, bag and her hat. Her shopping she had left in the car. Which was a pity because she realised she could have made significant progress with a bootee as she sat waiting for Valerie to make her appearance.

At last the show began, and, bored from the outset, Dottie leaned back and regarded her fingernails critically. She nudged her sister.

'Do you think I should get them polished a really deep red, or stick with a pale pink?'

'Shh!' said someone in the next box.

'I don't know. I should think Mother would have forty fits if you go for the deep red. She'll think you've become a lady of the evening...'

'Ssshhhh!' said the voice from the next box, with even greater urgency.

'That's rather why I was thinking of doing it. After all, she already has strong reservations about me working at Carmichael's, so...'

A head appeared round the partition, making both Flora and Dottie jump. It was the face of an elderly man, red with fury.

'Will you people please keep the noise down!' he bellowed. 'Kindly take your Mothers' Meeting elsewhere!'

Upon which, the door behind Dottie and Flora opened and an usher came in, saw the man and told him quietly but firmly that if he didn't sit down and be quiet, the police would be called and he would be ejected from the theatre, never to return. Outraged, but with no choice, the man sat back down. As the usher went out, he said to Flora and Dottie,

'I'm so sorry, ladies, if he starts up again, just let me know and I'll get him chucked out.'

'Thank you,' they said, and when he had gone, nudged each other and stifled giggles.

'Let's wait in the corridor,' Flora whispered. They gathered up their belongings and went out into the hall where the air was pleasantly cool even if the hall was somewhat gloomy. After only another ten minutes, they heard someone approaching, and a soft glow lit the way as she came along the corridor towards them.

'Good evening,' Flora said. The girl was extremely pretty and revoltingly young and slim. No wonder George had believed every word she'd told him.

'Good evening, madam,' the girl sad, and possibly because her customers were usually men, she looked rather suspiciously at the two of them, with their coats, hats and bags piled on the floor.

'Erm, you don't know us,' Dottie said. 'But we were here a few weeks ago, with my sister's husband. It was he who told you about the death of Archie Dunne.' The girl's face fought off an amazed look and found one that held a hint of surprise mixed with a dash of curiosity.

'Oh yes, poor Mr Dunne. Yes, I seem to remember something about that. What can I do for you?'

'Um...' Dottie said, thinking, now what is the best way to ask her if she was lying? Should I try to...

'You lied to my husband when you said you hardly knew Archie, didn't you?' Flora stated. She held up a hand as Valerie began to protest, 'Oh I know, believe me, I do understand. Obviously you didn't want to get into any trouble, and you probably suspected Archie may have been married after all. Naturally he would have told you he wasn't married, I'm sure they all do that. But after a while you no doubt began to wonder. Little things wouldn't quite add up. And you're a bright girl, you'd recognise the signs.'

'Well, I did just wonder, now and then...' Valerie admitted. She was looking from one to the other of them, like a rabbit caught in the glare of headlamps.

'Of course. But you couldn't be sure,' Dottie added, seeing where Flora was directing them.

'And so you probably thought you ought to follow him, just to make sure. After all, if he was really a married man, and just leading you on, you had a right to know.'

'Yes, you have your reputation to consider. You couldn't afford to lose your job.'

Valerie was looking upset. She craned forward over her tray of goods. 'That's right. I thought I might lose my job if anyone found out I was seeing a married man, and although the pay's not much, it makes a difference to me. It means I can get out of home, and my mum and dad always on at me and the younger ones to look after, always snivelling and wanting me to do things for them. I can't stick it any longer.'

'So you followed him home, after he'd been to see you?'

'No. Not right away, I didn't,' Valerie protested. 'He took me out a few times, and spent money on me, and it all began to seem a bit too good to be true, so...'

'So obviously you had to find out,' Dottie said, nodding sympathetically.

'It was when he took me to the flat,' Valerie said, 'I mean, I didn't really think about why he wanted me to go there. I know that was silly of me, but I just didn't think. He seemed so nice, and of course he was very good-looking. But he'd brought wine, and flowers, and had a nice dinner sent up, and so it didn't seem such a bad way to say thank you. But afterwards...'

'Afterwards?' said Flora. Valerie looked up and down the corridor. There were a couple of men coming along the corridor for cigarettes. She served them as quickly as she could, nervously fumbling with the change and the packets she handed to them. The men glanced at Flora and Dottie with a question in their eyes.

'Look, you've got to go,' Valerie whispered. 'If my boss comes along, I'll be for it.'

'We'll go in a minute, when you've told us everything,' Flora said. Valerie was almost in tears, and Dottie felt terrible.

'Look, please, I don't want to lose my job.'

'You won't,' Dottie promised with a smile, then continued with, 'So he led you on and spoiled you with gifts and then you wondered if it was all too good to be true.'

Valerie threw an anguished look about her again. 'Oh look, yes, all right,' she hissed, 'I did. So I followed him. He'd been here for the matinee, we went for a drink, then he brought me back here for my evening shift. But I'd asked for some time off, so I could follow him. I followed him back to the house. I saw that great big tall woman, his wife I suppose. She let him in and I saw the way she looked at him. Looked at him daggers, she did, and he stepped right round her like he was scared stiff of her, like he was scared to go in. I'll admit I felt sorry for him'

'But then you knew for certain he was married,' Flora prompted.

'Yes of course I did. So I told him I couldn't see him no more. He asked me to go to the flat with him again, said he wanted to explain. But I said no, said I couldn't see him anymore, not if he was married. And that was it. It broke my heart, saying no to him. He was so believable and so charming, but in the end...'

'And you never saw him again?' Flora said. Valerie shook her head. Someone was coming. Dottie looked along the dimly-lit hall then glanced back at Valerie who looked panicky. Aloud, she said, 'Certainly, madam, here are the matches. And your husband's cigars. Is that everything you needed?'

Along the hall, the shadowy figure had gradually assumed the form of a man in a cheap suit who stood watching them closely. Feeling that there was no alternative, Flora got out her purse and found the money.

'I'll just get your change, madam.' Valerie, with an apologetic look, again speaking very loudly and clearly. She reached into the pocket of her uniform and loudly clinked some pennies into Flora's hand.

'There isn't anything else I can tell you. Please don't come back here, I don't want to get into trouble. Now go!' Valerie hissed, adding more loudly, 'Thank you Madam, enjoy the rest of the show.'

Feeling under obligation to keep the charade going, they returned to their box and waited. Perversely, just as they took their seats in the darkness, the house lights came up for the interval.

*

Chapter Twenty

The persistent rain that had fallen all the day had now turned into sleet.

Night came early, the streetlamps were lit and it wasn't even four o'clock, and in spite of his greatcoat and hat, Hardy was chilled to the bone. He wanted nothing more than to go home and get warm. But he had one more call to make.

He mounted the steps to a gentlemen's club called The Old Standard, and opened the door to get in out of the weather.

Just inside, right by the window next to the front door, the doorman was standing, watching the street, his uniform dry and spotless, testament to the fact that few members had arrived or left that afternoon, so he hadn't needed to go outside and get wet.

'Good evening, sir,' the doorman said, and he couldn't resist a slight, matey smirk at Hardy's obvious relief at getting inside.

Hardy replied in kind and introduced himself, adding, 'I'd like to ask you a few questions.'

'Certainly sir,' came the amiable response, though some

of the matiness had disappeared.

'I believe this gentleman may have been a member here.' And he pulled out the now somewhat crumpled photograph of Archie Dunne, and handed it to the doorman.

'Is that...? Terrible business, terrible. I saw it in the evening newspaper. Yes, that is Mr Dunne, and he was most definitely a member here.'

'Had he dined here the night he died? Can you remember, it was late November.'

'Yes sir. I can be quite sure about that. Due to certain—um—domestic circumstances, Mr Dunne had been staying with us for perhaps a fortnight. Then he went home for two nights, and then lo and behold, there he was back again. I said to our membership secretary, 'well that didn't last long, did it?' And we laughed. I must admit I feel rather ashamed of that now. But of course, we didn't realise, we thought it was rather funny at the time. He had dinner here the night he died, having arrived at about seven o'clock with a small suitcase. Then after dinner he spent some time at cards with some of the other members. He went out at about half past ten. I offered to call a cab for him, sir, but as soon as we got outside, a lady came over. She had an umbrella and so Mr Dunne told me not to bother with the cab, he would walk. And he left.'

'With the woman?'

'Indeed.'

'Did you recognise her?'

'No.'

'Can you describe her?'

'I didn't see her face, it was concealed by a hat and the umbrella. But she seemed quite small and slender, I remember her head only just came up to his shoulder and he had to lean a little with the umbrella to keep it over both of them. She was wearing a rather fetching gold-coloured cloak. As I say, she carried the umbrella, but he took it from her and she took his arm. They walked off in that direction.' He paused here to lean forward and point towards the right. 'I fancied they were arguing, although I couldn't hear what they said, it was just the impression I got.'

'Did he seem surprised or angry to see her?'

'Perhaps a little surprised. I think he said something like, 'What on earth are you doing here?' or something like that.'

'And you didn't hear him address her by name?'

'No sir.'

'And you didn't at any point see her face?'

'No.'

'Had you seen her before, or since?'

'Not as far as I'm aware.'

'Did you form any idea as to where they were going?'

'Not at all, sir, I'm sorry.'

'That's quite all right. Thanks for your help.'

'Not at all sir. Goodnight.'

Hardy came down the steps and into the street. The weather was as bad as ever.

'That's it,' he said to himself, turning up his collar, 'I'm going home.'

When the two sisters cautiously emerged from the box forty minutes later, the corridor was empty. They followed the signs to the rear exit, hoping to leave the theatre without drawing too much attention to themselves.

Having achieved this goal, and reached the car, Flora turned to Dottie with a triumphant grin and said, 'We're so good at this sleuthing thing. We make such good detectives. Dottie, I feel we really have a talent for this sort of thing.'

Dottie laughed. 'We certainly have. Although we really have only confirmed what we already knew, we haven't added anything new.'

'But Archie was taking at least two women to that flat. What a dreadful philanderer!'

'Hmm. But it is nice to have confirmation of our suspicions and clearly Susan Dunne has something to hide.'

'Yes. What Valerie said about seeing him shrink past his

wife as she opened the door—I know we thought she was peculiar, but for her own husband to be so scared of her! One can almost see why he went elsewhere for comfort. Almost.'

'I've been thinking about what Valerie told us. I think we ought to do our duty and tell our favourite policeman—now an Inspector, no less—what we've learned,' Dottie said.

Flora halted the car and waited whilst an elderly couple crossed the road, and she turned to give her sister a teasing smile.'

'What?' Dottie demanded.

'Well he is rather gorgeous, Dottie. And so noble— giving up his studies to support his family, and all that pursuing law and order, keeping our streets safe for ordinary citizens. Apart from poor Archie of course. And now—as you say, an Inspector. Who knows how high his abilities might take him. He could be Chief Constable one day.'

'What on earth are you going on about? If you're implying—*mind that dog!*—if you're implying that I'm enamoured of the Inspector...'

'Of course you are. And I would be too, if I were a bachelor girl. Those eyes! That hair! Not to mention those massive shoulders. He's a bit too tall, perhaps, but I suppose beggars can't be choosers.'

In this way they returned to the Manderson home, and Dottie was reunited with her mother who seemed to still be under the impression that her heart was broken following the announcement of the Honourable Cyril Penterman's recent marriage. Flora quickly disabused their mother on that score.

'Dottie has better, newer fish to fry now, Mother dear.'

'Oh?'

Dottie marvelled that her mother could infuse one simple word with so much hope and longing. She immediately realised that her mother was mentally calculating what could be a better fish than an Honourable, and feared their mother was not viewing the situation in the same way as her daughters.

'No, Mother, I haven't fallen for an Earl.'

'But she has fallen for a policeman!'

'*No!*' Mrs Manderson gasped, clutching her pearls, and sank into a chair.

'Oh not a humble bobby on the beat, Mother, never fear. She's got her eyes on an inspector.'

'I have not!' Dottie laughed, half amused, half genuinely worried her sister thought it was true. Certainly her mother was believing this ludicrous tale of Flora's. 'Mother, I haven't! Flora! It was funny at first, but now, really, it's time to stop this nonsense. You know it's not true.'

'Isn't it true he gave you his handkerchief as a token of his love? Are you or are you not going to see him tomorrow to pour out your heart to him?' Flora challenged, laughing. Their mother was looking pale. Her hand, still hovering protectively over her pearls, was shaking. Flora administered a small medicinal sherry.

'I'm sorry Mother, I was just teasing Dottie. Though he is a very nice man and also rather delicious.'

'Florence! Kindly refrain from this vulgar talk. I assume it is William Hardy to whom you are referring?' Mrs Manderson began to recover herself.

'Yes, I am.' Flora smiled. 'I'll ring for tea, shall I?' She did so.

'But surely Mr Hardy is merely a sergeant?'

'He has just received his promotion to inspector. Apparently he is a very fine officer. And very highly thought of.'

'All the same...'

The telephone bell rang. A moment later Janet came into the room to announce that there was a telephone call for Miss Dorothy. Dottie therefore hurried away. They could hear the murmur of her voice though not what she was saying. Mrs Manderson leaned a little closer to her eldest daughter.

'And so is she planning on seeing this Hardy chappie or not?'

'Yes, Mother, that bit was perfectly true. We've—um—remembered—something that might be useful to him in his investigation.'

'It's very vulgar getting mixed up in all this crime. But she isn't really interested in this—this—Inspector Hardy?' Mrs Manderson pronounced his name in the manner of a woman trying to face up to a distasteful possibility. Flora had seen the same expression on her mother's face when she had been informed there were rats in the scullery.

Flora leaned closer to her mother and said softly, 'Actually Mummy, I rather think she is, she just doesn't realise it.'

'But a *policeman*.'

'I know, dear, but you wouldn't want her stuck with a bounder like Cyril and be unhappy all her life, would you? And Mr Hardy has got heavenly blue eyes. And he whisked out a handkerchief as soon as she needed it. He was very—gallant. I like the idea of a gallant man for our Dottie, don't you?'

'Well,' said her mother, sipping her sherry, and reflecting, 'a gallant man, even if he is a policeman, would be a catch. And a nice change after... And if you think Dottie really does, deep down...'

'Oh she does, Mother. Very deep down. And you know, I think he's going places. And don't forget, he's still frightfully young and an Inspector already. He could end up as Chief Constable. Possibly even a Peer.'

'Well,' was her mother's response.

Dottie returned. She looked worried.

'That was Susan Dunne! She was in a frightful state. She asked me to go over there. She said it's Leonora's evening out, and she pleaded with me to go over and see her. She was upset—actually weeping on the phone—and saying she must speak to someone. She begged me to go, any time after seven o'clock she said, as Leonora would be gone by then. She said she was sorry she didn't let us in earlier, she said she wanted to, but she was afraid.'

'Afraid of what?' Mrs Manderson demanded.

'She didn't say,' Dottie said, somewhat deflated, then

she turned to Flora, 'I said I'd go to see her, she sounded so desperate.'

'Shall I go with you?' Flora asked, then immediately added, 'Oh but I can't, George and I have guests this evening.'

'Well, if it's not too late, I'll pop in afterwards and tell you all about it. I don't suppose I'll be there for more than an hour or so. I wonder what she wants?'

'Good idea, I'm very curious about all this. If she gets too weepy, just tell her you're very sorry but you've got to leave. Don't just sit there and listen if she gets all maudlin.'

'I'm sure everything will be all right. Anyway, at least she's still speaking to me!'

The clock on the mantel chimed, and Flora leapt her feet. 'Blast! Look at the time, I really have to be going. See you later, girls, toodle-oo!' She kissed their cheeks and scurried out before either her sister or her mother had a chance to speak.

Mrs Manderson turned to her younger daughter. 'I do wish Florence wouldn't use those vulgar expressions. She didn't used to talk like that before she got married. I blame George and his family for this decline. They have such low standards.'

Dottie just laughed. 'Yes, Mother, quite right!'

The door opened and Janet came in with the tea tray.

*

Chapter Twenty-one

'I suppose you know you've lost me my job, coming here like this,' Valerie Knight said bitterly as soon as she came into the manager's office.

'Please take a seat, Miss Knight,' Hardy said. A sudden thought having occurred to him on his way home, he was now sitting in the manager's padded leather chair, and very comfortable it was too. Valerie Knight took a seat opposite him on the small wooden chair with the broken back. She was angry at being so publicly summoned to the office to speak to the police, and the tears in her eyes showed that her fear of losing her job was genuine. In a gentler tone, Hardy said, 'Don't worry, Miss Knight, I shall make it clear that you are simply being a helpful member of the public and that no guilt or misconduct can be attached to you.'

That helped. She nodded, leaning forward to say, 'What is it you want to know?'

'Tell me about Archie Dunne.'

She looked both annoyed and relieved. Any slight suspicion he still had of her now dissipated completely. 'Those two women earlier,' she said shaking her head, 'I knew they were trouble. I shouldn't of told them anything.'

'Well, you did, so why not tell me as well, then you can get back to work. How did you get to know Mr Dunne?'

'The usual way. He came to buy cigars off me a couple of times,' she said with a sigh. 'We got chatting. He was funny, and sweet. He said the show had given him an idea and wanted me to help him.'

'He said more than that, didn't he?' Hardy interrupted.

'Only that he'd had this idea from watching the show. It was Gay Divorce same as what's on still, and he told me he and his wife wasn't getting on, so I thought it meant he'd decided to divorce her.'

'And had he?'

'Well, sort of. I mean he wanted to get shot of her. I joked he could just strangle her and chuck her body in the river. He laughed and said if it didn't mean his neck he might consider it. He'd met someone else, he said, someone he wanted to be with. In fact, she was with him that night, I just caught sight of them as they were leaving. She was as young as me!'

'Do you know her name? What did she look like?'

Valerie shook her head. 'I can't quite—it was D something—short for something, I can't remember exactly what he called her. Sorry.'

Hardy ignored the plummeting sensation in his stomach and, carefully controlling his emotions he said, 'D something? And what did she look like? Tall and dark? Or shorter and fair?'

'Short and fair.'

'You're sure? It wasn't one of those two ladies who came to see you?'

Valerie Knight laughed, a gentle, teasing laugh that most men would absolutely find irresistible, Hardy thought. 'Oh it wasn't that tall pretty dark one that came here this afternoon, no. It was definitely a different woman. Don't you worry about that.'

Hardy felt exasperated with himself. But her information relieved his mind considerably, even though he already knew about the other D in Dunne's life, it was reassuring to hear it confirmed by another source. 'Do continue.'

'Well, so he said the show had given him this idea, and he asked me if I'd like to earn fifty quid. Before I could tell him what I thought of him, 'Oh,' he says, 'it's nothing like that, I wouldn't dream of suggesting such a thing,' he says.'

'So what was he suggesting?'

'He wanted to do a Brighton thing, he said. I was to wait outside his house one night when he came out, then link my arm through his, and he would kiss me on the cheek and we'd walk off down the road. It was all meant to be done so his maid could see and he hoped she'd tell her mistress—either that or perhaps his wife would see us herself. Then the second time, we was to be seen having dinner in some restaurant. And that was it. Well I wasn't going to turn down fifty quid just for that, was I, and dinner into the bargain.'

'So he wanted to compromise himself so his wife would divorce him and he could be with this other woman, D-something?'

'Yes.'

'A Brighton divorce, they call it. You pay someone to pretend to have an affair with you to keep the real person out of the spotlight. That's the main story of the show.'

'Yes,' she said, and looked down at her clasped hands. 'But of course, in spite of what I'd promised myself, and what he'd promised me, things did go quite a bit too far...' she hesitated and risked a glance up at Hardy's face, and looked away again. 'I wish—I wish I'd said no, but...You see I forgot it was just pretend. For a moment I thought he really liked me. I thought he'd forgot about this other girl and he'd marry me once his divorce came through. He kept buying me drinks and flowers, and when we went for dinner, he gave me a bracelet. And so I...' She stopped and bit her lip. A tear rolled down her face. 'I wish I hadn't,' she added in a whisper.

The silence pressed in about them. If he had known

Miss Knight better, he might have hugged her, but as a police inspector interviewing a witness, he couldn't do that. Nevertheless, he was human. As gently as he could, he said, 'You're not—in any—trouble, are you? If you are, I will help you. Just tell me the truth, Valerie.'

She gave a shaky laugh. 'No, nothing like as bad as that, thank God. But I feel so ashamed. What if my mum was to find out? Or me dad.'

'Archie Dunne was a notorious philanderer; he used women and threw them aside once he'd had what he wanted. Don't blame yourself, dear, you'll not get taken in again.'

'No, I certainly won't,' she said with a return of spirit, 'And at least I got my fifty quid and a posh dinner too.' She smiled at him.

'Could do with that myself,' Hardy agreed. 'So where did he take you?'

She told him the address and he noted it down, just as a matter of form, for his own records, although as soon as she'd said it, he recognised it as the same address he and Maple had already visited. As she was leaving, she said, 'You won't forget about talking to Big Ears, will you?'

'Big Ears?'

'The manager. I don't want to lose my job.'

'I'll talk to Big Ears, Miss Knight, don't you worry about that. Thank you for your help.'

'Will I have to go to court?'

'It's possible, but unlikely.' He followed her to the door, and held it open for her.

'I'm going to use the money to do a typewriting course, see if I can get a better job.'

'That's an excellent idea. Good luck, Miss Knight.'

Detective Constable Maple was patrolling the street, back in uniform, to avoid drawing attention to himself. No one questioned the presence of a bobby on the beat. He watched from the corner as a taxi pulled up. A young woman got out, and went up the steps to number 191.

Dottie got out of the taxi, paid the driver and turned to face Susan Dunne's house. She didn't really want to go in, not on her own, but on the other hand, Susan had sounded so thoroughly upset, Dottie hadn't liked to refuse her. But now she wished she'd insisted on Flora, or even her mother, coming with her.

From the street, the house looked cheery and welcoming—the bright electric light glowed through colourful curtains that Dottie instinctively knew her mother would think highly unsuitable, but Dottie herself thought most attractive. As she pushed open the rusty gate and went up the uneven steps to the front door, the sound of dance music reached her ears. Someone was listening to the radio.

However, when she arrived at the top of the steps, and put out her hand to take hold of the knocker, just like in a horror film, the door creaked slowly open by itself upon a dark hallway. Dottie felt an extreme reluctance to enter, the cheerful note had gone. In fact, as soon as the door had begun to move, chills ran down her spine and her scalp prickled.

Her stomach gave an uncomfortable lurch. She knew she should leave, she knew something was wrong. But to all outward—and sensible—appearances, there was no cause for alarm, other than the light being out in the hall and the front door standing open. She paused for a moment and took a calming breath. Her stomach lurched again, and she realised she had never felt this frightened before, and never on such small evidence.

She waited for her eyes to adjust to the low level of light, but even after a full minute, could still discern nothing. She took a step back again and looked about her, glancing up and down the deserted street and wondering. She could still hear the soft sound of a waltz, clearly coming from the drawing-room. She pushed thoughts of Cyril out of her head, crushing down a sudden memory of dancing with him, and she was cross with herself for thinking of him at a time like this. Her anger steadied her and she was able to think.

Perhaps she ought to try to find a neighbour, or go down the road to find a policeman walking the beat, and get him to come back with her. She need only say she was worried about her friend, or that she was nervous in the dark. She was fairly sure anyone would understand and offer to help her. Everyone knew that London policemen were the kindest and most helpful in the whole world.

But something determined rose up in her and told her not to be such a ninny. No wonder men think they can lie and cheat and go off and marry American heiresses if you go about being a delicate wilting little hothouse flower, she told herself. So she straightened her shoulders, put up her chin, took a good strong grip on her bag and put a smile on her face. She pushed the door wide open and called out, 'Hello Susan!' as she stepped into the hall.

There was no reply, but perhaps Susan had fallen asleep after her earlier emotion.

A sudden chime from a clock in the hall made Dottie jump, and she almost turned like a rabbit and ran. It was half past seven. She told herself sternly that she was being a child, and turning to close the front door carefully. she then put off her coat and hat and left them on the hall stand, spookily there like a skeleton in the dark corner beside the picture. She left her bag on the floor beside the stand, and smoothed her skirt and cardigan and patted her hair.

Ignoring the trembling, hollow feeling inside, she again called out hello, adding, 'I hope you don't mind me just walking in, but your front door was open, and I was a bit worried. I think the latch hadn't caught and wind must have blown it open.'

She pushed open the door to the little drawing-room at the front of the house. The music was louder now, and the electric lights of the room dazzled her momentarily, as she came in from the dark hall. She looked about the room.

Dottie stood in the doorway, frozen, unable to think or breathe.

It was—Susan. She was—sitting. On her settee, with her sewing beside her. Her throat—the blood.

Dottie stumbled back, gasping, she couldn't look away, her hand fumbling behind her for the door and not finding it. The radio played gaily on, the room warmed by the fire, and bright, and cheerful, but there on the settee...

Dottie became aware of a choking, gasping sound, and realised the strange sound, like a frightened child, came from her own mouth. Where was the door? She had to—had to leave.

But Leonora was there. She stood in front of the now-closed door. Dottie saw the long knife she held, and the blood on it, and the blood that was a slick mess all down the right side of her gold cloak. She had the appearance of a high-priestess conducting a sacrifice. She looked calm, yet her eyes glittered with repressed excitement.

'But...' said Dottie.

'Messy, isn't it? Yes, go over there, keep going back. That's right. Now sit. In that chair next to her. Oh don't be such a baby, she can't hurt you now.'

Dottie fell into the chair. It was a relief to sit, her legs didn't seem to want to hold her up any longer, and she stumbled. She turned her head so she didn't look at Susan's face tipped right back, her eyes wide in terror, even now in death, her lips drawn back in a grimace. The blood, thick and dark across her throat, and all down the front of her dowdy black blouse. Dottie squeezed her eyes shut and turned her head away, biting her lip to keep herself from making any sound.

Leonora's voice brought her back to reality.

'You know, for a few moments there you had me worried. As soon as you saw the door open, you almost went away again, didn't you?'

If only I had, Dottie thought. If only. If I live, if I'm somehow spared, I shall always, always follow my instincts. She couldn't speak, but she nodded her head in answer to Leonora's question.

'Yes, thought so! Bet you wish you'd run, Little Miss Do-Gooder, always poking your nose in where it's not wanted. Well, you've learned your lesson now, good and proper. Asking me if I'm all right. 'Oh are you sure you're quite all right?' You patronising cow! How could I be all right after what *she'd* done?' Leonora jabbed the knife in Susan's direction.

How tall Leonora was, Dottie thought suddenly, irrelevantly. Was it she whom the cigarette girl had seen? Hadn't she said something about Archie creeping past someone as if he was afraid? It wasn't Susan after all, but her maid. Susan was small, whereas Leonora towered.

Leonora was weeping suddenly, and saying, 'I loved him! Archie. Oh, I know he wasn't faithful, never would be faithful. But that didn't matter to me. I only wanted to serve him, my lord and master, my one true love. I lived just to make everything in his life more comfortable, more convenient. She didn't care a fig about him. Not a fig. From the moment they married, she nagged him and scolded him, she harped on at him night and day, and you could see it in her eyes—how she *despised* him! Her own husband. The one she had sworn to obey, to respect, to be a helpmeet unto. How dared she! After everything I'd taught her! *She* was the betrayer, not him! We're supposed to love them, to serve them, no matter what, always to be there to help and support. It's our wifely duty! But she didn't care for any of that. Her vows meant nothing to her. Nothing!'

She was screaming by now, tears and saliva running down onto her chin, dripping onto the front of her cloak, the hand holding the knife shaking violently. Dottie felt ill, her head swam. The thing that had been Susan beside her, the black-red gash yawning like a nightmarishly misplaced smile, and the thing that had been her pleasant young housemaid screaming and shuddering and sobbing in front of her.

'And you! You're no better. Taking up with first this one and then that. Flitting from one rich suitor to the next, never with one man long enough to gain his trust, always putting your own wants and needs first, never mind decent, modest behaviour.' The voice dropped now to little more than a whisper as she said, her tone one of offended pride and distaste, '*Flaunting* the colours. The

Queen's own colours in public. What right had you? You're not even one of us, you have no right—no—no!'

Suddenly she lunged at Dottie, and Dottie shrieked, and threw herself out of the chair. She fell onto Susan's feet as a burning stinging pain sheered though her upper arm as the knife's blade slashed at her.

But the room was alive, full, loud. Men shouted. Leonora screeched as a policeman took hold of her arm and forced her to drop the weapon. Simultaneously Dottie screamed as her hand touched Susan's cold, stockinged feet, and then arms came about her, lifting her up and away, a voice shushing her gently, an arm about her shoulders.

Somehow, Dottie didn't see how it happened, Leonora worked up her strength and wrenched herself free of the grip of the policeman who held her, she fell to the carpet, and snatched up the knife, driving towards Dottie, the knife scything wildly, but Inspector Hardy leapt backwards, taking Dottie with him, turning as he did so. Leonora's knife missed its mark, then she halted, and seeming at last to realise how the situation stood, Leonora gripped the knife, smiled at Dottie, then declared, 'For Queen Esther!' and plunged the knife into her own bosom, falling with a shriek to the floor, shuddering once, twice, and then she was still, her blood flooding out to become a spreading dark pool. Dottie fell in a heap on the floor. He lifted her to her feet, and his arms held her to his chest, and she gave full vent to the first attack of hysterics she had ever had.

She was led out into the street and helped into a waiting police car, where a greatcoat was wrapped around her shivering frame, and hot tea with a generous dash of something from a silver flask was put into her hands. Her hysterics fizzled out almost immediately, leaving her shivering with cold and tears still running slowly down her cheeks, and to add to her humiliation she had the hiccups. She sipped the tea. Gradually its heat and the alcoholic component warmed her and bolstered her nerves. Shouting still issued from the Dunnes' house, and lights were going on up and down the street, people began to peek around curtains and doors.

She found a handkerchief in the pocket of the greatcoat and she scrubbed her face with it. Then seeing blood on her right hand, she wiped it carefully, concentrating on each finger and nail, and knuckle, but refusing to allow her mind to dwell on the fact of the blood, or to wonder if it was her own blood, or Leonora's, or Susan's. The occasional tear or hiccup escaped her but she was feeling calmer. She was becoming aware of activity around her, and she only started slightly when the door next to her was opened and a gentleman in evening dress and carrying a carpet bag leaned in and said, 'I say m'dear, are you the young lady who's been injured? Been sent to take a look at you. Dr Garrett.'

She nodded, and guiltily tried to hide the cup. He simply smiled and got in beside her. 'Nothing like a cup of tea for a shock. Especially with a drop of something in it. Does the nerves good. Not much of an evening out for you, m'dear. What's your name?'

She told him her name, and her address, and the name of her parents, and he nodded as if satisfied, and quickly patched up the wound on her arm. As he worked he asked about a few people he knew and they discovered some mutual acquaintances. Dottie could have hugged him for the easy way he kept her mind off what he was doing. The wound was stinging tremendously and she felt she could hardly bear it, but by the time he had cleaned it and dressed it, the stinging had subsided to a dull throbbing ache.

'It's not as bad as it looks. It'll probably leave a thin scar, but at least it will be fairly easy to hide. And it'll just be a straight line, no puckering. Shouldn't be unsightly enough to put off any young chaps worth their salt! Change the dressing every day, and keep the wound clean. If your arm turns green or drops off, go and see your own doctor. Who is that, by the way?'

She told him. He made a note and promised to let him know what had happened.

'Now then, just get off home to bed, drop of brandy to help you sleep, rest tomorrow, the arm will be a bit sore for a few days, but otherwise you'll soon be back to normal.' He bid her goodnight, and as she pulled the greatcoat back around her, she noticed the crowd of on-lookers. She watched the comings and goings through the rain-spattered window of the car, she began to remember everything that had happened, and what she had seen. More importantly, she remembered the strange rambling things that had come out of Leonora's mouth, before she had—she had...

It was too fantastical, like something from some opium-ravaged Victorian epic. It wasn't the kind of thing that happened in an ordinary house in an ordinary street in an everydayish part of London. Dottie's teeth began to chatter, and the deep throbbing ache in her arm that must be what the doctor had alluded to when he'd told her it would be 'a bit sore' seemed to be worsening at every moment. She drank the rest of the tea, partly to warm herself and partly because she felt as though she might start screaming again. She was embarrassed by her earlier behaviour. Once again, she felt ashamed of her emotional reactions and felt she was of little use in a crisis. For goodness' sake, she had even fainted. Practically at Inspector Hardy's feet. Her cheeks flamed at the memory.

The car door opened again. A concerned face looked in at her. He smiled at her when he saw her looking up at him.

'Seen the doc?'

She nodded. 'Yes, all—all p-patched up. Nothing to worry about.' She tried to sound perky but failed miserably.

'Jolly good.' He seemed distracted, and why shouldn't he be, she told herself, he's got two dead bodies to deal with. He looked around, said something she couldn't hear to someone she couldn't see, then stepped back without another word and closed the car door. But he hadn't left her. He came around and got into the driver's seat, saying over his shoulder, 'I'll just take you home,' and he started the engine.

She felt guilty. 'Oh no! There's really no need, I can call a taxi. You're far too busy...'

'Don't be so bloody stupid,' he growled. So she leaned back in the seat and close her eyes. Because now, she had only just realised, the main drama of the evening was about to begin.

Arriving outside the Manderson home, he supported Dottie by her uninjured arm, up the steps to the front door of the house. He knocked.

'Oh dear,' Dottie said and bit her lip. He had no time to ask what she meant. Dottie took a step back. The maid who opened the door was pushed out of the way by Dottie's mother, who was not a happy woman.

*

Chapter Twenty-two

After the funeral, Muriel hugged her and they talked for a few minutes, and even Colonel and Mrs Moyer came over and thanked her for what she had tried to do—but to her mind, failed miserably, as she constantly reminded herself.

The Cyril Pentermans were there. Dottie noted that the new Mrs Penterman was very tall, very thin, and extremely elegant. She made Dottie feel childish, and somehow unfinished. Cyril tried several times to catch Dottie's eye but she refused to allow it, keeping her eyes very determinedly fixed elsewhere: the ground; her folded, gloved hands; the floral tributes or some spot about a thousand yards away. Anything to avoid giving him the opportunity to smile and act as though they were friends, as if he had treated her in a decent manner.

George drove Flora and Dottie home after the funeral, and the journey took them past the Dunnes' house, now standing empty, and as they turned into the end of the road, Dottie felt her heart begin to pound, and her stomach gave a violent lurch; although she managed to remain outwardly calm, her thoughts and feelings were in a whirl. And she heard Flora say to George in a low voice, 'George darling, you shouldn't have come this way.' Dottie leaned forward over the front seat to assure them it didn't matter a jot, but then there was the house, looking just as it always looked, or possibly even less inviting if that were possible, and they were past it and it was over. Her heart settled back again into its normal stately rhythm, and the taste of bile left her mouth, though her arm and shoulder ached as if in sympathy.

That afternoon she gave Flora the first pair of bootees and matching matinee jacket she had knitted for Bonzo. Flora was delighted and cooed over them, making George admire them too. Dottie was certainly pleased with them; the decorative pattern of the jacket had gone wrong at one point but no one would be likely to notice unless they really studied the pattern. She had started the set the morning after that night at the Dunnes' house, and she had felt consoled to be making something for the new baby. When Inspector Hardy had called to visit, he had found her sitting up in bed, knitting the baby jacket in soft pale yellow wool. He had given her the oddest look, a truly very odd look, which had made her blush to the roots of her hair, and that had been when the accident to the pattern had occurred.

He had stayed and talked somewhat uncomfortably for half an hour, with her mother there as chaperone, and then he had gone again. Another officer had called the following day to take her statement, and it had now been ten days since she had last seen the inspector.

As if reading her mind, Flora said, 'Have you seen Inspector Hardy since that night?'

Not wanting her sister to know about him calling to see her at the house, she simply said no, she hadn't seen him, adding, 'But I imagine he's very busy with bringing the case to an end. There must be a ton of paperwork involved. All those reports and things. There was really no reason for me to see him once I'd made my statement. He must be very busy with other cases by now.'

'No doubt,' agreed Flora with a sideways glance at her husband.

The next morning, she was at home on her own. Her parents were both out, her father at his club, and her mother was off doing good in the community somewhere. Janet helped her redress the wound, which had almost healed but had a tendency to get caught or rubbed by the fabric of her clothes.

Afterwards, Dottie wandered about the house aimlessly, bored, unable to settle to anything, uninterested in any of her usual pursuits, including the second baby jacket. She halted by the window in the drawing-room, the one that looked out upon the street. But it was not the street that she was seeing, but the scene that night in the Dunnes' house.

Several times the image of Susan, dead, and Leonora, screaming as she lunged at Dottie with that knife, had come to Dottie in dreams, and she had awoken, shivering in terror, her heart pounding, and had lain in her bed with the light on, afraid to sleep again.

But during the daytime she could think more calmly about what had happened. She wondered how things would have worked out if she had not gone to the Dunnes' that night. Would Susan still be alive? Would everything still be going along in its same strange—but living—manner?

As she stood there looking out at the street, she saw a black car pull up outside and Inspector Hardy got out. Dottie felt flustered, as if her breath had all been sucked out of her. He was running up the steps and knocking on the door. Dottie ran to open the door, and he came in, showering droplets of rain from his hat and greatcoat.

'I'll order some tea, or coffee, if you prefer,' she said. 'I'm afraid my parents are out.'

'It was you I came to see,' he said, following her into the drawing-room and shedding his coat and hat. 'I won't have any tea, if you don't mind, this is just a flying visit. I wanted to see how you're getting on.'

'Oh I'm all right. My arm is almost better. But I keep going over and over things in my mind. I can't seem to stop thinking about it. I keep thinking if I hadn't gone there, Susan, and even Leonora herself, would still be alive,' Dottie said.

'You mustn't think any of this is your fault,' he said. The gruff professional exterior seemed to have fallen away, and he was almost boyish in his earnestness as he leaned forward to impress this upon her. 'It is clear from the medical examination that Susan Dunne was killed almost as soon as she'd finished speaking to you on the telephone. Even if you hadn't gone to the house last evening, Susan Dunne would still have been dead.'

'But Leonora...'

'She must have overheard her mistress telephoning to

you. Even if she didn't know to whom Mrs Dunne was speaking, she could have probably guessed. But it made no difference—clearly Mrs Dunne intended to speak to someone and therefore she had to be silenced. As soon as she heard Mrs Dunne begging the person on the other end of the line to come to the house once Leonora had gone out, I'm afraid her fate was sealed.'

'Thank you. I'd completely forgotten you were watching the house. It's lucky for me you were. For one terrible moment, I thought...'

He looked at her, and she felt as though she was being scrutinised rather too closely. Then he leaned back in his chair and the air seemed to come back into the room, and he said, 'For one terrible moment, so did I. But as you say, we were watching the house. Constable Maple saw you go in and after a few minutes he decided to let me know. It's a good thing he did.' There was a lengthy pause then he added, 'It's possible even if you hadn't gone to the house, Leonora Simmons would still have made away with herself. None of her belongings were packed, so there was no indication she planned to escape.'

'The things she said, I can't decide if they were ludicrous manglings and mashings-together of lots of different bits of the Bible, like we used to learn scriptures at Sunday School, or if it was some lunatic stuff she'd made up in her own mind. All that stuff about living only to serve him. About duty and sacrifice. It was horrifying at the time, just watching her face, the way her eyes were practically rolling in her head, and listening to her voice as she shrieked it all at me. I've never seen someone so unhinged before. That was even more frightening than walking into the room and seeing Susan Dunne's dead body. Yet I still wanted to try and help Leonora. Though she'd said I was patronising. I didn't mean to be. I just saw how upset she was about Archie Dunne's death.'

'It wasn't my finest hour, I'm ashamed to say. I was already certain that Susan Dunne killed her husband, though we had no real proof. The maid backed up everything her mistress said. But although I'd noticed the maid was upset, it never occurred to me to wonder why or to think about what that might mean. I never once thought Susan Dunne could be in danger.'

'But why did Susan choose to kill him that night of all nights? It was so cold and wet? Why out on the street, when she could have killed him quietly at home and made it look like a simple accident?'

'We can only guess, with all the main witnesses dead. But it seems to me that she just couldn't take it anymore. He'd left her for several weeks, and gone to live at his club, then he came back, evidently there was some attempt at a reconciliation. And the night he died, he'd just left her again. And possibly she'd found out that he really did mean to divorce her for this other woman.'

'George's sister, Diana? Was he really going to marry her then?'

'I believe so. Mrs Dunne met her husband outside his club. He'd arranged to meet Miss Gascoigne at the flat, and was intending to take a cab there, which is why he wasn't wearing an overcoat or carrying an umbrella. But according to the doorman at the club, a woman, and I believe it was Mrs Dunne, met Mr Dunne outside and persuaded him to walk with her. They went in the general direction of the flat. I can only assume she'd insisted on him taking her to the flat to confront Miss Gascoigne, and had actually stabbed him once they got to the seclusion of Mortlake Gardens.

'So Susan definitely killed Archie? She must have cared a lot more about his philandering than she appeared to do.' Dottie coloured violently and broke off, not wanting to spell out the more sordid side of the affair. 'Did you find out anything more about the cloak?'

'That gold thing Leonora Simmons was wearing? Seems fairly certain that she just wanted to have something like her mistress's, something she no doubt paraded about in and fancied herself glamorous. A maid's life is pretty dull, you know, and her things weren't particularly valuable or of good quality. We know from what the doorman said that Mrs Dunne had one like it.'

'Are you sure that's all it was?' Dottie asked, surprised. 'I wondered if there wasn't something more behind it.'

'Well,' he said with a sigh, 'The case is closed now, due to Simmons' confession to you and the taking of her own life, and that's all my superiors are concerned about. There's no direct evidence that Mrs Dunne killed her husband, and in any case, she can't be charged now. Also there's the possibility that Simmons killed him in a fit of hysteria, and somehow her mistress found out about it. But there, it's all over and done with.' He reached for his hat and put it on.

Dottie wasn't satisfied. 'But why did he sing me those few lines from the song? It seems so odd. Why didn't he just tell me who had killed him?' She was biting her lip again, staring out of the window as she relived the scene that night in November.

'I can only guess, at this stage. Perhaps Archie knew he was running out of time? He knew he was dying, that help wouldn't reach him soon enough, but he also knew who stabbed him. He wanted the truth to come out about Diana, Valerie, and how he'd cheated on his wife time and again. But I think he felt disloyal giving his wife away. In spite of everything I believe he still loved her.' He smiled to himself as if he couldn't quite understand love so deep.

'Well we know she wasn't exactly an easy woman to live with,' Dottie agreed. 'Do you think that, in the face of death, he was full of remorse and guilt over his selfish actions? That he understood, even accepted her actions? Perhaps he even realised that Susan herself was in danger?'

'Whatever went through his mind as he lay there on the pavement, there was no time to put it all into words, so he just did the first thing that came to mind: he sang the lines from the song Night and Day and hoped that somehow the truth would come to light. I'm sure he wouldn't have wanted his wife to bear the penalty for murder. Perhaps he felt he drove her to it?' There was a quiet moment, then the inspector took up his greatcoat and got to his feet. 'I hope your wound continues to heal quickly, Miss Manderson. Once again, thank you for your help.'

'So you don't think there's anything odd about the picture and the cloaks and everything I told you Leonora said to me?'

He turned at the door. 'Well, as you've already pointed out, there were quite a few of those garments about. Seems they're all the rage. I don't think we need to go into that any further. And the rest of it, well, it's just a slightly odd religious view, but there's nothing in it, you know.'

'I'm not so sure...' Dottie said.

'I must go, I'm afraid. It's my sister's birthday today and we're going out to dinner and then the theatre. I've got quite a bit of paperwork to do before then.'

'I hope you're not going to see that show, *Gay Divorce*,' Dottie said.

He looked at her. 'We are as it happens. Why?'

'The song,' she said. 'The song Archie sang as he lay dying. It was from that show. *Night and Day*. Remember?'

'I remember you singing it to me that night. You have a delightful voice.' He paused again in the hall outside her room. 'Good day, Miss Manderson.'

'Oh please, call me Dottie. Miss Manderson is far too formal. After all, I still have two of your handkerchiefs.'

*

Chapter Twenty-three

Ten women sat about the long rectangular table. Candles lit the centre of the room, and the corners were lost in a kind of flickering shadow. There were two empty seats. The ten women, their heads and shoulders swathed in gold wool, bowed their heads whilst one of their number, the one seated at the head of the table, softly spoke a prayer. At the end of the prayer, she said, 'Amen,' and all around the table the women chorused the same word.

There was a pause then the woman at the head of the table said, in a marginally less hallowed voice, 'Finally, daughters of the Queen, let me remind you all, we are faced with two tasks this evening. First of all, it is a matter of gravest sorrow and disappointment to me, and to us all, that our two sisters should have destroyed one another through their refusal to remember our primary purpose: to serve our Kings, and our secondary purpose: to support our Sisters. We must remember, we are called to be modest, unselfish, and loyal above all things. We do not seek our own benefit nor to take status and position for ourselves. Let us learn this valuable lesson and never again allow deviation from our purpose to wreak such devastation upon our House.

'The second matter we must consider is this: these two empty seats amongst us must be filled, and we must decide who will fill them. If any of you knows of a woman, married or unmarried, servant or lady, who is of quality, goodness and purity of heart, let me know her name so that I may pray about the matter, and if it is seemly, interview them as candidates to be welcomed into our Household.

'It is with sadness that I have been forced to take another decision. We must destroy our robes. They have become too easily recognised by the heathen. Therefore, we shall divest ourselves of these soiled garments and put on new, clean vestments of modest black. One at a time, sisters, go behind the screen and remove your outer garment and lay it aside, and with joyful hearts, take up your new garment from the stand. I'm sorry this has had to happen, I know you all take great delight in the lustrous colour of our beloved Queen Esther, but the colour is sadly too easily remarked upon as we have lately become aware. I have purchased a supply of gold, jewelled clasps that we may use to secure and adorn our somewhat plain new robes. Sister, if you please, we shall begin with you.'

The sister immediately to the right of the woman at the head of the table got to her feet, walked behind the screen and presently came out, no longer clad in gold but in a cloak of black, the edges closed together at the throat by a small gold clasp with tiny round jewels of blue, red and green. She resumed her seat, then the woman next to her departed to perform the same transformation. Within ten minutes, they had all changed their gold cloth for black.

'Thank you, my dearest sisters. And now, we will end this meeting. As you know there will be no more meetings until the end of February. I shall contact you all with the precise date nearer the time. Let us say our closing prayer,'

The others joined their voices to hers and together they murmured the closing prayer of the Daughters of Esther the Queen:

'Good Queen Esther, bride of the King, help us to walk with modesty and self-sacrifice in this world of men, ever ready to perform any office, without reproach, criticism or demand. Help us to remember to serve our Kings selflessly, as you served yours, and by so doing, to preserve our nation in the day of reckoning. Amen.'

THE END

*

CARON ALLAN

Scotch Mist

Dottie Manderson mysteries: Book 3

a novella

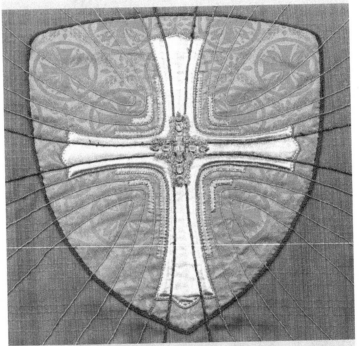

CARON ALLAN

The Mantle
of God

Dottie Manderson mysteries: Book 2